Killer Runway

A Bianca Wallace Mystery, 2
(A Cozy Mystery Novel)

Killer Runway

Bianca Wallace Mysteries, Volume 2

Daria White

Published by Daria White, 2021.

Killer Runway: A Bianca Wallace Mystery, Book Two
Copyright © 2022 by Daria White

PUBLISHED BY CRIMSON Fox Publishing
www.crimsonfoxpublishing.com[1]

FIRST EDITION
Cover Design by Vila Designs

---

1.   http://www.crimsonfoxpublishing.com

eISBN: 978-1-005277-13-0
ISBN (Paperback): 978-1-952667-71-8

Turner, Oregon

<u>Thank You from Daria</u>

Killer Runway
A Bianca Wallace Mystery, 2

Chapter 1

"I don't think I need a new outfit, Mel." Bianca perused the racks of shirts, jackets, skirts, and dresses in the clothing store. She caught a whiff of the sweet air freshener but followed her sister to the racks of dresses. Bianca eyed the rest of the customers inside, but the crowd average for a Wednesday afternoon.

Melanie pivoted with an emerald green cocktail dress in hand. Bianca tilted her head to the side. Not because of the dress, but because of her baby sister's haircut. Her dark brown curls barely touched her shoulders. Not a drastic change since her hair was only a few inches longer two weeks earlier, but the new style fit Melanie's youthful appearance. Smooth brown skin, slim in frame, but her joyous personality beamed from the inside.

Bianca kept her curls past her shoulders, though she contemplated a different color in the future. Natural black? Rich wine? Midnight blue? The last one, not so much.

"Well?" Melanie pressed. "What do you think?"

Bianca shrugged. "Not me."

"That's what you said about the leopard print dress. Which I think looked hot. If you don't wear it, I will."

Bianca giggled. "What would I look like wearing that?"

"A thirty-four-year-old woman who's confident in her body and doesn't mind wearing clothes to flatter her figure," Melanie said. Then she gave a soft smile, just as their mother, Deborah Wallace, would have done. "You look great. I'm not saying your taste in clothes is..."

Bianca folded her arms. Would she say *boring*? "What?"

Melanie held up her hand as if to defend herself. "I already said you look great. I just don't see the harm in switching things up." She passed by Bianca to another rack, while brushing against her shoulder. "Besides, what if someone notices? Like... Detective Sims."

Bianca gasped. "Melanie?"

"I mean, you've been seeing him—"

"Not like *that*. Only in the park and occasionally the gym." It had been that way the last few weeks since Martin's murder. Bianca didn't mind talking to the newest member in Edenville. It was refreshing talking to a man and having a pleasant conversation. Sure, his gray eyes allured her. The way he licked his lips made her stomach quiver, but the man was attractive. So what?

Melanie shook her head, clearly not believing her sister. "Sure. What are you going to do when I'm gone? Sure, my last assignment rescheduled, but I'll be leaving again soon. If it weren't for me, sis, you'd never go out."

"I go out." Bianca admitted. Occasionally, when she felt like it or something in town interested her.

Her baby sister eyeballed her. "*Alyssa* has been on more dates than you have."

Bianca pointed at her sister. She wouldn't admit the truth to Melanie, even if Bianca's teenage daughter had more dates with her current boyfriend than she'd had since her divorce from Alyssa's father. "I'm going to let that one slide."

Melanie sighed. "Okay, maybe that was a bit much, but all I'm saying is: Enjoy yourself, sis."

"I do," Bianca said. "In my own way. When I want to branch out, I will at my discretion." She turned to her sister, serious. "Just because my life isn't what you think it should be doesn't mean I don't enjoy myself."

Melanie bobbed her head, the corners of her mouth lifting. "I know. I'm sorry." She pressed a hand to her forehead. "I know I can be pushy." Her eyes bugged. "I am becoming Mom."

Bianca laughed. "I love you both, so no worries, but when I tell you I'm okay, believe me."

Melanie winked at her, only to raise her eyebrows and lean forward.

"What?" Bianca directed her own attention to the front of the store.

A woman walked in alone, carrying a black purse. She was at least five-eight, slim, honey skin, and long, dark brown hair with highlights.

Melanie handed the emerald dress to Bianca. Her pace quickened to the woman ahead of her. "Sherry! You made it!"

Bianca watched as the woman made eye contact with her sister. She squealed along with Melanie, only to open her arms for an embrace. Sherry? The name sounded familiar but didn't ring a bell. Then again, Melanie traveled more than Bianca did as a journalist, so her sister met new people all the time. Bianca returned the dress to the rack, occasionally glancing at the two women who hugged, squealed, and hugged again. Then Melanie waved Bianca over.

Adjusting her purse on her shoulder, Bianca walked over to the duo.

"Sherry, I want you to meet my older sister, Bianca. Bianca, this is Sherry Wilson. We went to high school together."

So that was it. Bianca extended her hand. "Pleasure to meet you." Had they met before?

Sherry beamed. "I remember spending the night at your house."

Bianca snapped her fingers as she thought back. She recalled a young girl that had worn glasses, had had pimply skin and long pigtails in her hair. Sherry had obviously come into her own. Smooth skin, petite figure, and flawless makeup. "Wow. You look... amazing."

Sherry flipped her long hair with a giggle. "Thank you."

Melanie eyed her friend. "I'm assuming you've given up sweets. We loved cookies and cream."

"I splurge now and then, but I am on a healthy eating plan," Sherry said. She refocused her attention on Bianca. "I think Melanie said you'd gotten married and had a baby."

"Yeah," Bianca continued. "I married out of high school. I have a teenage daughter who's dating now, so I'm trying to get used to that." She pointed between her sister and Sherry. "Have you two kept in touch this whole time?" Had Melanie mentioned her lately? Then again, her sister had a life outside of her. Was that why she pressed Bianca to get out more?

"We try. It's easier with social media." Melanie looped her arm through Sherry's. "It's nice to have a friend with whom you can pick up where you left off."

Sherry smiled. "I agree. I'm a model, and I travel all the time, so it's harder for me to make friends compared to when I was in high school."

"And…" Melanie shrieked. "She's in the fashion show this weekend!"

That was it! She'd seen Sherry's name associated with Clique Classic's fashion show. Bianca had designed the fliers, pamphlets, and banners for the event. They had posted them around town, on top of the newspapers, including online. The opportunity came as a referral from another company she'd worked with the previous year. They had raved about her talent to where Bianca got the opportunity of a lifetime for Wallace Designs.

She even gasped once she realized the notoriety working with Clique Classic would bring to her business. While she didn't recognize the names of top designers or the few models, she couldn't deny the sleek fashions. Bianca got two free tickets to attend the show. Perhaps it wouldn't be a bad idea to buy a new outfit since she was going anyway to take pictures for her portfolio.

"Yes, I'm excited, but I wanted to come early to catch up with you. It's been too long. How come you're not covering the show again?" Sherry asked.

"You know I haven't covered a fashion show since my early years in journalism," Melanie said.

Sherry nudged her shoulder. "Fashion doesn't have enough edge for you anymore."

Melanie shook her head. "I'm not saying I didn't like it, but I wanted a little more depth." Then she turned to face Bianca and looked back at her friend. "If you have a moment, I could use a favor."

"What?" Sherry asked.

Melanie reached a hand out to her sister. "Bianca needs help to pick out an outfit for the fashion show. Maybe she'll listen to an expert in fashion."

"Mel?" What would Bianca do with her?

"Just some friendly advice." Melanie tilted her head to the side.

Bianca squinted her eyes at her sister. "Fine." She faced Sherry. "She picked out an emerald green cocktail dress, but I don't think it's me."

Sherry bobbed her head. "That's what's most important. You want to pick an outfit that extends your personality. If you're not comfortable, there's no point in wearing it."

Melanie stepped past them both to a nearby rack. "I think this will be perfect." She held up the long-sleeved leopard-print dress she'd tried to convince Bianca to buy earlier. "Don't you think?"

Sherry tapped a finger to her thin lips. "It's cute, but..." Her eyes perused the store further, only to gasp at a black-and-white peplum dress. "This." She took it off the rack and held it up against Bianca. "This is gorgeous. You can never go wrong with the classic black-and-white dress. Choose any color for accessories and the perfect pump to match."

Melanie stood next to her friend. "Should her hair be down or in an updo hairstyle?"

Bianca couldn't help but feel she was on one of those fashion help shows on the TLC network. Her lips parted to reply, but a simple black dress captivated her eyes. Sheer sleeves. Walking towards the outfit that called out to her, she picked up the hanger. Mesh panel. Mock neckline, long sleeves. Knee-length, followed by a fitted waist.

"Sis," Melanie said as she stepped over. "Why didn't I see that?"

Bianca held the dress to her chest. "I saw it first."

"It's perfect." Sherry then walked over to the nearby shoe rack. "And these will go with it" She pointed to the leopard print pumps.

"What is it about leopard print you two can't get past?" Bianca asked.

Melanie and Sherry giggled.

Bianca only shook her head. She walked to the fitting room with her dress and the leopard-print shoes in hand.

Chapter 2

Late Thursday afternoon, the following day, Bianca sipped from her cup of herbal tea. Veronica, her virtual assistant, talked about Bianca's scheduled meetings through the screen on Zoom. After posting a virtual assistant job listing online, Bianca interviewed the twenty-six-year-old a week later. Veronica was efficient in word processing, communication, and her computer skills. Not to mention her pleasant personality made it easier for Bianca to work with. Today, her assistant pulled her blonde hair into a messy bun with a black-and-white polka-dot headband. Black mascara accented her dark blue eyes and red lipstick covered her medium full lips.

"I pushed back your virtual meeting with the real estate company to next week as requested," Veronica said.

"Great." Bianca set her cup on her desk and leaned over to scratch Casper, a Beagle, who was asleep at her feet. "What else?"

"I finished the presentation for James Buffet." The business tycoon who had reached out for Bianca's services, thanks to Chad Lee's recommendation. Bianca would reach out to the honeymooning couple later, since they'd extended their trip. She didn't blame them and was glad they were happy despite the arrest of Chad's mother.

"Great." Bianca directed her attention back to her assistant. She opened her planner on her tablet. "I hope I'm not forgetting anything."

Veronica shook her head through the screen. "That's it for today. Anything else you want me to take care of?"

"I'll shoot you a message." Bianca closed her calendar and brushed back a loose curl from her face. "That's it, Veronica. Thank you."

Her assistant smiled. Then she left the meeting. Bianca ended the meeting on Zoom just as Casper stirred at her feet. His collar jingled as he used his back paw to scratch behind his ear.

"Need a walk?" Bianca asked.

He barked.

Changing out of slippers and into tennis shoes, Bianca grabbed her keys and headed for the front door.

"Mom?" Alyssa called out from the hallway.

Bianca stopped in her tracks. Facing her daughter, she answered, "Yes?"

"Can we do lasagna tonight instead of spaghetti?" she asked. Dark brown eyes like her mother, smooth brown skin, and curly hair. The faint freckles remained on her nose.

Bianca showed a satisfied smile. "Ask your Aunt Mel. She's the one who's cooking tonight."

"I called, but she didn't answer," Alyssa said.

"She's probably still out with her friend, Sherry. I guess they need time to catch up." Bianca secured the leash around Casper's neck. "She'll be back, so ask her then. I'm sure she won't be long."

Alyssa nodded and headed back to her room.

Bianca exited the front door, locking it behind her. Walk around the neighborhood? Or take the car to the park? Walking around the neighborhood sounded better. Then again, if she went to the park, what were the chances of running into Detective Sims again? It seemed as if he always showed when Bianca was around.

Bianca shook her head, pacing down the sidewalk with Casper in front of her. When her phone buzzed inside her pocket, she smiled at the picture of her mother. Pixie haircut, round face, and fine lines around her eyes. Her mother's smooth brown skin glowed and Bianca prayed she would still take care of herself, as her mother did at age sixty. "Hey, Mom?"

"Hi, sweetie. I'm calling to let you know I can't make dinner this evening with you all," her mother said.

"Okay. No problem. Anything wrong?"

Her mother cleared her throat. "Oh, nothing."

"Nothing, huh?" Should Bianca dig into her mother's personal life? Would this have anything to do with Luther Burkes? No harm in rattling her mother a little. "Got a hot date?"

"Bianca Wallace!" her mother exclaimed.

She covered her mouth to stifle her giggles. "Can't blame me for asking. As if you wouldn't if I canceled plans on you."

"Honestly, I don't know who's worse. You or Melanie."

"Melanie knows already?"

"I sent her a text since she didn't answer the phone. How many kissy face emojis should a person send?" her mother replied.

Bianca laughed harder.

"I will see you girls' next time. If I *choose* to give you details then, that will be my choice," her mother said.

"Have fun, Mom." Bianca added.

Her mother sighed. "I know you and your sister mean well." A giggle escaped her. "I just didn't expect the two of you to remind me so much of..."

"You?" Bianca answered.

"Exactly," her mother said. Both of them laughed this time. "Anyway. Are you excited about the fashion show this weekend? This is a tremendous event for Edenville."

"I think so. I have an outfit, so no problem there," Bianca said. She followed behind Casper once more, passing through the large trees in the front yards of her neighbors. Today, the blue sky was free of clouds and the sun glowed.

It wasn't quite summer in Edenville, but it would be soon. Temperatures ranged between eighty to ninety degrees. If not hot, it would rain, although there weren't storms forecasted for the last week. Bianca would take it along with summer, taking its time to arrive.

Alyssa would leave to visit her father. Malcom and his wife, Hope. Bianca squared her shoulders as she paced along the sidewalk. How would Hope treat Alyssa? Would they get along? Would Alyssa like her? Bianca wouldn't tell her daughter to be uncivil, but a stepmother would be new for her.

Casper barked, disrupting Bianca's thoughts. He dug his paws into the grass. Thank goodness it was an empty lot and not one of her neighbors' yards.

"Looking for something?" she asked him.

He barked again, and since he came up short with whatever he was looking for, he trotted again ahead of her. Bianca shook her head slightly, smiling to herself. Then Melanie's words came to mind. Perhaps she was right about Bianca enjoying herself and taking more time for fun. With Alyssa leaving, she wouldn't want to lock herself in her home waiting for her baby girl to return.

"What can I do?" Bianca asked, grateful that no one was around to hear her talk to herself. Attending the fashion show would be fun. What else? Bianca chewed at her bottom lip. Something fun? Perhaps trying a new activity?

Like what? The flutters in her stomach increased. She knew she didn't have to figure it out all in one day. Thank goodness.

Deciding to return home, she nudged Casper back toward her house. He must have been ready too, since he didn't resist. Her keys jingled, opening the front door once she arrived. She caught Alyssa in the living room, sitting on the couch, watching reality TV. Bianca didn't care about the scripted drama series, but Alyssa found it entertaining. Once she unleased Casper, he sprinted to her daughter's side.

"I guess he missed you," Bianca said to Alyssa.

Alyssa scratched the dog behind his ears. Then she faced her mother. "We may have a… problem with dinner tonight."

"What?" Bianca asked.

"We don't have any cheese or sauce."

Bianca shook her head. "No, I went to the store last week." Walking to her pantry, she opened the doors. Scanning the shelves for the sauce, she didn't see what else Melanie needed to cook. Then Bianca moved to the refrigerator, opened it, and squatted to the floor to check the bottom drawer. A *tsk* escaped her mouth. "You've got to be kidding. I made a list."

"I can call Aunt Mel and let her know," Alyssa said.

Bianca shook her head. "No. I'll go. She hasn't seen this friend of hers in a while, so I'm sure they're still hanging out." After making a quick trip to her bedroom to change and to grab her purse, Bianca returned to her living room. She asked Alyssa, "Is there anything else we need?"

Her daughter shook her head.

She pointed to her. "If I'm on my way home by the time you think of something, I'm not going back inside."

Alyssa giggled. "Fine, Mom."

Bianca smiled, heading to the garage for her car.

BIANCA TAPPED HER FINGERS on her lips. Staring at the contents in her grocery basket, she wondered if she was missing anything else. Pasta for the lasagna. Check. Marinara sauce. Check. Cheese. Check. Twisting her mouth as she pondered, nothing else came to mind.

She pushed her cart forward, listening to the music through the speakers. Then she paused. She knew this song. Her lips parted as Janet Jackson's "Come Back to Me" played. Bianca couldn't help but laugh. She hadn't heard the song in years. Shaking her head, she walked to the checkout area. The bleep of items being checked out caught her ears next.

The store wasn't too crowded, despite it being a late Thursday afternoon, but Bianca waved at the familiar faces. Ms. Ella, the woman who owned the floral shop, was one of them. Ivory skin, lean, and narrow pink lips. She didn't have a hat on today, although the town knew the middle-aged woman for wearing a hat with almost any outfit she wore.

After checking out, Bianca grabbed her bags and walked to her royal blue Kia Soul. Opening the trunk, the plastic bags rustled as she placed them on the floor. Loud voices flooded her ears. Was someone shouting?

Turning on her heels, she spotted two men arguing ahead of her. One was tall, bald, athletic, while the other was a few inches shorter, stocky, with a buzzed haircut. Bianca looked away. Perhaps they were arguing over a parking space. Was it that serious, though? Then again, arguments over trivial matters weren't too uncommon in today's world.

"And you keep away from Sherry!"

Bianca's ears perked. Sherry? Melanie's friend Sherry? No. Too much of a coincidence. Bianca turned her head. Which one had said it?

The stocky man inched forward to the taller man. "Are you threatening me?"

The tall man didn't flinch, but his fist clenched at his side. "I'm telling you. Keep *away* from her. It's over."

Did Sherry have a stalker? Bianca held back her gasp. Did she know these men were talking about her? Was she in trouble?

The shorter man raised his hands in a surrendered gesture. His demeanor appeared calm compared to the taller man. "No need to get hostile."

The taller man pointed to his face. "Don't patronize me."

"I'm not doing anything to you. I came to have a civil conversation, but I guess you're not up for it. I'm going to be the bigger person before things escalate. I'll see you around." Then he stalked off to his car, champagne in color.

"Bianca?"

She jerked at the sound of her name, but when she saw who it was, she breathed easier. Detective Sims. Lamar. His gray eyes never ceased to make her fingers tingle. Although she had to get used to him calling her "Bianca." It had taken him a while since he was fairly new in town, but after she'd helped him solve his previous murder case, he'd warmed up to her.

Bianca pressed a hand to her chest. "I wish you wouldn't do that."

He chuckled. "I thought something was wrong, so I wanted to check."

Today, he wasn't in uniform. Was it his day off? Dark jeans, a gray T-shirt that complemented his brown skin, and not the mention the stubble on his chin that lined his jaw perfectly. Bianca licked her lips, willing her body to get a hold of itself.

"I'm fine, thank you," she assured him. Had he heard the argument? Bianca looked again, but both men were gone. "I was just... getting ready to head home."

He bobbed his head.

"What are you getting?" She gestured to the entry doors of the grocery store.

He stuffed his hands inside his pocket. "I'm not sure. I'm not the best cook in the world."

"Let me guess. Takeout?" she teased him.

He laughed, revealing his bright smile. "Sometimes, but I'm working on my culinary skills."

She grinned. "Well... spaghetti is easy to make. Unless you overcook the pasta."

He shook his head. "I didn't say I was *that* bad."

She exhaled. "Good. I've seen some posts on social media that even I'm like, *how did this person mess up that recipe?*"

"Like what?" he asked, intrigued.

"I've seen burnt grilled cheese sandwiches, pasta stuck to the ceiling, and I don't even know how one person ruined the stove with cheese." She covered her forehead with her hand. "I was embarrassed for them."

Detective Sims only laughed. She joined in with him.

"That sounds terrible," he said.

When her phone rang, Bianca reached for her purse, still hanging on her arm. "I'm sorry."

He shook his head. "Don't worry. Take it. I won't keep you."

Bianca spotted her sister's name. "It's Melanie. I'm sure it won't take long." She answered and put the phone to her ear. "Yeah, Mel?"

"You're at the store?" she asked.

"Yeah. Alyssa said we needed some things for tonight. You had fun with Sherry?"

"It was amazing! So glad we could meet up. I'm on my way home now. Just checking in with you. Are you leaving now?" Melanie asked.

"I am. Just talking to a friend," she said.

"Who? Judy?" Judy Long owned R&J's Restaurant and Bakery in Edenville with her husband Richard Long. Though in her late forties, she married ten years her senior. Bianca thought of the redhead with green eyes as a close friend and mentor, especially with advice about Bianca's love life. Bianca didn't care to hear it, but she listened. The age difference didn't matter between them, since the friends were kindred in spirit.

Judy and Richard's business was getting back on track, especially after being in debt to his deceased stepbrother. Martin. His murder made headlines in town, and when she found out he was blackmailing Richard, she wondered if his own stepbrother committed the crime. Thank goodness he didn't.

"No." Bianca's scalp prickled.

Silence.

From the corner of her eye, Detective Sims wasn't standing too far away from her, scrolling through his phone. He hadn't left? Did that mean he wanted to keep talking to her? Bianca swallowed.

"Bianca?" Melanie pressed further. "Never mind. I think I know who. And if it's who I think it is, invite him over for dinner."

"What?" Bianca exclaimed.

"Everything okay?" Detective Sims asked.

"Yes," Bianca said.

"Perfect," Melanie replied. "Tell him seven-thirty and don't be late."

"What?" Had Bianca heard that right? "No, Melanie. Melanie?" Nothing. Great. Now Melanie was expecting him to come over for dinner. "Just great."

"Bianca?" he repeated.

"Um... I don't know if you want to cook still, but my sister apparently thinks you should join us for dinner."

He tilted his head to the side. "Really?"

Bianca bobbed her head.

"What do *you* think?" He inched closer.

Bianca's breath caught in her throat. "I mean... you're still sort of new in town. Plus, you *saved* our lives not too long ago." Why was she justifying this? Why couldn't she say he didn't have to come, wish him well, and go home?

"So... this is an official *thank you* dinner?"

"If you want to call it that. Or just a friendly dinner," Bianca said. Why did he make her feel like a bumbling teenager?

Detective Sims grinned. "What time?"

"Seven-thirty works for us," Bianca said. "Do I need to send you my address again?"

He shook his head. "I remember the way." Then he took a few steps backwards. "See you tonight." Finally, he turned and headed inside the store.

Bianca exhaled. What had she just done? Why wasn't she too freaked out about him coming to dinner?

Chapter 3

Melanie left the cooked lasagna in the oven to keep it warm. Bianca stared at the table. Four plates, glasses, and napkins, with each plate having its own set of silverware. When Bianca glanced at the clock on the wall, the ticks only made her muscles twitch even more. Detective Sims would arrive in thirty minutes, and after changing her outfit three times, Bianca settled for a strapless, floral, knee-length dress with her wedged heels.

"Would you stop fidgeting?" Melanie said as she sliced the garlic bread at the counter. "You're acting as if this is a date."

Bianca narrowed her eyes at her sister. "Hilarious. Thanks to you, I'm not wearing yoga pants."

Melanie eyeballed her. "No. Some things we just don't do when guests come over."

Just like their mother. Bianca's shoulders slumped. Casper lapped at his filled water bowl and wasn't Alyssa finished getting ready for their guest. Wringing her hands together, Bianca walked to her daughter's room. She tapped on the door.

"Come in," Alyssa said.

Bianca entered her teenager's room. She'd stacked a few books on her desk, but her laptop was closed. Alyssa sat at the foot of her bed. "Something wrong, Mom?"

Was anything wrong? Was it only Bianca's nerves that made the hairs on the back of her head stand at attention? This wasn't a date, but why did it feel as if she were bringing another man into her daughter's life? No one had come over for dinner before. *It's nothing.*

"Just checking on you." She folded her arms over her chest.

Alyssa nodded, but didn't say a word.

Bianca walked closer. "Everything okay?"

"I don't know. I think so. He hasn't..." she said.

Who? "You mean... Kendrick?"

Alyssa nodded. "I guess with me leaving to visit Dad this summer... I don't know if that's a good or bad thing."

Bianca sat next to her daughter. "Have you two talked about it?"

"Not really. I guess I've been avoiding it. Things have been so great between us. I don't want to ruin things."

"How would you ruin it, sweetie?" Bianca asked.

"Well... I'm wondering about the distance. Me in California and him here in Texas. I enjoy spending time with him at school and when we hang with friends on the weekends."

Bianca draped an arm around her daughter's shoulders. "You don't have to be together all the time. That's not always healthy. Sometimes you need space. You're still your own person, and so is he."

Alyssa sighed. "Why is this so complicated?"

"It doesn't have to be. Remember what I told you?"

"Be myself."

She brought her closer to her in a side hug. "That's my girl."

"Mom?"

"I know. You're getting too old for hugs." Bianca pulled back, despite the twinge in her chest. Her baby was growing up. Alyssa would need her less.

"No. I'm sorry." She faced her. Her brown eyes shined. "Thanks for always being there."

Bianca tapped a finger on her daughter's nose. "Always."

When the doorbell rang, Bianca flinched, hoping Alyssa didn't notice. Casper barked.

"Mom. Are you okay?" her daughter asked.

Bianca cleared her throat. "Sure. Why wouldn't I be?"

Her daughter folded her arms. "Mom?"

"Finish getting ready." She stood to her feet, heading to the door, but stopped and turned around. She pointed to her daughter. "I don't care what your Aunt Mel says—be on your best behavior."

Alyssa mimicked, zipping her lips.

Bianca's eyes widened. "I mean it." Entering the hallway, she willed her stomach to stop jumping, but hearing Detective Sims' deep and husky voice only made her stomach quiver further. "Breathe," she whispered to herself. "It's just dinner."

"So glad you could make it," Melanie said.

Casper stood on his hind legs at Detective Sims' feet. The detective bent to pet the dog, giving him what looked like a nice massage along his back. "Thanks for having me." Then he straightened and spotted Bianca. His smile returned. "Hi."

"Hi," she said.

"Sis, why don't you show Detective Sims the guest bathroom so he can wash up for dinner?" Melanie suggested.

Bianca gestured to the hallway. "Follow me."

He did. "Nice place. Glad I'm not here with a gun in my hand like last time. I can finally see the house."

Bianca would never forget the night that had almost turned deadly, when Priscilla Davis had pointed a gun at her. Thank goodness Melanie had called Detective Sims. "Me too. To think that wasn't too long ago." She pointed inside the half-bathroom. "There you go."

He moved past her. "Thanks."

She caught a whiff of his cologne. Woodsy this time around, and becoming one of her favorite scents on him. "I'll give you a minute."

Bianca walked back to the living room and spotted Melanie in the kitchen.

"Not bad, huh?" Melanie said. "It's different seeing him this relaxed. Though I know he needs to be serious about his job."

"This is not a big deal. Remember that," Bianca reminded her.

Melanie's eyes softened. "I know. It's just dinner. I won't start anything."

Alyssa's laugh caught Bianca's ears, and she saw her daughter walk down the hallway alongside Detective Sims. So far, so good. She wasn't terrorizing him with a teenage attitude. While Alyssa had her moments, she was, overall, a good kid.

"Smells amazing," Detective Sims said.

"Dinner's ready," Melanie announced, with the lasagna pan in her hand. She placed it on the table. "Alyssa, you're next to me, right?"

Bianca held back from commenting, but she wondered if her mother had put Melanie up to this arranged dinner. She turned to Detective Sims. "Have a seat, please."

He did, and Bianca slid into the seat next to him. As she scooted herself forward, her knee brushed against his. "Sorry about that."

"Don't worry about it." The corner of his mouth lifted into a soft smile.

"Shall we say grace?" Melanie suggested. Extending her hand to Alyssa, Bianca's daughter reached for the detective's. Bianca placed her hand in Detective Sims' hand as well. She ignored the tingles up her arm and by the time her sister had finished saying the blessing, Bianca cleared her throat. How was she going to get through dinner with him this close to her?

"Great as always, Auntie," Alyssa said.

"Thank you." Melanie nudged her niece's shoulder.

"This is incredible," Detective Sims added. "I haven't had a homecooked meal like this in a long time."

"It's our mother's recipe," Melanie said.

"You both cook?" he asked, gesturing between Bianca and her sister.

Bianca swallowed before answering. "I do, but Melanie's lasagna tastes better than mine. Although I will say my best dish is our mom's chicken fried steaks."

"Agreed," Alyssa chimed in. "The best."

"Thank you." She winked at her daughter.

"So do you have family in town, detective?" Melanie asked, before sipping the tea from her glass.

He shook his head. "Not in town. My mom lives in Waco with my stepdad. I visit when I can."

"Why did you move here?" Alyssa asked.

Bianca said, "You don't have to answer that." She didn't want him to feel as if they were prying.

"No, I don't mind answering. The best way I could put it is... I needed a change. What used to work for me didn't anymore, so I made the move," he explained.

Was there more to the story? Like a relationship gone sour? Bianca wouldn't ask.

"Well... I wouldn't live anywhere else, so you picked an amazing place here. We rarely have... too many crimes," Melanie said. Then she tugged at the collar of her shirt. "I think Martin's murder was a rare thing. Hopefully, it was."

"I hope so too," Bianca agreed. At the sound of buzzing, she noticed Alyssa taking out her phone. "Phone?"

"Mom, it's Kendrick." Her eyeballs widened, as if pleading with her to let her take it. "Can I finish dinner in my room? Please?"

Bianca sighed. "Go ahead." She could make an exception now and then, but they would need to have another talk. She didn't want her daughter to get too caught up in a boy.

"Thank you. Excuse me. Nice to see you again, detective." Alyssa picked up her plate. She hurried to her room, with Casper following her.

"You too," he said.

"Watching her makes me feel old." Melanie groaned.

Bianca giggled. "Why?"

"I can't believe she's almost grown. What are you going to do?"

"Buy a gun if any more boys come over." Bianca gasped, facing Detective Sims. "Not that I would injure them on purpose."

He chuckled. "Self-defense is not murder, Bianca, but I will watch you."

She swallowed. Watch her? No. It meant nothing. Even if it did, harmless flirting was just that—harmless.

By the time they'd finished their meal and cleared the table, Melanie insisted she could clean the kitchen herself. "Would you like some coffee?" she asked Detective Sims.

He shook his head. "No, thanks." Then he checked his watch. "I need to head out, anyway. Thank you for dinner. It was great."

"I'll walk you to the door." Bianca walked in front of him. Alyssa came out of her room with her empty plate in hand.

"Bye, Detective Sims," she said. Casper's paws padded on the hardwood floors.

"Goodnight, Alyssa," he replied with a wave.

Bianca opened the door and led him to her porch. An astounding display of stars filled the sky, and she was grateful for the cool breeze. "I hope my family wasn't—"

"I enjoyed it, so no worries." His gray eyes sparkled.

Bianca's breath caught again.

"It got me thinking, though."

"About what?" She rubbed at her arms, but it wasn't the chill of the night that gave her goosebumps.

"Your chicken fried steak." Then his smile got bigger.

She laughed. "We'll see."

He bobbed his head. "I guess we will." He paused for another moment, tucking in his bottom lip. Then he said, "Goodnight, Bianca."

"Goodnight."

He descended the few steps to the walkway, and Bianca watched him proceed to his car. Then she turned her back on him and went inside.

THAT FRIDAY EVENING, Melanie and Bianca visited Sherry at rehearsal before the fashion show the next night. Passing by security guards with black caps and dark blue uniforms, they entered through the doors and proceeded to the ballroom. What a transformation. Bianca couldn't believe how they converted the space to a full stage and runway for the models. Cushioned chairs lined both sides of the stage and a podium was on the right side of the room.

How many people were attending? Would more celebrities show? According to Melanie, Sherry had invited them to watch their last rehearsal before the big event.

Bianca's eyes drifted to the stage and the runway, being held up on stage blocks. She spotted a few men and women taking turns on the walkway. A woman with long, auburn hair, tall, held up her hands to stop the models.

"Let's run through it once more." She motioned them to walk back towards her. She had to be the backstage manager or the producer of the show. Glancing over to one table, covered in black tablecloth, Bianca spotted the various charities the show was donating fifty percent of their funds to. Helping Hands, which fed the homeless, a children's hospital, and a cancer treatment center. Bianca touched a hand to her chest. She could never turn down supporting a good cause.

"I didn't expect this," Melanie said, leaning in closer so her sister could hear her.

"Me, neither." Bianca stepped forward. People crowded the place, and the voices ranged from loud talking to murmuring. There was a mixture of sweet perfume and cologne in the air.

Her eyes glanced at the banners for Clique Classic. A logo of golden letters where the Cs overlapped each other. She had given the logo a contemporary touch, and the elegant scripting of the letters gave it a balanced look.

"Critiquing yourself again?" Melanie teased, nudging her shoulder.

"I don't critique my work." Bianca denied the notion, despite the perfectionism that creeped out of her. Still, she pulled in a deep breath. Who knew how much publicity this would give Wallace Designs? Bianca would take plenty of pictures tonight for her portfolio and have Veronica add them to the photo gallery on her website.

Melanie laughed.

Stepping to the side, Bianca bumped into a woman. "Excuse me."

Balancing once again on her feet, she saw the woman's face. Red, long hair. Sea-blue eyes. The woman wore a blue paisley-patterned jumpsuit complementing her petite frame. With her makeup as flawless as it looked, Bianca had to wonder if the woman was a model in the show.

"So sorry," she said.

"No, forgive me," Bianca added. "It's a little crowded in here."

The woman extended her manicured, slender fingers. "I'm Paris Deveraux."

"Bianca Wallace. This is my sister, Melanie Wallace."

The women took turns shaking hands.

"You're in the show?" Melanie gestured at her outfit.

Paris giggled. "I am. I'm part of the ending, so I'm looking forward to closing it out with a *bang*." She flipped her hair. Her confidence clear.

"We look forward to it," Bianca said.

"I think Sherry's part of the opening, so it's going to be fantastic!" Melanie added.

"Oh... Sherry." Paris' face dropped. "You know her well?"

"I've known her since high school," Melanie said.

Paris forced a smile. "How nice." Then she walked away without another word.

"Okay..." Bianca raised her eyebrows. Obviously, Paris didn't care for Sherry.

"Well, regardless of what beef there is going on between the models, this is going to be so much fun tomorrow night!" Melanie bounced on her toes. "Let's find Sherry."

Bianca and Melanie pressed through the clustered groups of people. By the time they made it backstage, she made eye contact with another petite woman with long, dark brown hair pulled into a low ponytail. Red-rimmed glasses rested on her narrow nose. She had olive skin and a mole on her right cheek.

"Excuse me," Melanie said to the woman. "Do you know where we can find Sherry Wilson? I'm a friend of hers."

The woman tilted her head. "Melanie Wallace. Right?"

"Yes," her sister confirmed. "This is my sister, Bianca."

"Nice to meet you," Bianca said with a smile.

The woman gestured for them to follow her. "I'm Sherry's stepsister, Jacqueline. She's expecting you."

"Sherry told me about you at our brunch," Melanie said. "She said you were running errands, but you could have joined us."

"Well, my errands took longer than expected. Being her personal assistant is no simple job." Jacqueline paused in front of the door and knocked.

"*Who is it?*" Sherry exclaimed.

Bianca blinked. Sherry sounded irritated. Was this a bad time? "We can come back later."

Jacqueline shook her head. "Give me a minute, won't you?" She walked inside, leaving Melanie and Bianca in the hallway.

"She sounds upset," Melanie pointed out. "Maybe it's best we see her after the show. I'm sure she's under stress."

"Maybe." Bianca heard the women's voices, but the closed door muffled them.

Jacqueline opened the door and exhaled. "Come in. Sorry about that." She gestured for them to come inside Sherry's dressing room.

"We don't want to intrude," Bianca said.

Sherry waved them inside. "Sorry about that. I couldn't find my ring." She held up her right hand. Nothing fancy, but a simple gold band with what looked like a small, emerald cut stone. "I hardly ever take it off. My mother gave it to me, so it means a lot since she's gone."

Bianca sat in a nearby chair. "I'm sorry to hear that. What was it?"

"Breast cancer." Sherry's eyes shined, but she didn't cry. "Anyway, I'm glad you two could visit before things get really crazy around here."

Melanie pointed outside the door. "It gets worse?"

The women laughed. Jacqueline gave a faint smile, but she said little.

"So I have a request for you." Melanie continued.

"Mel, I don't—" Bianca tried to stop her, but her baby sister overruled.

"What is it?" Sherry leaned in as if to get in on the secret.

"I told you about my niece. I know the show is for ticket holders only, but is there any way we can bring her? I know she'll love meeting you."

Bianca shook her head since her daughter never expressed to her the desire to attend the show. Was this another moment Alyssa only shared with her aunt?

"Are you kidding me?" Sherry beamed. "Of course. I can work something out with Giselle. She can even meet up with me after the show. I'd love to meet her."

"Thank you," Bianca said. "I can't imagine why Alyssa didn't tell me."

Melanie nudged her shoulder. "I'm the cool aunt. Besides, it's not as if we kept it from you. I mentioned it to her last night before bed. You were working late in your home office."

Bianca couldn't deny it. She thought she heard giggling from Alyssa's room, but thought nothing of it. She knew how close her sister was to her daughter.

"Anyway." Melanie reached for her friend's hand. "I know you don't have to, but thank you. I think this will be a great experience for Alyssa."

Sherry gave a soft smile. "You're a great aunt, and I hope she enjoys it. I love my career but..."

"What?" Melanie released her hand.

Sherry continued. "Trust me, I love what I do, but it's not all glamorous. I live out of a suitcase. Sometimes I wonder what it would be like to have a normal life. Maybe in a small town like this." She smiled at Melanie. "I'm sorting a lot of things out right now, but I'll tell you soon."

"There's more than what you've told me already?" Melanie laughed.

Sherry winked at her, but her smile was faint.

"You like Edenville so far?" Bianca asked.

"I like the slower pace." Then she shrugged with a laugh. "Maybe one day. Who knows? Maybe I'll share my experiences in a book."

That'd be an interesting read. Not the first time a celebrity wrote a book.

"I can't see Aiden living here, though," Jacqueline chimed in.

The women turned to look at her. Who was Aiden?

Sherry cleared her throat. "That won't be an issue anymore."

"You went through with it, didn't you?" Melanie asked. Went through with what?

Sherry rubbed the back of her neck. "Yes, I broke up with him. You were right. We're in two very different places."

"You didn't tell me," Jacqueline pointed out. Then she inched closer. "Why am I just now hearing this?"

Sherry's tone turned serious. "I'd rather not talk about this now. Okay?"

Her stepsister flinched, as if her words stung.

When a buzzing sound took over the room, Sherry grabbed her phone and handed it to Jacqueline. "Put her on speaker."

Jacqueline took her phone. "Hi, Mom."

"Should we go?" Melanie whispered to Sherry.

Her friend shook her head. "She's only calling to check up on me."

Bianca swallowed because of the bite in Sherry's voice. Perhaps it was better if they left, but she followed her sister's lead.

"I heard that," an alto voice replied through the phone. "I hate when she gets like this."

"It's my nerves, Joan," Sherry said. "You know that well enough by now. Is there something you wanted?"

"How are you, Mom?" Jacqueline asked.

"I'm fine, just checking on my girls," Joan said. "Are we excited? I hear this new clothing line is going to be the next big thing! Did your father call you?"

Sherry forced a smile. Was she annoyed? Was it the stress of the upcoming weekend alone? Not excited to see her dad? Bianca wrung her hands together in her lap.

"I can't talk to him now," Sherry said.

Joan continued. "But he's coming to see you, dear. He's taking time out of his busy schedule to see his top model daughter."

"Are you sure *he's* not up to something?" Sherry asked, her voice full of suspicion.

"Is it the show? You always get antsy before a show." Joan asked.

Jacqueline interjected. "Mom, can we call you back later? I have some last-minute things to do for Sherry."

"I *called* to talk to her, but like always, she's giving me the runaround," Joan commented with a hint of annoyance in her own voice.

"Sure, Joan. Nice to hear from you." Sherry flipped her hair, crossing one of her lean legs over the other.

"I'll call you later, Jacqueline. Hopefully, your *sister* will be in a better mood." She hung up.

Jacqueline handed Sherry's phone back to her.

"Everything... okay?" Melanie asked, gesturing back and forth between the two stepsisters.

"Don't tell me you and your family get along all the time?" Sherry pointed out.

Bianca glanced at Melanie. "We've... had our share of differences, especially growing up."

Melanie held up a hand. "I will admit, she came through for me when I got my first boyfriend. Bianca caught him under the bleachers in the gym with another girl."

Sherry snapped her fingers. "I remember him. Didn't you dump food on his head in the cafeteria?"

Melanie tucked a tendril of hair behind her ear. "Not my finest moment."

They laughed. All except for Jacqueline, who forced a smile.

Bianca chimed in, directing her comment to the stepsisters. "I'm sure you two have some memories you can laugh about now." She didn't understand why she wanted to diffuse whatever tension was in the room, but why did her heart go out to Jacqueline? Was she the failure in the family, as opposed to Sherry's successful life?

"None that I can think of right now," Sherry commented. "She's an excellent assistant, though. Expecting almost my every need."

Jacqueline gave a faint smile. Then she cleared her throat. "Do you need anything now?"

"Can you get me something to drink?" Sherry asked her.

"Fine." Then Jaqueline walked to the door. "I'll... be back." She closed the door behind her.

Melanie tilted her head to the side at Sherry. "I thought you two were getting better."

Sherry waved her comment away. "I've tried, but I'm tired. I realize all we have in common is my father married her mother. I can't trust her with anything else." Sherry sighed. "Sorry. I've said too much. I didn't mean to drag you two into my drama."

"Maybe you two can make up," Bianca said. She hoped so. Having a sister was one of the biggest blessings in her life. It was too bad when others couldn't experience what she had with her family.

"It's best that we keep it professional," Sherry explained. "My dad is... well, we have our moments. Joan, I can tolerate her, and Jacqueline gets her job done, but... I can only do so much. So I've expected that not all families are close, even if it's blended like ours."

"Things can change for the better, right?" Melanie pointed out.

"Maybe, but I gave up on that dream," Sherry said. When a buzzing noise filled the air again, she reached for her phone again. "Why won't he stop calling me?"

"Aiden?" Melanie asked.

Sherry exhaled. "I hate to rush you two, but I have a lot to do before the show tomorrow."

Bianca stood to her feet. "Sure. No problem."

Melanie walked over and hugged her friend. "Call me if you need to talk."

Sherry gave her a faint smile. "I will."

Melanie followed behind Bianca outside the door.

"I hope she's okay," her sister said.

"It got me thinking." Bianca nibbled at her bottom lip.

"About what?"

"You saw how Jacqueline responded when Sherry didn't tell her about the breakup?" Bianca pointed out.

"Yeah. She looked disappointed, but Sherry says they're not close," Melanie said.

They continued past the crowd in the ballroom and to the front doors. How much had Sherry shared at her lunch with Melanie?

"What else did she tell you?" Bianca asked.

Melanie rubbed at her shoulder. "Only that her father *begged* Sherry to hire Jacqueline."

Bianca's eyebrows raised. "Really?" What was the story behind that?

"Where is she?" a bass voice said from behind them.

Bianca turned around. Melanie stopped in her tracks as well. A man headed to the front doors, but the security guards stopped him. She didn't know his face.

One guard held up his hand to the man. "Sir, only names on the list can enter the venue. This is a closed event for ticket holders only. I'm sorry, but your name's not listed."

"Who is that?" Bianca whispered to her sister.

Melanie whispered back, "I don't know. Your guess is as good as mine."

"But I have to see Sherry Wilson," the man continued. Olive skin, mussed sandy brown hair, a square jaw, and only five-nine.

The other guard asked the man, "Is she expecting you?"

The man answered, "We have *business* to discuss." Was that a smirk on his face?

Business? Like what? Bianca's heart pounded at the anticipation.

"We should go," Melanie said as she retrieved her phone from her purse.

"Who are you calling?" Bianca wondered.

"Sherry." Melanie took a few steps back. "Sherry? There's a guy outside wanting to see you. No. I don't recognize him, but he said you two had business. So far, security won't let him in. Do you—oh? Okay. If you say so. See you tomorrow." Melanie hung up and returned her phone to her purse.

Bianca watched as the man stalked off back to his car. The same car at the grocery store. Champagne color, but she noticed this time it was a Chevrolet Impala. "What did Sherry say?"

"It's not anybody she knows," Melanie said. "I don't know who this guy is, but Sherry wasn't meeting anyone."

Bianca wished she knew who the person was. Something was brewing and her gut told her it wasn't good.

Chapter 4

"Excuse me." The following Saturday evening, Bianca pressed through the crowd at the fashion show, following Melanie and Alyssa to their seats. She hadn't expected to be this close to the stage, but Melanie had said Sherry not only got an extra ticket for Alyssa, but upgraded all their tickets. Music blared through the speakers as people murmured and talked before the show started. Sweet perfume mixed with crisp cologne filled the air.

Bianca took care not to fall in her leopard print five-inch heels, but she had to admit that she loved her outfit. With red lipstick, flawless makeup, and her hair in loose curls in a half-updo style, Bianca felt confident. Her lungs expanded to the fullest in a deep, satisfying breath.

Alyssa's style a choice was wearing her aunt's black and gray block colored sleeveless dress with three inch black heels. Bianca winced. Getting used to her daughter looking more like an adult every day was challenging, but she managed as best she could.

"Here we go." Melanie pointed to their seats. Her outfit included black pumps and the leopard-print sleeveless dress she'd tried to get Bianca to buy. She'd straightened her hair, and the bright light made her locks shine all the more. Melanie sat, followed by Bianca and Alyssa. "I'm excited!"

"Me too," Bianca added. Casper was safe and sound with her mother. Bianca smiled, ready to enjoy a night out with her sister and daughter.

Alyssa grabbed her phone. "I have to go live on my Instagram!"

"Right now?" Bianca thought a simple Facebook page was enough for her, but Alyssa had over one thousand followers on her Instagram page.

"Why not, Mom?" Alyssa fluffed her loose curls as she stared at herself on camera. "Chloe still won't believe this! I promised I'd take pictures with as many celebrities as I could."

Bianca held back her laugh. Her daughter and best friend were definitely part of the new generation that had to post everything on social media. Bianca barely recalled her excitement when she got her first cell phone.

Melanie then squinted her eyes at her. "Aren't you glad you came, sis?"

"Yes," Bianca admitted. "You were right." She nudged her shoulder. "And it's good for business."

Bianca perked up when a familiar tune played through the speakers. "Dance with Me" by the R&B group 112. "Do you remember this one?"

Melanie raised her hands in the air. "Yes!" Then she shimmied her shoulders as she danced to the beat.

Bianca snapped her fingers to the tune. "Takes me back."

"Who is this?" Alyssa asked, her face scrunched in confusion.

Melanie giggled. "Don't worry about."

When Bianca's phone buzzed inside her purse, she wondered if it was her mother. Was something wrong? No. It wasn't her mother. It was Nicole. Bianca didn't want to miss the opening of the show, but she wanted to see her friend, who was FaceTiming her.

Looking around to make sure the show wasn't about to get started, Bianca answered. "Hey, married lady." She waved through the screen.

Nicole smiled. Long blonde hair, blue eyes, and a bright smile. Her best friend held her arms out as if to hug the world. "Hey! I've missed you."

"I miss you too." Bianca called out, despite the chattering of voices in the background.

Nicole's forehead wrinkled. "Where are you, all dressed up?"

"Fashion show with Melanie and Alyssa." She turned her phone so they could say *hello*.

"Hey, Nicole," Melanie said, still snapping her fingers at the music.

"Hi Aunt Nicole." Alyssa waved with a beaming smile.

Nicole laughed. "It looks like you're having fun. I just wanted to say *hi* real quick. Alyssa, is that lipstick?"

Alyssa wrapped an arm around her mother's shoulders. "Aunt Mel and I talked her into it. Like it?" She puckered her full lips, glossed with plum lipstick.

"I can't get used to it." Nicole touched a hand to her chest.

"I can't either." Bianca changed the subject. "How's the honeymoon?" she asked, despite the background noise.

"Great. Remember how I said we extended our trip?"

"Yeah," Bianca replied.

"Well, we're heading to London," Nicole said. Her eyes danced. "It's been amazing, Bianca."

"I'm happy for you." She blew her a kiss through the phone. "Tell Chad I said *hi* and I'll see you both when you get back."

"Bye, Nicole," Melanie added.

Alyssa waved goodbye too.

Nicole blew a kiss back. "Bye." With that, she hung up.

"She looks happy," Melanie said.

Bianca stuffed her phone back inside her purse. "I'm glad, especially after everything they went through."

"Where's the restroom? If I go now, I won't miss the beginning of the show." Alyssa stood to her feet.

Melanie pointed to the opposite side of the ballroom.

Bianca stood too. "I'll go with you."

Alyssa shook her head. "I can find it myself. Don't worry. I won't get lost." Excusing herself past the other attendees in their row, Bianca watched her daughter press through the crowd.

"She's almost seventeen, Bianca." Melanie reminded her.

Bianca returned to her seat. "I know, Mel. It's just unnerving. She's almost seventeen, has a boyfriend, and close to graduating high school."

A *hmm* escaped Melanie's lips. "I know. I still can't believe it, but enough of that. We're here to support Sherry and have some fun!"

Bianca giggled at her sister's enthusiasm, forgetting the empty nester syndrome that was creeping up her spine. Once 112's song concluded, the lights dimmed. A shush took over the room, and Bianca crossed her legs. Melanie practically squealed in her seat. Spotlights and special lighting highlighted the catwalk. Then Bianca heard a woman's voice over the microphone.

Thanks to the camera zooming in, Bianca could get a better look at the image on the monitor. The woman was curvy, with long, strawberry-blonde hair and a bright smile dancing across her full face. Though she had only talked to her through Zoom when she hired her, Bianca recognized Giselle Porter. "Welcome, ladies and gentlemen. I'm your host, Giselle, and I'm happy to present to you this evening, our Clique Classic fashion showcase!"

The audience applauded and cheered.

"Amazing!" Melanie squealed.

Giselle continued. "We'll be including our classic pieces this evening. "I'm also pleased to announce that since the scenery of this Edenville has struck me, I want our models to have their pictures taken around town after tonight's first show! So... we're going to be in Edenville for the next month!" The crowd cheered again.

"All month? That's amazing!" Melanie exclaimed to her sister over the applause.

Bianca's lips parted, speechless. Imagine how much publicity a month-long fashion event would bring to the town? Were more models attending? That would be a perfect networking opportunity for Bianca, since she did the graphics for the fashion show. Giselle already wrote a five-star review on her website. It was a matter of time before new clients came Bianca's way.

Giselle said, "For tonight, we're going to give you a preview of our upcoming summer line!"

More cheers and whoops erupted from the crowd. Bianca giggled at the excitement. While she purchased nothing from Clique Classic herself—too out-of-the-box for her simple taste—the clothing line had a few items that piqued her interest. When she spotted Alyssa making her way back to her seat, Bianca stood to her feet. She noticed Alyssa looked back a few times, but she didn't break her stride. When her daughter reached her, she touched her arm.

"Everything okay?" she asked her.

Alyssa shrugged. "Sure I guess. I thought I saw... I'm sure it was nothing." She sat in her chair and adjusted in her seat.

"What? Something happen?" Melanie leaned over to hear.

Bianca sat next to her daughter. She didn't know why her mind returned to the man from the day before. Sandy brown haired man who'd been looking for Sherry. "What did you see?"

Alyssa shook her head. "I couldn't tell Mom. Like I said, it was probably nothing. There's a lot of people here, anyway." Alyssa tucked a curl behind her ear, and while Bianca didn't want to accuse her daughter of not telling the truth, her mother's intuition sensed there was more to the story.

"Here we go!" Melanie pointed to the stage.

Bianca refocused and joined in the cheering as the first line of models came from behind the sheer curtains. Hands on their hips, the women walked the catwalk as if they owned it. Black and white were their colors. A platinum blonde wore a block-colored dress, black and white. The other woman's hair was jet black, long, and she was wearing a striped black-and-white dress.

"I love the stripes," Melanie chimed in her ear, despite the loud music.

Bianca pointed to the platinum blonde. "I think I like hers better."

Melanie nudged her shoulder as the next set of models joined the stage. The first two exited.

Giselle continued. "Short and sweet is the cool, summery look here, ladies and gentlemen. Our models are wearing khaki elastic shorts with red-orange jungle print tops, which look so cute with their open necks and cap sleeves. You can't go wrong in this simple yet stylish outfit."

The audience applauded once more.

Alyssa's mouth dropped. "I love it!"

"Not bad," Bianca commented, although she couldn't see herself in red-orange. Covering her mouth, she stifled her giggle.

"There's Sherry!" Melanie exclaimed while pointing towards the stage.

Bianca smiled while admiring Sherry's outfit. Her knee-length, pearl-white dress with a jewel neckline was breathtaking. Her shoes? Red pumps. The camera zoomed in on Sherry's face briefly, showcasing her flawless complexion. Bianca had to ask her about the red pumps. The height of the heel was perfect.

"Is she okay?" Alyssa asked.

Bianca blinked, focusing back on Sherry's face. The model touched a hand to her forehead for a moment, but then placed a hand on her hip. She continued her model walk, swaying to the runway music.

"If you're looking for an ensemble on a special night out, you'll love this sleek yet stylish pearl white dress," Giselle said.

Bianca stared at Sherry. The woman lost her balance but tried to play it off. She forced a smile and continued.

"Something's not right," Melanie said.

"I know." Bianca couldn't pinpoint it, but despite Sherry's flawless makeup, she looked pale. Sherry's hand returned to her chest again, as if to catch her breath. She shook her head slightly, as if to shake off the feeling. By the time she stood in front of Bianca and Melanie, she swayed. Some crowd members stood to their feet, along with Bianca and her sister.

"Sherry?" Melanie called out to her. "Are you okay?"

Sherry didn't answer. Her lips parted, and she wobbled in her heels. Could she not breathe?

Giselle paused. "I... think one of our models may need a break."

"Sherry?" Bianca called her name this time.

"Mom? What's going on?" Alyssa asked, practically frozen in her seat.

Sherry's eyes only rolled to the back of her head. Then, as if in slow motion, Bianca's eyes bugged as the woman fainted off the stage, causing a loud shriek to erupt from the audience. Both Bianca and Melanie held their hands out to catch her. A security guard who came out of the corner of her eye behind Sherry also helped to break her fall.

PLOP! Bianca fell back in her seat, along with her sister. Alyssa's screams rang in Bianca's ears, along with some of the audience members. What had just happened?

"Uh..." Giselle began, obviously not expecting a model to faint. "Excuse me, ladies and gentlemen. We have a minor emergency that requires a brief intermission. Please, everyone, remain calm and stay in your seats. Is there by chance a doctor in the house?"

Bianca adjusted in her seat, careful not to let Sherry's head drop from her lap. She brushed her long hair away from her face. Her eyes were closed and her mouth was parted. "Sherry? Sherry, can you hear me?"

"Sherry? It's Melanie!" her sister called out while touching a hand to the model's arm. "Sherry, you need to wake up." Melanie's bottom lip trembled.

"What's wrong with her?" Alyssa's eyes rapidly blinked, as if to process what she'd just seen.

"Is she breathing?" a woman behind them asked.

"Get her some water!" another woman called out.

"Ms. Wilson?" the security guard said as he knelt before them, focusing on Sherry. "Ms. Wilson?" He spoke into his walkie-talkie. "We need an ambulance out here immediately. A model has passed out, and she's not responding."

Pressing two fingers to her neck, Bianca checked for a pulse. Nothing. "Come on, Sherry."

"No. This can't be happening!" Melanie exclaimed. "No!"

"Let me through. I'm a doctor," a tenor voice said.

Bianca raised her chin, facing the other man pressing through the crowd. Then he knelt before her. This wasn't Edenville's doctor, Dr. Maxwell. This man was younger, with dark blue eyes and spiked brown hair. He reached out his hand, just as Bianca had, to check Sherry's pulse.

He sighed. "Help me get her on the floor."

Bianca and Melanie did as the doctor had requested. Alyssa didn't move at all, but her eyes remained glued to Sherry.

The security guard straightened to his feet, holding his hands up to keep the crowd back. "Ladies and gentlemen, please stay calm. We have a doctor here. Don't crowd her, please."

"Do we know you?" Bianca asked the young doctor.

"I'm filling in for Dr. Maxwell at the clinic. He's visiting relatives in San Antonio with his wife this week," he said as he lifted Sherry's chin. "I'm Dr. Nash." Leaning over, he performed CPR, breathing air into Sherry's lungs.

"Sherry, wake up," Bianca whispered.

Dr. Nash pressed his hands to the woman's chest. "One. Two. Three. Four. Five."

Nothing. Sherry didn't respond. Dr. Nash tried again.

"Is she...?" Alyssa asked.

Bianca's head turned back and forth between her sister, Alyssa, and Sherry's limp body. She was living in a nightmare. The crowd watched without looking away, despite the security guard giving Dr. Nash space.

"I'm sorry." Dr. Nash sighed, dropping his own chin. "I can't get a response. She's... dead."

"No!" Melanie shouted. The crowd shrieked again.

Bianca's stomach plummeted, heartbroken for her sister. Judging by the sirens outside, the ambulance had arrived. Reaching out for her sister, whose shoulders shook as her body trembled, Bianca hugged her. Some girls' night out this had turned out to be.

Chapter 5

Bianca held both her sister and daughter close as they rested their heads on her shoulders. The ambulance had arrived not too long ago, and the paramedics had covered Sherry's body on the carpeted floor. Low murmurs filled the room.

"I can't believe what just happened," Melanie whimpered.

"I'm so sorry, Mel." Bianca didn't know what else to say to comfort her sister. If only she could take her home, but they had yet to be questioned by the police.

Melanie raised her head. "I mean... we just saw her. We talked with her yesterday. How did this happen?"

"Was she sick or something?" Alyssa asked.

Bianca's sister shook her head. "Not that I know of. She was healthy, and happy, as far as I knew."

Bianca bit her bottom lip. What about the man who visited Sherry? She didn't see him at the fashion show. Then again, had it been natural causes?

"Ladies," a familiar voice said.

The women turned to face Detective Sims. A dark blue suit was his attire for the evening. He stood solidly on his feet, as if ready to perform his job. Bianca knew he would.

"Detective." Melanie sniffled.

Alyssa only bobbed her head.

He cleared his throat. "I can't imagine what you must be feeling. I'm told the deceased Sherry Wilson collapsed in front of you."

"Practically on top of us from the catwalk." Melanie pointed ahead of her to the stage.

Alyssa straightened from her mother's embrace, folding her hands in her lap. If only she could take her home now.

Detective Sims pulled out his notepad and pen. "Can you tell me what happened?"

"She... She..." Melanie's voice choked.

Bianca took her hand and faced Detective Sims. "Sherry walked out on stage. I saw her touch her forehead, but she pushed through whatever she was feeling. When she approached us, she wobbled. Something wasn't right, but when we called her name, she didn't answer. I couldn't tell if she was choking or having trouble breathing. Her eyes rolled back, and she fell off the stage."

Detective Sims jotted down on his notepad. "I know this is hard, but witnesses say you were friends. How long?"

Bianca squeezed her sister's hand to reassure her.

Melanie rolled her shoulders back. "Since high school. Before we moved to Edenville from Atlanta, Georgia. We've kept in touch over the years."

"Any sickness or ailments?" He continued.

Melanie answered. "The most I saw her do was take a Tylenol for a headache. She was fine."

"Did she have any enemies that you know of?" he asked.

Bianca released a deep breath. That clarified that the police considered murder. Who wanted Sherry dead? Bianca kept her thoughts to herself. At least for the moment, but the possibility of murder piqued her interest.

Melanie shook her head. "No. Only that she just recently broke up with her boyfriend. When we went to lunch this week, she said they were at a crossroads in their relationship."

"Such as?" Detective Sims pulled up a chair and sat in front of them.

"She wanted to get married. Aiden, her boyfriend, told her he wasn't ready, but she didn't want to wait any longer," Melanie explained. "They'd been together for almost two years. She wanted more, and he wanted to keep things the same."

Bianca's mind raced with possibilities. First the men outside of the grocery store, engaging in an argument that had appeared to be about Sherry. The breakup, and another man appearing the day before her death. Regarding Aiden, was he heartbroken about their breakup? Would he have got back at Sherry for leaving him?

"Do you know Aiden's last name?" Detective Sims asked.

"I think Sherry said..." Melanie chewed at her bottom lip as she pondered. "Carlyle." She snapped her fingers. "That's it! Aiden Carlyle."

Detective Sims continued writing. "Anything else?"

"There was a man..." Bianca interjected. "Yesterday, we came to see Sherry here, and as we were leaving, there was a man demanding to see her."

"Can you describe him?" he asked.

"Mussed sandy brown hair, five-nine, and olive skin," Bianca said.

Her sister, Alyssa, and Detective Sims stared at her.

Bianca looked between all of them. "I remembered. So what?"

"Mom, can we go home?" Alyssa's slackened face proved she'd seen enough. Bianca's heart squeezed, wishing she could have spared her daughter from seeing a dead body.

Detective Sims sighed. "Not yet, Alyssa, but we're almost done. Okay?"

She bobbed her head and Bianca appreciated his soft tone.

He faced Bianca once more. "Anything else that comes to mind?"

"The... the day we invited you for dinner. There were two men arguing in the parking lot when I was at the grocery store. Something like, 'Stay away from her,'" Bianca added.

"*What?*" Melanie exclaimed.

Bianca shrugged. "I didn't know. I heard them say 'Sherry,' but I wasn't sure it was the 'Sherry' we knew. How could I have known?"

"I'll look into it." Detective Sims closed his notepad.

At the sound of ringing, Melanie retrieved her phone. "It's Mom."

Detective Sims gestured at her to take it. "Go ahead. If I have any more questions, I'll be in touch."

Melanie nodded and stood to her feet, answering the phone.

When Alyssa stood, she cleared her throat. "Can I go to the restroom? I need a moment."

"Sure," Detective Sims said.

Bianca stood. "Honey, are you—"

"Mom, I'm fine." Alyssa walked off without another word. Bianca wrung her hands together in her lap, watching after her daughter. The heaviness in her chest increased as she recalled how Sherry had fallen to her death.

"Bianca?" Detective Sims said.

She sighed. "I think I'll be okay for now. I need to get my daughter home, and I can't imagine what's going on in my sister's head." Running a hand down her neck, she processed her thoughts out loud. "It doesn't make sense for a healthy woman to fall dead like that."

"People of all ages die of natural causes," he said. Then he stood. "Let me know if you think of anything. Okay?"

Bianca's lips parted. "Unless..." If it was natural causes, then why did he ask if Sherry had enemies?

"Bianca?" There was a slight warning in his voice.

Her eyebrows raised. "She was... poisoned."

He inched closer. "Bianca, I don't need you spinning theories here."

She eyeballed him. "Remember the last time you said that?"

He grimaced, but his eyes weren't cold. "Yes, you helped catch a killer before, but that doesn't mean you need to make it a habit of getting involved in police business. I'm sorry about your sister's friend, but we'll handle this."

She folded her arms over her chest. "But what if—"

He exhaled through flared nostrils. "I won't say it because we know nothing yet. Once we investigate, we'll have more answers. Until then, take your sister and daughter home."

"But you will look into—"

He held up his hand to stop her. "I'll look into it. Go home and get some rest. And no spinning theories."

Bianca looked back at Melanie, who wiped at her eyes while talking on the phone with their mother. "Fine. I won't spin theories." At least not for now. The feeling returned. The gnawing in her gut when she knew something was off.

BIANCA DIDN'T BLAME Melanie for staying home from church the following day. While their mother had insisted on staying with her, Melanie had assured them she would be okay at home alone. Their mother was still bringing dinner, so they wouldn't miss a Sunday meal together as a family.

Once service had dismissed, soft music played in the background as the members of Edenville Community Church chatted with one another. The sun beamed through the stained-glass windows. Bianca smiled and shook hands with fellow members, but it didn't keep her from thinking about Melanie. Plus, she couldn't get past the possibility of Sherry being murdered.

"Do you think we should head home now?" Alyssa asked. She didn't mention the fashion show herself, and judging by her unusual quietness, Bianca figured the night before was on her daughter's mind.

Bianca bobbed her head. "Yeah. Let's go." Staring ahead a few rows forward, Bianca gestured to her mother that they were leaving. Her mother nodded, mouthing, "See you later."

Bianca drove in silence. Alyssa cleared her throat a few times, but didn't ask questions. Because of the publicity of the fashion show, everyone in town had heard the news of Sherry's collapse.

"How long was Aunt Mel friends with this woman again?" Alyssa asked, playing with the hem of her plum, knee-length dress.

"Since high school," Bianca answered.

"Were they best friends?"

"They kept in touch as much as possible. I think it's easier when you're younger, but as an adult, you have to be much more intentional in your relationships. You can grow apart and not even know it," Bianca explained.

Alyssa bobbed her head. "I hope Chloe and I will stay friends."

Bianca replied. "I'm sure you two will be best friends for life."

"I hope so," Alyssa said.

"I'm... sorry you had to see that last night." Bianca focused on the road, stopping at a traffic light.

Alyssa didn't respond.

Bianca tried again. "If you need to talk, I'm here. Okay?"

"I know, Mom." Alyssa turned her head to look out the passenger window. "I just... still see..."

Bianca reached a hand to her daughter. Alyssa's fingers wrapped around hers, but she didn't face her. The light turned green and Bianca's engine hummed as she pulled forward.

"Mom, I..." Alyssa started, but paused. She still hadn't made eye contact, and while Bianca didn't want to push, she waited for her daughter to open up to her.

"Yes?" she replied in a soft tone.

Alyssa shook her head. "Nothing. It's fine."

There was something up. Bianca didn't know what, but she would be patient with Alyssa. When her daughter was younger, all Bianca had to do was open her arms, and Alyssa would run to her embrace. Tears filling her eyes, she would tell her mother everything.

Things had changed now that Alyssa was a teenager, so Bianca was learning to give her needed space. Yet Bianca would press if the situation was life threatening to her daughter. Until then, she wouldn't press now. Alyssa always came around, despite her silent episodes.

Pulling into the driveway, Bianca hit the button for the garage door of her farmhouse. Her eyebrow raised at the charcoal sedan. Jordan? Had he called her while she'd been in church? Had she missed his message that he was coming over?

"Uncle J is here?" Alyssa asked, unclicking her seatbelt. A soft smile crossed her face. At least something perked her mood a bit.

"I guess so." Bianca cut the engine and reached into her purse. No messages from Jordan. She'd been grateful he'd fully recovered from his head injury, and even though he'd gone back to work on his books, he had said he was taking his time since he'd been in the hospital.

Jordan suspected Priscilla Davis in her husband's murder, Martin Davis. Then she had her secret lover, Paul, to follow Jordan and attack him with a golf club. Priscilla had taken the golf club from her brother-in-law, Richard Long, weeks prior and blackmailed his wife Judy since the couple had a $41,000 debt with their restaurant and bakery.

Priscilla had been hysterical at Martin's memorial, but it was all a charade. What gave her away? The blood stains on her gloves, and when she came to pick up her anniversary video from Bianca, it all came together. Thank goodness the police came in time, as Bianca didn't plan on being held at gunpoint by a woman she'd thought was a respected citizen in Edenville.

Bianca cleared her throat. "Let's head inside." She followed Alyssa, only to find Jordan at the dining table with Melanie. Her sister was still in her pink polka dot pajamas with pink slippers and pulled her hair into a low ponytail. Her face was makeup-free, and judging by her heavy eyes, she'd had a rough night.

"Hey, Uncle J," Alyssa said.

Crew haircut, full dark brown beard, and muscular in build. His eyes beamed at the sight of Bianca and her daughter. "Hey, Alyssa." Standing to his feet, he opened his arms for a bear hug. Alyssa complied, wrapping her arms around him. He lifted her off her feet for a moment, but when her feet touched the floor, she embraced him a second time.

"I'm glad you're here," she said.

"What are you doing here?" Bianca waved her phone at him. "You didn't say you were coming over."

Jordan moved past Alyssa to embrace Bianca. "I heard what happened. I came to check on you all."

Bianca patted his back. When she pulled away, she stared at her sister. Alyssa draped her arms around her aunt's neck and closed her eyes. Melanie patted her cheek in return, though a sniffle followed.

"How is she? How long have you been here?" Bianca asked.

"About thirty minutes," he said. "She told me Sherry fell into your lap."

Bianca bobbed her head. "Did you know her?"

Jordan shook his head. "I've heard about her in tabloids and social media, but we never met. So far, the police think natural causes?"

"Yeah, but..."

Jordan raised an eyebrow. "But what?" He pointed at her. "What's going on in that curious mind of yours?"

Bianca pulled him to the side. Thank goodness Alyssa kept Melanie company. Casper was asleep in the corner in his doggy bed. "I just don't think it was natural causes, but nothing's official yet from the police."

Jordan folded his arms. "And what will you do when it's official?"

"I don't know. I wasn't trying to get involved last time."

"I'm glad you did." He rubbed at his head. "You practically saved my life."

Bianca beamed at him. "I don't want a repeat of that, if you know what I mean."

Jordan looked back at Melanie. "I hate seeing her like this. She's distraught."

"She said they tried their best to keep in touch. I think the fact that we had only talked to her twenty-four hours earlier is the most shocking of all," Bianca said.

Jordan bobbed his head. "What clues do you have? I hear this fashion event is staying longer in town."

"Yeah. At least for a month. So far I saw two men arguing, mentioning her name, and there was a man looking for her the day before at the rehearsal."

"That's not much to go on," Jordan said.

"I know." Bianca pulled her bottom lip in. "Wait. You have an agent. Right?"

"Sure, what does that have to do with anything?" Jordan shrugged.

"Networking. Would a modeling agent cross over into the book world?"

"If a model wanted to write a book, I guess," Jordan said. "But…" He paused. "My agent has mentioned a few names before that he's worked with. He's pretty well known in the industry. Carl Blunt."

Bianca noted the man's name in her head. Was there a connection to Sherry's agent? She would search to see. "You've been his client for how long now?"

Jordan tilted his head as if to give it some thought. "At least four years. He never hesitates to meet new clients."

"I vaguely recall Sherry saying something like, 'writing my experiences in a book,'" Bianca said.

Jordan folded his arms. "It's possible. I'm assuming you want me to ask my agent if he knew her manager or something."

Her smile grew. "That would be great."

"I'll see what I can do." Then he checked his watch. "I would stay longer, but I got to get back to work. I'm on a deadline."

Bianca hugged him again. "Thanks for coming."

"You bet." Then he turned and faced Alyssa and Melanie. "Ladies, I'm heading out."

Alyssa walked over to the kitchen island and grabbed an apple from the small wicker basket. She bit into it but waved.

Melanie hurried to his side and hugged his neck. "Thank you so much."

Jordan lingered in her embrace for a moment, but then he pulled back, clearing his throat. "Anytime."

Melanie gave him a faint smile and walked him to the door. Once he left, she turned and faced Bianca.

"I'm going to change." Alyssa tossed the apple core in the nearby trashcan and walked past them to her room. Casper scratched behind his ears. Then he trotted over to his water bowl.

Bianca almost followed her, but she held back. Alyssa would talk eventually.

"How are you holding up?" Bianca asked her sister.

Melanie shook her head. Then she walked over and plopped on the couch. "I'm not."

Bianca sat next to her, taking her hand in hers.

Her sister slouched further in her seat. "It doesn't make sense to me, Bianca. Sherry's dead. I couldn't sleep well last night because all I could see was her collapsing."

Bianca noticed the TV was on but muted. She reached with her free hand to turn it off, but when a breaking news report flashed on the screen, she perked up. Then when Sherry's image came on screen, she turned up the volume. Staring at the anchorwoman, a strawberry blonde with arched eyebrows and thin lips, Bianca tuned in along with Melanie.

"Good afternoon, Edenville. I'm Marilyn Hopkins with breaking news of the terrible tragedy that happened at the Clique Classic Fashion show yesterday. It shocked fans of the rising clothing line when twenty-nine-year-old model Sherry Wilson collapsed on stage during the show. They pronounced her dead at the scene with no immediate answers as to the cause of death. We now have reports from Edenville's Police Department that the coroner found traces of poison in her system. It is the official cause of death."

"What?!" Melanie exclaimed, jerking to attention in her seat and releasing Bianca's hand.

Bianca covered her own mouth. She'd had her suspicions, but had prayed she'd been wrong. Not this time. She'd been right. Poison killed Sherry.

"Bianca?" Melanie shook her head slightly, as if in shock. "Who would do such a thing?"

"I don't know."

Marilyn Hopkins continued. "The police are currently investigating, but we have named no suspects yet. We'll keep you up to date on this tragic story. I'm Marilyn Hopkins and this is our breaking story on EDV News."

Bianca muted the TV. "This just got worse."

"We need to find out who did this." Melanie faced her sister. "Will you help me?"

"Mel—"

"Remember how you felt when the police accused Nicole?" Melanie's eyes, still red, teared up again. "Someone *murdered* my friend. Whoever did this can't get away with it."

All Bianca could hear was Detective Sims' voice in her head. *Let the police handle it.* Yet her heart broke for her sister.

"Sherry didn't deserve to die, Bianca." Melanie shook her head. "No one deserves to die like that."

Bianca embraced her sister. "I'll do what I can." She patted her back, hoping she could keep that promise. The next thing to do would be to figure out how to investigate without stepping on Detective Sims' toes.

Chapter 6

The following day, Monday, Bianca met up with her mother in downtown Edenville. During her lunch hour, she agreed to have some mother-daughter time. Melanie buried herself in work, and Alyssa wouldn't be home from school until later in the afternoon. Casper would keep Melanie company in the meantime.

"I should get special pricing since I'm your mother," Deborah Wallace said with a wink.

Bianca laughed. Her mother had hired her to create special invitations for her upcoming matchmaking event in town. A calligraphy font had been Bianca's first choice for the invites, but after sending her mother a preview, at her request, her mother preferred a handwritten design. Bianca went back to work and found the perfect font to give her mother's invites the personal touch she had desired. She wanted all of her customers satisfied, including her mother, who was Wallace Designs' biggest cheerleader. The finished product included the handwritten font, her mother's heart logo in the top center on a cream background.

Though she knew her mother was teasing her, she loved rattling her. "Weren't you the one who taught me how to take care of business? Family or no family?" Bianca asked.

Her mother groaned. "Just like you to throw that back in my face." Then she smiled. "They look amazing, by the way. Great job, as always."

She looped her arms through her mother's as they paced down Main Street.

"Thanks for coming with me. I wanted to talk to you alone about your sister," her mother said, pausing in front of the jewelry store.

Bianca bobbed her head.

"Did she say much after I left yesterday after dinner?"

"No. She went to bed early. She hardly does that," Bianca informed her.

"She's going through a lot. Even when she told me on the phone, I couldn't believe it. Now the word's out about this poor woman being poisoned. What's become of this town?"

"Things happen all over the world, Mom. You know that."

"I know. It's just... disturbing. How's Alyssa?"

"Not talking about it." Bianca had hoped on their drive to her school that Alyssa would mention what was bothering her. Instead, her head stayed glued to her cell phone. "I'm giving her time, but I know it affected her."

"My poor grandbaby," her mother said. "Well... I'm sure when she's ready, she'll talk to you. That's something she wasn't expecting, so I'm sure she needs time."

Bianca rubbed at her brow with her free hand. "And Sherry had been so nice to get Alyssa an extra ticket. Melanie couldn't wait to introduce Alyssa to Sherry. I still can't believe that happened."

"And the report on the news?" Her mother huffed. "Poisoned? I remember Sherry being such a sweet girl. Who would dare do this?"

"I had my suspicions something was wrong when Sherry fell, but the police..." Bianca stopped.

Then her mother eyeballed her.

"What?"

"Are you getting involved again?" Her mother unhooked her arm from hers. "Bianca Wallace, don't get the idea that you can solve this case. You got away with it last time, but don't make this a habit."

Bianca sighed. "I haven't asked questions, if that's what you mean." She didn't reveal having Jordan looking into Sherry's agent for her.

Her mother's face softened. "I know you mean well. I'm... just protective."

"I know. I wouldn't expect nothing less from you." Bianca wanted to say more, but a man through the window inside the jewelry store caught her attention. Tall, bald, and athletic. The man from the grocery store parking lot. He was talking with the cashier. "Mom? Do you mind if we..." Bianca rubbed at her wrist, thinking of an excuse to go inside. "Check out some bracelets inside?"

Her mother's forehead wrinkled. "Um... sure. If that's what you want. I'm glad you've taken your mind off investigating."

Far from it. The bell jingled above them. Bianca walked closer to the locked display cases. Earrings made with rubies, diamonds, emeralds, opals, and sapphires shined in the bright lighting.

"I'd like to return this," the man said to the brunette cashier.

Since Bianca saw her mother perusing the bracelet bangles displayed on silk scarves, she inched closer to hear the conversation.

"Certainly, Mr. Carlyle. Do you have your receipt?" the cashier asked.

Carlyle? Was this Aiden Carlyle? He reached into his pocket for his brown leather wallet. Retrieving a small piece of paper, he handed it to the woman.

"Now I remember." The brunette's eyes lit up. "You came in last week. This is one of our best emerald cut rings. You were proposing, right? Let me guess, you want to exchange it for a better diamond. Is your fiancée coming? Sometimes couples decide to pick the ring together!"

"No," he snapped. Clearing his throat, he softened his tone. "I'm not getting married. She's... dead."

The woman gasped. "Oh, no. I'm so sorry. I'll process this for you right away."

Bianca kept her back turned as she listened. Melanie told her the reason for the couple's breakup was Aiden hadn't wanted to get married. Did he change his mind? Did he regret losing her and wanted to make amends? It didn't matchup going from not wanting to propose to see him now with a ring. How soon did he purchase it after the breakup?

"Thank you." Aiden's expression was slack, and his lips pinched together in a grimace.

Bianca's mind raced with questions. Melanie said they dated for two years. Aiden's reluctance to get married caused the breakup. Did he... propose and Sherry turned him down? Did the rejection drive him to—?

"Can you hurry, please?" He barked.

"One second, sir," the cashier said. She kept her demeanor professional despite his attitude.

"Someone's in a hurry," Bianca's mother said.

"Looks like it." Bianca kept her eyes glued to Aiden. His fingers tapped on the glass counter, and his tongue poked his cheek. Not the reaction she expected, but perhaps this was his response to Sherry's death. Sure, people grieved differently, but shouldn't he look distraught since someone killed the woman he loved?

"What about these, sweetie?" Her mother held up a few golden bracelets. One was on the thin side, while the other was wider. They sparkled underneath the bright lights inside the store. "I think they'd go perfect with your skin tone."

Bianca turned her head and stared at them both. "Nice. I like them." When the bell jingled, Bianca jerked to look at the door. She sighed. Aiden walked out.

"Or we could try the silver ones." Her mother returned the gold ones to their station and then eyed the silver selections. "Let me see." Her mother tapped her fingers on her lips.

Bianca pulled out her phone and typed in Aiden's name. Thank goodness he was the only Aiden Carlyle who appeared in the search engine. There he was. Actor. Model. As she perused his biography, she read how his career hadn't taken off until he'd started dating Sherry.

Then she found an interview with Sherry and Aiden in *Her Side*, a magazine famous for printing women entrepreneurs, latest fashion trends, and inspirational quotes to inspire women.

Bianca read the writer's introduction. *"I have with me a power couple taking the modeling industry by storm!"*

Judging by the picture of the couple with their arms wrapped around each other, they looked happy. Then Bianca saw the date. This interview had taken place three months prior. Skimming farther down, she searched for Aiden's answers in the interview.

"I'd been struggling earlier in my career. Nothing went well for me, but when I landed my first big commercial, they paired me with this amazing woman. I knew then she was special and my life wouldn't be the same."

Bianca tilted her head to the side. Had there even been a sincere connection between them? She didn't want to assume the worst, but had Aiden only dated Sherry to further his career? Scrolling farther down the screen, she noticed another picture. The couple was holding hands and smiling, but the smile didn't appear to reach Aiden's eyes. His stare appeared blank and emotionless.

Still, the man had bought a ring for Sherry. He'd planned to propose to her. Had even that been an act? Was his tone with the cashier a simple mistake, or did he have a temper? Did Sherry know this? Was there more to breaking up on top of his lack of commitment?

"Bianca?" her mother called out.

Bianca locked her phone. "Yes?"

"I said, which one?" her mother asked. Then she reached out a hand and touched her shoulder. "Are you okay? You seem a little flustered."

Bianca shook her head. "No, I'm fine." She wouldn't tell her mother. Not after the almost-lecture she'd gotten. "You know what? I don't need a bracelet today. I can always come back."

Her mother raised an eyebrow. "Are you sure?"

Bianca smiled, hoping her answer would satisfy her mother. "Yeah. It's not like I don't have any to choose from." She shrugged. "I'm not planning anything big where I'll need a new one."

"Uh-huh," her mother said.

Bianca blinked. "What does that mean?"

"Oh... nothing, but keep in mind you may have some place to go or perhaps get dressed up if you ever wanted to hang out with someone special." Her mother winked at her. "Anyway, let's go." Her mother waved goodbye to the cashier and Bianca followed her out the door.

Though her mother hadn't mentioned Detective Sims, Bianca knew he'd crossed her mother's mind.

THE STARGAZE HOTEL. That was the name Melanie had given Bianca, as the hotel Sherry had been staying in while in town. After dropping her mother off at home, Bianca didn't mind taking some time before picking up her daughter from school to see if there was any information she could find about Sherry and Aiden. Then there was Paris Deveraux. Though she had no proof yet, it floated in her thoughts, since the woman's dislike for Sherry was clear.

Checking her phone, she read the text from her sister.

Room 219.

Bianca exited her car, paced to the automatic doors, and entered the lobby. Her wedged shoes clicking against tiled floors, she walked past the wooden marble-covered front desk and cushioned chairs for new guests. Approaching the elevator, she pushed the button to go up.

The elevator pinged, and she entered once the shiny metal doors opened. Thank goodness she was alone. She could think out loud.

"Aiden buys a ring for Sherry, but they break up. He returns the ring and practically yells at the cashier." Next. "A man shows to talk to Sherry at the rehearsal, but she didn't know him according to Melanie." Lastly. "Paris doesn't like Sherry. She's poisoned and falls from the runway." A *tsk* escaped her lips. "What happened backstage?"

The elevator pinged once she reached the second floor, and she now walked on the nylon carpet. When she reached 219, she knocked. Melanie had said Jacqueline had been there when she'd arrived to meet Sherry for lunch. Would she answer? Would she be willing to talk to Bianca?

Jacqueline answered. She blinked for a moment, as if she didn't recognize Bianca.

"Hi, I'm Bianca Wallace. Sherry and my sister, Melanie—"

She bobbed her head as if the memories had come back. "Yes, I remember. Sorry. Can I help you?" Her long, brown hair hung freely around her shoulders, but she still wore her red-rimmed glasses.

"I'm here on behalf of my sister. She would have been here, but with everything... I came to see if you were all right," Bianca said.

Jacqueline nodded and invited her to come inside her room. Walking past the luggage stand, a large mirror, and the TV on the wall, Bianca sat at the cushioned chair in front of the wooden desk.

"I appreciate it, especially since you hardly know me," Jacqueline said.

"I know, and I don't mean to make you feel uncomfortable," said Bianca. "To be honest, I'm still shocked at what happened."

Jacqueline spoke in a flat voice. "Things happen and there's nothing we can do about it."

Not quite the response Bianca had expected. "I am sorry for your loss. I can't imagine what it's like to lose a sister like that."

"*Stepsister*," Jacqueline clarified. "The woman hated me, as far as I could tell. As hard as I worked for her, she never appreciated it. I wasn't a sister. I was her personal assistant. Someone she could order around, and I couldn't find a job anywhere else, so I put up with her stuck-up ways." She paused, taking a breather. "Forgive me. I've said too much."

"Sometimes we need to vent," Bianca said, although she couldn't deny the woman's hostility.

Jacqueline bounced on her toes, wrapping her arms across her chest. She looked upward at the ceiling. "My mother was no help, either. She was always trying to get Sherry to like her." She shrugged. "I don't know why. To impress my stepdad maybe."

Bianca didn't reply. If Jacqueline was opening up, she didn't want to stop her.

Scratching at her eyebrow, Jacqueline continued. "Sometimes I felt pushed aside, and I was her *own* daughter." She sighed. "I guess she figured the more she tried to get along with Sherry, the more she could earn my stepfather's love."

"Was their marriage strained?" Bianca asked.

Jacqueline shook her head. "Not that I could see, but I remember a few arguments when I was younger. Sherry would act out to get her dad's attention, but my mom would stick up for her. I was..." She stopped. "I mean, I saw no tension between Mom and my stepdad, but she never did that for me. It wasn't as if they played Sherry and me against each other, though. We just never got along. Oil and water. We had our moments, but we were never friends, even though I... always wanted a sister."

A twinge hit Bianca's heart at her words. "I'm sorry."

Jacqueline teared up, sitting on her full-sized bed. "I had just talked to her. She'd met with someone right before the show started."

Bianca's eyes widened. "Did she say who?"

Jacqueline shook her head, removing her glasses for a moment to wipe her eyes. "She was in a hurry to get ready for the show. Giselle didn't tolerate tardiness."

Bianca bobbed her head.

"But even though we didn't get along, whoever did this needs to pay. I wouldn't be surprised if it was Paris."

"Paris." Bianca's suspicions confirmed.

"Paris Deveraux. She's staying here too. Fourth floor, I think. She was Sherry's archrival. I don't know how Sherry did it, but she beat Paris every time in landing the highest-paying modeling gigs. They started their careers practically around the same time in their late teens, but the press loved Sherry." Jacqueline huffed. "I don't know why, though."

More information to look into with Paris Deveraux. Still, Aiden Carlyle wasn't off the hook with her yet.

"I'm sorry," Jacqueline said. "You came here to offer condolences, and I'm here rambling." She forced a smile, wrapping her arms around her middle once again. "Thank you, and thanks to your sister. I hope she's getting through this as best she can."

Bianca smiled back. "She's trying."

Something buzzed behind her on her full-sized bed. "I'm sorry. That's my phone. I have to get it." Leading Bianca to the door, she said, "Thank you again for your kindness." With that, she closed the door.

Bianca stared at the number plate for a few moments. She heard Jacqueline's voice through the door, despite her voice sounding muffled.

"I know," Jacqueline said on the phone. "No. I can't do that now." A groan surfaced. "What do you want me to do? She's dead!"

Bianca gasped, but when she heard another door close inside, she couldn't hear Jacqueline anymore. Did she take her call in the bathroom? Bianca snapped her fingers, annoyed that she couldn't hear the rest of the conversation. She turned to head for the elevator.

And then there were two suspects. Or three. Jacqueline didn't seem too heartbroken over Sherry, despite the few tears she'd shed. What did she mean by that last comment, "what do you want me to do. She's dead."

Even when the ambulance had carried Sherry's body away, Bianca didn't recall seeing Jacqueline. What story had she given the police? Had there been arguments between the stepsisters that anyone else witnessed? Not to mention Sherry had met with someone before the show. Who?

Bianca pushed the button again for the elevator. Taking her phone out once more, she searched for Paris Deveraux's name. Red hair. Sea-blue eyes. Slim and trim, and a bright smile in almost every picture Bianca saw. Was this fashion beauty queen capable of murder, or was this the case of the evil stepsister gone too far?

Chapter 7

That Monday evening, Bianca sprinkled seasoned salt and onion powder on the sliced chicken breasts on her cutting board. Alyssa was in her room doing her homework, with Casper by her side. Bianca still didn't ask questions when she picked her up from school earlier. Once again, Alyssa glued her eyes to her phone. Melanie appeared to be in a better mood. She'd traded her pajamas for her dark jeans and an off-the-shoulder top. Her hair remained pulled back in a low ponytail.

She walked past her sister to grab a few plates from the upper cabinet.

"What are you thinking?" Bianca asked her.

Melanie sighed. "I can't... seem to get past this. It doesn't seem real."

"I get it, but remember, it takes time. Don't worry. I'm sure the police are doing everything they can to find out what happened," Bianca reassured her.

"I still want to know who Sherry met before the show," Melanie added.

Bianca had waited until Alyssa had been out of the room to tell her sister about her theories. First Aiden, then her conversation with Jacqueline, and now Paris Deveraux.

"Who has the strongest motive?" Melanie leaned against the counter with her arms folded.

"Not sure. First there's Aiden. Sherry dumped him and perhaps he thought a proposal would win her back."

Melanie asked, "But why kill her if he really loved her? Sherry would have told me if Aiden proposed to her. Unless... something else was going on and she wasn't ready to talk. She could have her quiet moments."

Bianca shrugged. Maybe she met him before the show to talk things through a day before? Was it after she and Melanie left the rehearsal? Perhaps he proposed and Sherry didn't get the chance to tell Melanie yet due to focusing on her job. Was it not that important to her since she and Aiden were through, anyway? Did she brush him off, happy to move on with her life?

Maybe Aiden got angry enough to plan to kill her? What if he slipped the poison to her before the show? Under the pretense of making up or agreeing to be friends, he slipped her poison somehow right before the show?

"So, how do you think the killer poisoned her?" Melanie wondered.

"Maybe she ate something or... drank something." Bianca thought back to their last talk with Sherry. "Remember, we were in Sherry's dressing room the day before?"

"Yeah? And?" Melanie replied.

"She had Jacqueline get her something to drink." Bianca placed the chicken breasts on a pan, wiped her hands, placed the pan in the oven, and set the timer to cook.

Melanie straightened. "Do you think Jacqueline... Oh, Bianca."

"I don't know." Bianca moved to the sink to wash her hands. "It's possible since Jacqueline was her assistant. I'm sure she did her share of getting drinks for Sherry. Running errands. Keeping her schedule in order. Not to mention her attitude."

Melanie shook her head. "But you said so yourself: She cried when you talked to her today. Why would she—"

"Do I have to mention Priscilla Davis? Her tears fooled me too," Bianca pointed out.

Melanie pressed her hands against her temples and rubbed her head. "This can't be happening."

"This is far-fetched, but what if Jacqueline... I don't know. Envied her sister? She said they weren't close, and I don't think overall she was happy," Bianca said.

"I wonder what she told the police," Melanie added.

"I know Detective Sims won't give out that kind of information." It was best she left him out of her findings for now.

Melanie's hands dropped to her side. "So we have Jacqueline possibly envying her sister. So she poisons her drink with what?"

Bianca retrieved her phone from the dining table. Opening Google, she searched "poisons soluble in liquids." Too many possibilities. Biting her lip, she added, "Tasteless." She didn't think Sherry would have drunk something if it had tasted funny.

"Oh, no." Melanie exclaimed, staring at the screen.

Bianca read out loud. "Arsenic."

"The news didn't name the poison, did it?" Melanie asked.

"No, it didn't."

"Okay, so... we have Aiden and Jacqueline as possible suspects. What about this other guy you saw at the grocery store? And the man outside during the rehearsal." Melanie paced the floor.

"I don't know their names. I only know what they look like. Do you remember meeting anyone else when you were out with Sherry?"

Melanie replied, "She mentioned Aiden, and we talked about Jacqueline. The only other..." She snapped her fingers. "Her manager."

Bianca perked. "Right. Can't forget him." She needed to follow up with Jordan too.

"Hunter... Hunter something. Anyway, she said she was leaving him and hiring someone else. After managing her career for five years, she wanted someone new," Melanie explained.

"Did she say why?"

Melanie replied. "Only that she wanted to branch out more. Act and even nonfiction writing. I thought she was joking about the book, but she was serious turns out. At first he didn't think it was the right move for her, and Sherry never enjoyed being told what to do."

"So... he changed his mind or something?" Bianca wondered.

"Sherry just said she didn't want to work with him anymore," her sister said. "She was looking for someone else."

"Uh-huh." All of this new information played in Bianca's head like the end credits to a movie. Typing into her phone again, she included Hunter's name along with Sherry's. Bingo. Hunter Graham, thirty-eight years old, and he'd been in the managing business since 2011. Scrolling through his list of clients, Sherry appeared to be his top one in the last five years. "I wonder if that was it." Another suspect to add to her growing list of perpetrators.

Melanie blinked. "What?"

"Think about it, Mel. She tells him she's leaving him. He gets revenge on her. She was his top client." Bianca tapped her phone against her hand. "We need to narrow this down. There are too many scenarios. And I can't forget Paris, but there's not much there either. We know she didn't like Sherry, but even Jacqueline mentioned her too. "

"I don't see how we're going to piece this together," Melanie added.

Bianca walked over and hugged her sister. "We will."

Casper barked, and Melanie pulled back from her sister with a faint smile. Then she bent down to pet their dog.

"Everything okay? How are you, Aunt Mel?" Alyssa asked, her brow wrinkling.

"Getting there," Melanie said, straightening to her feet.

Bianca directed her attention to her daughter. "Sweetie, can you make the salad?"

Her daughter nodded and walked over to the refrigerator. When Alyssa stood in front of the counter, her gaze flitted around the kitchen, never settling on an object for long. This wasn't the Alyssa she knew. Quieter than usual. Bianca's eyebrows drew together. If only her daughter confided in her. Soon enough, she knew she would.

Hearing another buzz, Bianca watched her sister grab her phone from her back pocket. Her smile grew at whatever message she'd received.

"Can I ask you something?" Bianca squinted her eyes at her little sister.

Melanie didn't reply. She only used her thumb to type what must have been her reply.

"Mel?" Bianca repeated.

"What?" She flinched, jerking her head up to meet her sister's gaze. "Did I miss something?"

"Are you distracted by someone?" Bianca's lips twisted into a grin.

Melanie laughed. "What? No. Why would I be distracted?" She walked over to the table to sit.

Bianca followed. "Does this have anything to do with Jordan coming over to see you yesterday?"

"He was being nice," Melanie reassured her.

"Have you been talking to him outside of him coming over?" She pressed a little further. Not quite payback for how Melanie had been riding her lately about Detective Sims, but Bianca was curious.

Melanie played with her stud earring. "He's funny. A gentleman, and we've talked a few times. That's all."

"That's all, huh?" Bianca wasn't convinced, since her sister was avoiding eye contact.

"That's all."

Bianca opened her mouth for a rebuttal. Nothing. "Fine."

"I'm finished," Alyssa said, setting the salad bowl at the table.

"Thank you, sweetie," Bianca said.

Alyssa adjusted her headphones in her ears. "Mom, I know it's a school night, but can I hang out with Chloe? I need... to get my mind off things for a while. There wasn't much homework today, so I'm caught up."

Melanie sat back in her chair. "I'm sorry, Alyssa."

She shook her head. "It's not your fault, Aunt Mel."

Bianca gestured at the salad. "Don't you want to eat something at least?"

Her daughter shook her head. "I'm not hungry now. Besides, I can get something with Chloe later if I need to."

Bianca wouldn't fight her on leaving the house. Perhaps that's what Alyssa needed to unwind. "Okay, but remember your curfew."

"I will. Thanks." Alyssa turned and walked down the hallway and back to her room.

"I'm trying not to worry about her," Bianca said, once her daughter was out of sight.

"I shouldn't have suggested she'd go." Melanie rested her chin in the cup of her hand as her elbow rested on the table.

"No." Bianca warned her. "This is not your fault. There's no way you could have known. Plus, it was a friendly gesture for Sherry to get another ticket."

Footsteps interrupted them, and Alyssa returned with her light gray jacket covering her gray short-sleeved shirt. The finishing touch to her outfit was flower patterned leggings and flat shoes. "I'm gone, Mom. Chloe's outside."

"Tell her I said hi. Be safe," Bianca said.

"I will. Bye Aunt Mel." Alyssa waved with no smile on her face.

Bianca's sister waved back. "Bye honey." Casper barked after her once she closed the front door behind her.

Once Alyssa left, Bianca and Melanie tried talking about other topics for a bit to get their minds off of things, but they inevitably had to focus on Sherry's death again. There was nothing else on their minds for long the past few days.

Now Bianca had three mysteries to solve. One involving a murder. The other involving her sister and Jordan Thomas. And finally, what was on Alyssa's mind?

WHY DIDN'T I WEAR FLATS? Bianca's heels burned although she loved her wedged heels, but they weren't the best choice when walking in downtown Edenville. She flew solo later that same Monday evening after dinner. Alyssa was hanging out with Chloe still, Melanie had work to catch up on, and her mother had a date with Luther Burkes. Casper stayed at home, keeping Melanie occupied. Though she'd insisted she was fine, Bianca knew her sister was grieving her friend's death.

An occasional horn honked from the cars driving past her on the main street, and pedestrians strolled along the sidewalk talking to the people they knew. Bianca paused in front of R&J's restaurant and bakery. Gazing through the large glass windows, Bianca smiled at the evening crowd. Thank goodness Richard and Judy's business hadn't gone under as they'd feared.

Proceeding down the sidewalk, Bianca winced. Perhaps it was time to return to her car for her flat shoes. Yet if she walked all the way back, she might as well head home. Deciding that the numbness in her feet wasn't worth continuing her walk, she pivoted towards the direction of her parked Kia Soul.

Then she stopped in her tracks. Detective Sims was exiting Richard and Judy's restaurant. She also recognized Detective Atkins, dark brown skin, goatee, and stocky built. He was out of uniform, along with Detective Sims. A few others exited the restaurant, including three women. The women said goodbye to them, leaving them standing in front of the restaurant window. When a woman with shoulder length brunette hair eyed Detective Sims, a slight growl escaped Bianca's throat. She denied the tiny spark of jealously over the handsome detective.

Clearing her throat, she wondered if she could sneak past without being noticed. Her forehead wrinkled. Why? She could say *hello* if Detective Sims made eye contact with her. Bianca rolled her eyes, annoyed at herself for the irrational thoughts racing through her head.

"Bianca?"

He'd spotted her. Smiling, Bianca greeted the group. "Hi. Nice to see you again. You too, Detective Atkins."

Detective Atkins smiled, making the laugh lines on his slim face more noticeable. He'd grown a small afro since the last time Bianca had seen him, parked outside of her house, monitoring her stalker.

"You alone tonight?" Detective Sims asked.

Her lips parted at the sight of his gray eyes, as they always seemed to do. "Yeah, just taking a walk downtown." Her gaze lifted, noticing the sun had set. "Heading home now."

"Not so fast," Detective Sims said. "I'll walk with you." Then he directed his attention to Detective Atkins. "See you in the morning."

The men fist-bumped. "I'll see you then." Detective Atkins then acknowledged Bianca. "Goodnight, Ms. Wallace."

"Goodnight," she said. Tilting her head to the side, she walked in step with Detective Sims. "You don't have to walk with me, you know."

He shrugged. "I know. Just being... neighborly."

She gestured at R&J's place. "How was the food?"

"Incredible. Best place in town, I think."

Bianca bobbed her head. She held back a whimper, knowing it wasn't much farther to her car. "I agree. Not to mention the pastries. Sometimes I stay away because I know what'll happen if I'm too close to the donuts."

"They're your guilty pleasure?" he asked with a sparkle in his eye.

She grinned. "I wouldn't say that, but I have a sweet tooth. Don't you?"

He replied. "I indulge every once in a while." Then he patted his toned stomach, which wasn't hard to miss in his fitted T-shirt. "Can't eat too much of it. I have to stay in shape for the job."

"Catching criminals. Killers." She raised her eyebrows.

Detective Sims sighed. "If this is your way of asking me about the case, forget it, Bianca."

She blinked, placing a hand to her chest. "You think I was digging for information? Why would I do that?" she teased.

He inched forward. If he stepped any closer, he'd be a breath away from kissing her. "I haven't known you long, but I think we can agree you can't stay away from a mystery."

Bianca licked her lips. "Touché. And... I think we can also agree that you can't talk me out of it."

His mouth twisted into a grin. "Where's your car, Bianca?"

She pointed to it, relieved to know her feet would be free from the heels. Her car beeped after turning off the alarm. Opening the passenger door, she leaned to grab her flat shoes on the floor. Once she'd made the switch, she breathed easier. "That feels amazing."

Detective Sims laughed. "Okay."

She eyeballed him. "I almost walked barefoot to the car."

He folded his arms. "Why didn't you?"

"Are you kidding? I don't do that. Unless I'm at the beach or something." Bianca closed the passenger door and locked her car once more.

"When was the last time you went to the beach?" he asked.

A twinge of pain passed through her chest. She didn't mind talking about it, but the memories were hard. "It was, um... my honeymoon. My parents sent us to Hawaii."

Detective Sims bobbed his head. "I see."

"The last time I went somewhere tropical was a few years prior to our divorce. Alyssa loved making sandcastles and splashing in the water. After we split, it didn't... feel the same. I haven't traveled like that for a while."

He gave her a soft smile. "I'm sure you're making new memories now."

She smiled back. "Yes, I am. Taking it one day at a time."

Looking past her across the street, Bianca followed his gaze to the ice cream truck. "Dessert?" he asked.

"You didn't have any earlier? I told you about Judy's pastries."

He winked at her, gesturing for her to follow him.

Bianca's grin grew wider as she fell in step with him again, taking care to look both ways as she crossed the street. His choice, strawberry ice cream. Bianca decided on half chocolate and half vanilla. Finding a secluded bench, they sat down to indulge in their treats.

"You seriously don't like strawberry ice cream?" he teased her.

Bianca waved her plastic spoon at him. "Don't judge me. We all have our preferences."

He chuckled. "Fine. I won't hold it against you."

"Is this your day off?" she asked.

He shook his head. "No. I had an early morning, but when my co-workers invited me out, I figured why not?"

So that was it. How often did he go out with his co-workers? Did he notice the brunette eyeing him too? Not that Bianca cared too much. Detective Sims' smoldering eyes were tough to ignore. Bringing herself to the present moment, Bianca swallowed the smooth ice cream, relishing in the chill it brought. A moan escaped her mouth.

"Enjoying yourself?" he asked.

"I do what I can. That's why I don't mind going places, even if it's by myself," she said.

"I can respect that."

"You can? Some people think it's a bad thing. It's almost as if they feel sorry for me when they see me alone," Bianca explained. Her eyes bugged, and she swallowed another spoonful of ice cream. "That may have been too much. I didn't mean to say that."

"You're fine, Bianca," he said. "I'm sure you know by now, but it doesn't matter what people think of you."

"What about you? Have you ever cared what other people think?" Bianca wondered.

"I can think of one time." His face slackened and his lips tightened. "Anyway, I worked my way through it. Came here." Then he stared at her. "And like you, I have the chance to make new memories."

Bianca's chest heaved. Her mind couldn't help wondering. Was he referring to a previous relationship? What memories did he want to forget? She never pried too much into his personal life, despite the notion to inch closer to him and ask. Would he tell her? Taking another spoonful of ice cream, she willed her stomach to stop quivering. "I'm happy for you."

"Thank you." He didn't stop staring.

Bianca's body temperature rose and the ice cream wasn't helping. Swallowing the last of her treat, she stood to her feet and tossed the Styrofoam cup in a nearby trash bin. "I should get home."

"Early riser?" he asked. He did the same and tossed his cup into the trash.

"No. I'm not a morning person, believe it or not," she admitted. "It's one of those things I've disciplined myself to do. I'd rather stay in bed."

He fell in step with her again, walking her to her car. "Maybe you need a vacation? Start traveling again."

A *hmm* escaped her throat. She'd never considered that. "Perhaps. That's *if* I can convince my sister to go with me."

"I mean for you." His eyes focused on her face once more. "Why not do something just for you?"

Bianca's shoulders drooped. "That never crossed my mind. I guess it would be the perfect time. My daughter is spending the summer with her dad. My sister will probably be gone on another assignment." Then her mother crossed her mind. But Deborah Wallace could take care of herself.

"It's your choice, but think about it. It might be a good idea," he said.

Bianca parted her lips. "Thank you. I will."

He bobbed his head. "Goodnight, Bianca."

She fiddled with her keys in her hand. "Goodnight."

She wouldn't stare, so she turned her back on him. Yet her fingers tingled. She never thought with his tough exterior that he would buy her ice cream. Thank goodness he hadn't sat too close to her on the bench. He may have heard how fast her heart had been beating.

Bianca rubbed at her forehead. How was this possible? Were these actual feelings developing, or was he just being nice? When was the last time a man had flirted with her? Was she oblivious to his interest? *Was* he even interested in her? Bianca blew out her cheeks.

It was time to go home. There was enough going on in town with a murder. Her personal life would have to wait. Then again, how long had it been on hold already? Bianca groaned. She wouldn't solve anything standing by her car.

Unlocking the door, she slid into the driver's seat. Cranking the engine, she pulled out of her parking space, only to be stopped by a red traffic light. Turning her head to the left, she noticed an illuminated sign in front of what appeared to be a vacant building. *Office space for lease.*

Bianca tapped on her steering wheel and pulled ahead as the light turned green. Office space? With business picking up, she wondered if it would be best to work outside of the home rather than her office.

What were the pros? A place for clients to meet her in person? That would give Bianca her home office back. Having local clients visit her at home was nice in the beginning, but with her reputation growing outside of Edenville, she was missing home being home. Veronica couldn't meet with her, since she lived four hours outside of Edenville, but that would change once she moved into town, once her lease on her apartment was up in two months' time.

Having a presence in the heart of downtown, where many of her clients would be, that was the plus. Bianca's nose wrinkled.

What about her dog, Casper? She could find a dog sitter in town or have him stay with her mom's dogs, Jasper and Horas. Melanie could take him too when she wasn't on a writing assignment. Then again, he could come with her if she had to bring him. A lot to consider with this new venture. Was it a good idea?

Chapter 8

The following Tuesday morning, Bianca hit the *snooze* button when her alarm went off on her phone. Her eyes squeezed shut, but it was no use. She was awake. The sunlight peeked through her curtains and she pushed back the covers on her queen-sized bed. Rubbing at her eyes, she stood and shuffled her feet to her main bathroom. After showering and dressing for the day, she was happy to meet Alyssa in the kitchen washing her own plate.

"Ready?"

"In a sec." Alyssa wiped her hands with a nearby dish towel. "How's Aunt Mel doing? Any better?"

"One day at a time." No sense in hiding her curiosity. Her gaze remained focused on her daughter. "How about you?"

Alyssa stared back at her mother as she folded the dish towel, placing it back on the counter. "I'm... getting there."

"I can't imagine how it shocked you. It took me off guard too." Bianca hoped she brought some comfort to her daughter.

Alyssa wrung her fingers together. "It's nothing I can't get over. I'm sorry about what happened to Aunt Mel's friend. I... looked forward to meeting her backstage."

A thought popped into Bianca's head. Why didn't she remember before? "Didn't you tell me you saw something that night? When you went to the restroom before the show started?"

Alyssa looked away, staring at Casper, who was gnawing at his rabbit chew toy. "I don't remember, Mom."

"Are you sure? If you do, we can always go back to the pol—"

"Mom, can we just go? I really want to get to school. I want to... take my mind off things. Please?"

No sense in pushing harder than she needed to. Bianca gestured to the door that led to the garage. "Sure. Let's go then."

Alyssa grabbed her backpack and then bent to pet Casper. "Keep Aunt Mel busy, huh?"

He barked and wagged his tail.

Bianca smiled and grabbed her keys. Alyssa slid into the car next to her, and Bianca pulled out of the garage to the street. Bianca opened her mouth to speak to Alyssa, but collected her thoughts instead. *She needs more time than I thought.* Not to mention, it could have been typical teenager mood swings. Were there other things on Alyssa's mind instead? Her relationship with Kendrick, perhaps? Nothing to worry about too much.

Brushing a curl behind her ear, Bianca recalled how Detective Sims had stared at her the other night. She swallowed as she straightened in her driver's seat. Not quite what she planned on thinking about. Yet, she hadn't been expecting to sit next to him in the moonlight, or her body temperature to rise despite eating her ice cream.

"Mom?" Alyssa's voice broke through.

"I'm sorry. You said something?" she asked, stopping at a red light.

"I said Chloe and I will be staying a little late after school today. With finals coming up, we formed a study group with some other kids," her daughter explained.

Bianca couldn't help but tease. "Will Kendrick be there?"

Alyssa's pupils dilated. "Uh... maybe."

"Sure. Just make sure you focus on studying and nothing else."

"Mom, we'll be in the library. No harm in that," Alyssa countered with a tilt of her head.

So it was typical teenage behavior. Why did Bianca worry again? Simple, she was a mother. "Uh-huh. I've had my share of fun in high school in the library. You think you're getting away with the librarian, not looking," Bianca said. Then she gasped.

"Mom!" Alyssa's mouth dropped. "Don't tell me you and Dad got kicked out of the library."

Bianca swallowed. How would she dig herself out of this hole? "Not exactly. It's... not as if we were making out. Just a few lingering... kisses. Next thing I knew, we had to separate and... leave for the day."

"Wow," Alyssa replied. "I don't know if I'm grossed out or surprised that you really used to be my age."

Bianca came to a red light, giving her an opportunity to eye her daughter. "I'm not that old. I keep telling you that. One day, you'll be my age with kids and then you'll understand what I'm talking about." She pointed to her daughter. "Not before you finish college, though."

Alyssa raised her hands in a gesture of surrender. "I won't. You can relax on the grandkid talk."

Bianca turned at the red light and into the parking lot of Edenville High School. Despite the cars in front of her, she pulled up next to the curb. "So three-thirty or four this afternoon?"

"Four thirty works. I'll text you if we finish early or I can ride home with Chloe." With that, Alyssa slid out of the car, waving goodbye.

Bianca waved back, and using her rearview mirror, she looked behind her for a clear view. She pulled out of the parking lot, only to hit the steering wheel once she remembered. She had agreed to bring croissants for the teachers. As part of the PTA, the rotation fell on her once again. Bianca didn't mind, since it gave her a chance to have one of her friend's baked goods.

"Shoot." Perhaps her mind had been too occupied with her daughter and Detective Sims. Thankfully, she knew where to go, so she headed toward R&J's Restaurant and Bakery. Judy never failed to have what Bianca needed, whether it was for the teachers or her own sweet tooth.

Parking and dashing out of her car, when Bianca opened the door, the bell chimed. Her eyes locked with Judy behind the counter. Thank goodness it wasn't a long line, although it was still early. Her green-eyed friend waved, and she returned the gesture.

Tapping her foot to the floor, a middle-aged couple caught her eye at one of the small tables. Holding hands across the table from each other, Bianca wondered by their downturned faces what had happened. Salt-and-pepper coifed hair covered the man's head. His thick eyebrows were noticeable, and he was husky for his small frame.

The woman seated across from him had a long face and sharp features, especially along her jawline. Silky brunette hair barely touched her shoulders, and if it weren't for her wrinkly neck,

Bianca would have guessed the woman was younger. Finally approaching the counter, Bianca smiled at her friend.

"What can I get you?" Judy asked, her red hair pulled into a tight bun.

"Please tell me you have croissants," Bianca pleaded.

"You know I do." Judy sing-songed her response.

Bianca giggled. "I don't know about you sometimes," she further teased.

Her friend waved her comment off. "You love it, and we could use some cheer in this town with all that's happened." Then her friend stared past her. "You see that older couple over there?"

Bianca didn't turn around. "I saw them when I came inside. Hope they're okay."

Judy shook her head. "That's Clark Wilson. Sherry's father. I think that's the stepmother too."

Bianca blinked. No surprise that they would show up. There'd been a death in the family. "They talked to you?"

"He said they were on vacation, but I've seen his name enough online to know who he is. Richard loves politics, so he knows who's in office, regardless if they're a big name or from a small town."

"What do you know about Mr. Wilson then?" Bianca asked.

"He's a mayor back in their small town, Cliffston, Georgia, outside of Atlanta. His first wife died when Sherry was small, but he remarried when she was a teenager. He's very private, but has the reputation of keeping his campaign promises."

It all came back to Bianca. She recalled Sherry's father, who at the time was a city council member when they lived in Atlanta, Georgia. He was mayor now? Even if it wasn't in

Atlanta, good things were obviously benefiting his career. Did he move to a smaller town in Georgia before or after Sherry made it in the modeling world? Bianca had even remembered Melanie getting a letter from Sherry, entailing information about her new stepmother. Bianca didn't stay home much longer after that, since she moved to California after her marriage to Malcom.

"What about the new wife?" Bianca handed Judy her debit card.

"That's the only story I know that made headlines. Their town is small but known for holding up traditional family values. Any type of scandal and you're through. Although I don't think their marriage started off on a scandal. People were just surprised he remarried since he was so distraught after his first wife passed away. His new wife's name is Joan." Judy handed her back her card.

Bianca placed it back inside her wallet. "All of this from a small town."

"I think you've lived in Edenville long enough now to know plenty of things happen in small towns. They're just not as well-publicized as the big cities," Judy said.

Bianca pivoted to face the couple. They weren't talking. Only holding hands. "I wonder," she whispered to herself.

"Here you go." Judy handed her a white box filled with croissants.

Bianca took it. "You're a lifesaver. Thank you." Backing away from the counter, she took her time heading to the door.

"I just can't believe it."

Bianca slowed her steps while listening to Clark Wilson.

"Who would do such a thing to Sherry?" he asked his wife.

"I don't know, dear," Joan said. "Hopefully, the police will have some answers. I... know I didn't always get along with her, but I am so sorry."

A mirthless laugh escaped his lips. "You two were like oil and water sometimes."

"I think we'll be here a while packing her things. Jacqueline said Sherry never packed light when working a gig." Joan added.

"She always said 'there's an outfit for every occasion. I can't wear the same outfit all the time.'" Her father sniffled. "Even when she was little, she insisted on packing her entire closet when we traveled for vacations. I guess that... started her love for fashion."

Knowing she couldn't eavesdrop too much longer, Bianca headed out the door to her car. Joan hadn't gotten along with Sherry. Not a total shock to Bianca, since she heard their phone call and Sherry's comments at the rehearsal. Blended families took time to gel, but apparently the stepmother and daughter butted heads. Bianca blew out her cheeks, knowing she had to drop off the croissants and get back home to start her work day.

Chapter 9

That same Tuesday evening, Bianca and her sister walked into the gym with their yoga mats. Music blared through the speakers, and she heard the grunts and heavy breathing of others exercising. The air smelled of antibacterial cleaner, rubber mats, and sweat.

"I think we fit in well. What do you think?" Melanie asked.

Bianca tied up her unruly brown curls, ready to workout with her sister hoping to run into Aiden Carlyle. "You're sure he'll come here?"

Melanie nodded while stretching her legs. "Sherry said he was a gym fanatic. He never missed a workout. If he's still in town, which I'm sure he is, if Clique Classic is, he'll be here. Plus, she told me he preferred the evening workouts over the mornings if he could help it."

Bianca stretched her arms. Alyssa and Casper were spending the night with her mother. No need to worry over them.

"I'm glad it all came back to you," Bianca said. "What else did Sherry say at your lunch?"

Melanie's mouth twisted, as if she were trying to remember. "I remember her talking about Aiden. Jacqueline. That's all, to be honest."

"Nothing about her manager?" Bianca wondered.

Her sister shook her head.

Bianca had to follow up with Jordan. It slipped her mind again, especially after seeing Sherry's father and stepmother at Judy and Richard's restaurant and bakery. Then her lips parted at the sight of a tall man entering the gym. No doubt since she saw him at the jewelry store. Aiden Carlyle. Dark shirt popping with muscles, basketball shorts, and sneakers were his fitness attire. Bianca stretched into a lunge.

"How do you want to do this?" Melanie whispered.

Bianca watched further as he headed to the locker room. He didn't stay long, then walked out and headed for the weights.

"I think I have it," Bianca said. "You go first since I'm sure he'll recognize you. I'll come in a minute or you can say, 'I want you to meet my sister.' We'll keep an eye on him since I've witnessed his *temper*."

Melanie blew out her cheeks. "Got it. Not to mention... plenty of witnesses here." She walked casually over to where Aiden stood.

Stretching her legs some more, Bianca watched, and when she saw Aiden hug Melanie, she breathed easier. Perhaps he would be open to talk. Then her sister waved her over, and Bianca joined them to play her part.

"I want you to meet my sister, Bianca Wallace. Sis, this is the *famous* model and actor, Aiden Carlyle," Melanie said, touching a hand to his arm. Her sister apparently knew how to stroke his ego.

Aiden's bright smile grew. "I wouldn't say 'famous.'" He extended his hand to Bianca. "Nice to meet you. Pleasure."

"You too." Bianca noted his firm grip. "It's not often a well-known model comes to Edenville. How do you like it so far?"

He bobbed his head. "It's quiet. Not like New York. That's where I met..." His jaw clenched. "Sherry."

"I'm so sorry," Melanie said. "I can't imagine how you feel."

He nodded. "I wasn't there. I was meeting with my manager. I didn't hear about it until I watched the news."

A meeting? Wasn't he in the fashion show with Sherry? Why would he pass up an opportunity to be showcased in Clique Classic's upcoming success? What was so important? Even Bianca didn't sit on the chance when Giselle emailed her with an offer to work together after the referral she'd received.

Bianca also wondered where Aiden was meeting with his manager. She saw him in the grocery store parking lot. So with him in Texas, would his manager, whether he was in a larger city like New York or Los Angeles, bother to come to a small town like Edenville for a meeting? Unless... was it a virtual meeting? Bianca met with Veronica over Zoom regularly. Was that the case with Aiden?

She dug deeper. "It was a shock to all of us," Bianca added. "The police say it was... poison. I know it's probably none of my business, but I can't help but wonder: Did you know anyone who wanted to hurt Sherry? She seemed too nice to have enemies."

Aiden cracked his knuckles. "If they did, they got past me. I would've stopped whoever it was. Sherry didn't deserve that. She was too smart. Too beautiful. Too... She was amazing. If only Hunter saw that."

"Hunter? As in Hunter Graham?" Bianca raised an eyebrow. Based on her own research, Bianca knew he may have been bitter towards Sherry for dropping him.

"He claimed he knew what was best for Sherry's career, but she was too independent. They clashed constantly," Aiden explained.

"You didn't witness any arguments, did you?" Melanie asked.

Aiden rubbed his chin. "There was one. Though we'd broken up, I didn't see the harm in talking to the guy. He's here scoping for new clients, especially with Clique Classic's month-long fashion event after the show. Sherry wasn't the only well-known model on board. I caught Hunter at the grocery store. I told him to stay away from Sherry. He didn't seem fazed by me warning him. Hunter *always* gets what he wants."

Again, Bianca was taken aback by Aiden's news. Though she'd witnessed the disagreement between the two men, Hunter was calm compared to Aiden's temper. Did she not see until now that the man with him was Hunter? Come to think of it, when she Googled him, his hair was thicker in the pictures. A contrast to the buzzed haircut she noted in the grocery parking lot.

"Was Sherry scared of him?" Melanie asked.

Bianca didn't think so. There was nothing she saw to fear.

Aiden didn't answer.

Melanie leaned in. "Aiden? Something wrong?"

"I don't think she went through with it, but I heard talk of a... restraining order," he said.

Bianca flinched. Detective Sims had to know this already. Was Hunter Graham even on his list of suspects? Should she tell him? He had to have interviewed Aiden too, especially since he was a recent boyfriend of Sherry's. Yet Bianca didn't think Aiden would cover for Hunter and keep that away from the police. The men obviously didn't get along.

"When? I don't remember her telling me that." Melanie's forehead furrowed.

"Sherry kept a lot to herself," Aiden said. "Even some things from me."

Bianca asked, "I'm curious if you're in the month long fashion event going on in town?"

Aiden said, "I am. Why?"

"No reason, but I'm wondering why you weren't in the show too. It's interesting you'd have a meeting on the launch night. Wouldn't all the models in Clique Classic be involved with everything?"

Aiden's eyes shifted, and a vein engorged in his forehead. "It couldn't be helped. It was an important meeting."

"Did you see Sherry at all before the show?" Melanie asked. "I'm sure—"

He stopped her. "I'm sorry. I think I'm going to skip the gym today. Excuse me, ladies. Have a good evening." He walked to the locker room.

"Wow," Melanie exclaimed. "He didn't want to answer you there, did he?"

"Exactly, and it's possible Sherry filed a restraining order against Hunter. What took things that far for her to even think about doing that?" Bianca replied.

Her sister's eyebrows raised. "You disagree?"

Bianca folded her arms across her chest. "Hunter just seems so... mild mannered. I'm telling you, he was calm during that argument with Aiden at the store. Plus, he doesn't think Sherry went through with the restraining order."

Melanie walked beside her to their yoga mats. "Then maybe she didn't go through with it. I would have definitely remembered Sherry telling me something like that." She sighed. "Or... maybe I didn't know her as well as I thought I did. I remember saying, 'I'll tell you more soon,' but... I thought nothing of it. What did she want to tell me, Bianca?"

Bianca touched her sister's arm. "We all have some things we keep to ourselves. I'm sure she had her reasons."

Melanie replied, "We'll never know now, Bianca. She's gone."

Bianca sat on her mat. "I wonder where we can find this Hunter Graham." She faced her sister. Then Bianca jerked, as an idea had popped into her head. "Jordan." Finally, her memory benefited her.

Melanie grinned, but Bianca wouldn't tease her sister about Jordan. At least not now.

"What about him?" her sister asked.

"I remember him telling me his agent was well known and never ceased to network. I'm sure he knew this Hunter guy. I've been forgetting to follow-up but not anymore," Bianca said. "I remember our conversation last time he was at the house."

Melanie's forehead wrinkled. "You think it'll help?"

The women turned, watching as Aiden walked through the glass doors with his gym bag.

"It's worth a shot." Bianca grabbed her yoga mat. "Let's go. We weren't working out, anyway."

Melanie giggled, taking her yoga mat in her hand. When they arrived at Bianca's car, they slid into their seats and locked the doors. Bianca cranked the engine, gesturing to her sister.

"What?" Melanie's eyebrows furrowed.

"Call Jordan now. We can't sit on this too long," Bianca said. "And put him on speakerphone."

"Melanie reached into her jacket pocket and took out her phone. She didn't scroll for long, and when she put her phone on speaker, Bianca heard the loud rings.

"Hey, Mel," Jordan greeted her. "Are you okay?"

"Yeah, I'm with Bianca. We have you on speaker. Is this a bad time?" she asked.

"No. Just finished a writing session. Why? What's wrong?"

"Didn't you tell me that your agent knew pretty much everyone in the industry because of his networking?" Bianca asked.

"Yeah, I talked to him yesterday. Just didn't call you yet," Jordan said.

"Well? Does he know Hunter Graham?" Bianca continued.

They heard him sigh through the speaker. "Well... I was right. With a name like Sherry Wilson, she was one of Hunter's top clients. My agent said a friend invited him to a black-tie event about a year ago in New York. A few celebrities showed up and he met Hunter there. How does he look now? Carl claims he had thick hair back then."

"Buzzed haircut." Bianca answered.

"Right. Just looked him up now with Sherry's name on the internet." Jordan continued. "Carl claims there was an argument, but nothing serious. Nothing life threatening. Security guards escorted the other man out. Not Hunter."

First the grocery store parking lot and now this story from Jordan. Hunter Graham didn't appear to have a history of irrational behavior. Would he have gotten violent and killed or orchestrated the poisoning of Sherry? Bianca couldn't picture it, but she wouldn't write it off just yet. "What else do you remember?" she asked, leaning one elbow on the console in her car.

"According to Carl, though he was good at his job, hardly anyone stayed with him as a client," Jordan added.

"Including Sherry." Melanie sighed. "This just keeps getting better, doesn't it?"

"Aiden said he's still in town scouting new clients." Bianca commented.

Jordan continued. "I remember Carl mentioning a Paris... Paris something. Not a standard last name. She's a model, though."

"Paris Deveraux?" Bianca pointed out.

"That's it!" Jordan confirmed.

"Didn't we meet her the day before too?" Melanie said. "She was nice until we mentioned Sherry."

"I think she's a client of Hunter's too. As far as I know, they still work together," Jordan said.

Bianca made a mental note. *She's staying here too. Fourth floor, I think.* "Stargaze Hotel."

"What?" both Melanie and Jordan said at the same time.

Bianca explained. "Jacqueline, Sherry's stepsister, told me that Paris was at the same hotel. Fourth floor. I wonder if we can find Hunter there too."

"Worth a try," Melanie agreed.

"Just be careful, you two. Haven't we had enough close calls to last a lifetime?" Jordan said.

Melanie gave a soft smile. "I'll be careful. Uh... I mean, we both will. Don't worry."

"Good to know," Jordan replied. "Knowing you two, something is about to happen."

Bianca replied, staring at her sister, noting her slip in her wording. "We will."

Melanie hung up and returned her phone to her jacket. Placing her hands in her lap, she looked forward.

"What was that?" Bianca gestured at her.

Melanie faced her and blinked. "What do you mean? I said bye."

"The *I'll be careful*." She reminded her sister. "Sounded like you needed to reassure him. What's up with that?"

Melanie cleared her throat. "He's a friend who's concerned. No need to read into anything."

Bianca smirked. "Okay. I'll let it go." She pointed at her. "But the next time you want to lecture me about Detective Sims, remember this conversation. I let you off the hook."

Melanie's mouth dropped. "Seriously?"

Bianca put the car in drive. "Seriously."

Chapter 10

Bianca leaned against her mother's kitchen counter. Though she and Melanie looked for Paris at the Stargaze Motel, the hotel staff wouldn't give them any information. She had a part of the Clique Classic's month-long fashion event too. Bianca finally assumed Paris wasn't at the hotel for the moment, so she and Melanie returned home.

Family dinners never failed to happen with Bianca's mother, and this time, even though it was on a Wednesday night, Melanie came with her and Alyssa to their mother's house. Despite her downturned features, at least her sister was trying, and that was all Bianca could hope for. The timer pinged on her mother's stove and Bianca pivoted, grabbed the oven mittens, and opened the door. The heat surrounded her face, but she took out the pan. Today's meal was her mother's chicken and rice recipe.

"Smells amazing," Bianca said, placing the pan on the stovetop.

"I have a surprise for you tonight." Her mother pointed out.

"Mom, what did you do?" Bianca wondered, placing the mittens back on the countertop.

Her mother waved her comment away. "You'll see, and I think you'll like it."

Bianca grinned. She cleared her throat before asking her next question. "Is Luther Burkes coming over?"

Her mother grabbed the plates inside the cabinet. "What makes you think he's coming over?"

Bianca tilted her head to the side. "Mom?"

Deborah Wallace placed the plates on her kitchen island. "Is it that obvious?"

Bianca's grin grew. "The question is: do you genuinely like him?"

Her mother's eyes beamed. "I do, Bianca. He's... a wonderful man and I enjoy getting to know him." Her mother pressed her hands to her cheeks. "I didn't think I'd be dating again at this stage in my life. I didn't expect to... lose your father."

Bianca's heart sunk, and she walked over to embrace her mother. "But I know he'd want you to keep living. He wouldn't want you to hold back when you could have something amazing."

Her mother patted her back. "You're right, sweetie." Pulling back, her mother dabbed at her eyes. "He was such a selfless man. He gave his life to protect his family and his community. Your father was one of the best men I knew. And loved."

Bianca linked her arm through her mother's. "I'm happy for you. Mr. Burkes seems like a good choice for you."

"We're taking things slow, but I'm too old to play games," her mother pointed out.

"Not *that* old," Bianca said.

Her mother raised an eyebrow.

"Let's say *mature* or... *seasoned*," Bianca suggested, but a giggle escaped her lips.

Her mother chuckled. "Take the food to the table. I can't with that sense of humor of yours."

Bianca used the oven mittens once more to carry the pan to the table, finding Melanie and Alyssa in conversation. Casper, along with her mother's dogs, Jasper and Horas, golden and dark brown Yorkies, were reclining in the corner. "Dinner's ready."

Alyssa smiled along with her sister. At least they were both in a better mood tonight.

"Here are the plates," her mother said, walking in behind her. When the doorbell rang, the dogs barked and immediately hurried to the door. She placed a stack of plates on the table. "I'll get that."

"I wonder who that could be," Melanie teased.

Alyssa cupped her cheeks. "I still can't believe Grandma is dating."

"Are they exclusive now?" Melanie asked.

"She didn't say anything about that to me. Only that she's happy," Bianca answered.

Melanie folded her arms on the table. "Well... that's all that matters."

"Come in," Bianca's mother said to Luther as she guided him into the dining room. She faced Bianca, along with Alyssa and Melanie at the table.

"Good to see you again," Bianca said to him.

Luther Burkes gave a slight bow, though her mother's arm looped through his. He trimmed as always his beard, and Bianca noticed the laugh lines around his eyes. "Good to see you all again."

"Please sit." Bianca's mother directed him to a dining chair.

Luther instead looked at her mother. "Where are you sitting?"

Bianca's mother pointed to her seat. Luther pulled her chair out and waited for her to sit down first.

"Always the gentleman," Melanie commented. "I love it."

Luther chuckled. "I learned a thing or two in my years about how to treat a woman. Although I've learned a lot from the young women too. Getting used to the modern days but keeping up with the traditions I feel are important."

"Such as?" Bianca asked. She passed the plates down to everyone to serve themselves.

"I have a granddaughter about Alyssa's age. Apparently, she wants to be so independent that she says 'I don't need a man.'"

"What does your daughter say to that?" Bianca's mother asked him.

Luther sighed as he served his plate. "She's... never cared too much about what I think. Things haven't been the same since her mother left."

Bianca's mother took his hand. "You don't have to talk about it if you don't want to."

He gave a faint smile. "Don't worry about it. That was a long time ago. I do my best to stay in touch with my daughter and granddaughter, but relationships are a two-way street."

"They don't talk to you at all?" Alyssa asked.

"Only on holidays and birthdays," Luther said.

"That's sad," Melanie added. "You don't have to go into details, but I am sorry to hear that."

"Me too." Bianca chimed in. When her phone rang with Mary J. Blige's ringtone "Just Fine," that meant only one person was calling. Her ex-husband. Malcom Holmes. Had something happened? He'd only been calling when it had something to do with Alyssa. Bianca appreciated that. She didn't care to reminisce about the good old days of their once marriage.

Bianca stood and walked over to the basket sitting in her mother's window. Her assumptions proved correct.

"Bianca?" Her mother didn't care for phones during their meals.

"It's Malcom, Mom. It may be something important. He doesn't call that much anyway," Bianca explained.

Alyssa perked up. "Dad?"

Bianca wondered if her daughter suspected they would talk about her. Though Malcom knew of their daughter's relationship with Kendrick, his protective side always surfaced. Or did she share with him about Sherry's death at the show? Did she open up to her father before her own mother?

"Yes." Bianca answered. "I won't be long."

"Fine, but we're saying grace when you finish," her mother replied.

Bianca excused herself to the kitchen and answered. "Hello?"

"Hey," his bass voice greeted. "You have a minute?"

"Sure. Why?" she asked, her skin prickling with curiosity.

"I know we agreed Alyssa would leave to visit the weekend when she gets out for the summer, but I need another week. I have a project at work and I don't want her to come and I'm too tied up," he said.

Bianca breathed easier. "Sure. No problem. Thanks for letting me know. Have you told her yet?" she said.

He answered, "No, I wanted to check with you. I'm working on being... considerate."

Perhaps he *had* changed. Communication hadn't been his strong point during their marriage. "I'll let her know. I have to go, though. Family dinner."

"Family dinner?" Malcom sighed. "That's the thing I miss. The family getting together. I didn't appreciate it then, but I miss them now. Don't get much of that anymore."

Bianca wouldn't dare rehearse the past. "Yeah, well, you know how my mother is about phones at dinner, so... I'll let Alyssa know. Talk to you later."

"Thanks, Bianca. Bye." He hung up.

Bianca ended the call and exhaled. So Malcom missed her family's dinners. When she'd told him about them, when they'd gotten married, he'd found them silly. He hadn't thought a family needed to see each other every single week or more. He'd said he'd wanted his own life with her outside of her family. He'd come from a different background. Love was understood, not spoken of, between Malcom and his parents, and they weren't as close-knitted as Bianca's family was.

Malcom had never said he'd envied her relationship with her sister and parents, but the flaring nostrils, thinning mouth, and twitching hands couldn't have been denied. Bianca shivered, hoping to shake away the past for good. Then again, it was part of her story. She couldn't wish it away.

"Bianca?" her mother called out.

Exhaling once more, Bianca joined her family and Luther at the table.

"DON'T WORRY, BIANCA," Luther Burkes said. "We'll give your car the works today."

"Thank you." She beamed at her mother's potential suitor, Luther Burkes. Was it official between them? Her mother hadn't announced it, but Bianca had a fluttery feeling in her stomach that something was going to happen between her mother and Luther.

It was long overdue, in Bianca's opinion. How would her mother tell them? Surely, she knew that both her daughters wanted her to be happy, and if Luther was her second chance, Bianca wanted her mother to go for it.

Go for it. Not the advice she wanted to hear for her own personal life. Bianca licked her lips as the charming Detective Sims came back to her mind.

She focused back on where she was. Late Thursday morning, the day after their Wednesday family dinner, Bianca glanced over Luther Burkes. He wore his usual jumpsuit for his work attire. His salt-and-pepper hair still covered his head, and Bianca could appreciate a man with a well-groomed beard. How would Detective Sims look when he was older? *Not again.*

Bianca choked and patted her chest. *Not the time.*

"You okay, Bianca?" Luther asked. "Do you need some water?"

Bianca grabbed her bottle from her cup holder. "I have one. Thank you." She sipped slowly as her chest heaved. Her breathing returned to normal after a few more sips.

Luther's furrowed brow didn't look too convinced, but he didn't ask any further questions. "Okay. You can pull forward."

Bianca bobbed her head, rolling her window up. She still smelled the wet concrete mixed with the soapy chemicals.

Taking care not to hit the gray Mercedes-Benz ahead of her, she eased her foot off the brake, allowing her car to coast in neutral.

Opening a browser on her phone, she typed in Sherry Wilson's name. The top story? "Model Falls to her Death." Thank goodness they had taken the video down. No one needed to see her die like that.

The screams of shock still lingered in Bianca's ears. Melanie was getting better, but Alyssa still kept what she was feeling to herself. Scrolling the internet for more information, Sherry saw a few photos of Sherry with Aiden, along with Paris Deveraux.

Scrutinizing the photo with Sherry and Paris, she noted the photo was an advertisement for a perfume collection. Both women stood in long, satin evening prom dresses with spaghetti straps, cowl necks, and high slits, their silhouettes all lined, full length hem with neutral high heels.

How often had they worked together? Bianca hadn't gotten the impression that Paris had liked Sherry that much. Then again, Bianca had worked retail jobs in college and some of her co-workers she hadn't liked, but she'd put up with them for her paycheck to help support her, along with Malcom's work-study job.

She jerked when she heard a tap on the hood of her car. One of Luther's employees, a young man, spiky black hair, robust, no older than twenty-five, motioned for Bianca to park to the left underneath the bay. She did, only to pull up next to the gray Mercedes-Benz. Since she'd signed up for the works today, Bianca cut the engine and stepped out of her car.

Casper's hair had collected once more in her back seat, so a thorough vacuum was exactly what her Kia Soul needed. Thank goodness the open bay shielded her from the beating sun. The woman a few feet away from her stood with her phone in her hand. She recognized the silky brunette hair along with the strong jawline. Bianca knew that face... in Judy and Richard's place. She was taller than Bianca had assumed, at least five-eight, with a curvaceous build.

Bianca tapped her foot on the ground. If this was who she thought it was, how could she strike up a conversation? Then she noticed the leopard-print satchel hanging off the woman's arm. It complemented the woman's light blue jeans and short-sleeved black blouse.

"Love your purse!" Bianca exclaimed, widening her eyes for emphasis.

The woman tilted her head to the side and blinked. Then she focused on her satchel. "Oh, yes. Thank you."

"Where did you get it?" Bianca asked. "Or are you new to Edenville? I don't remember seeing this in stores here."

The woman, Joan, if she remembered correctly, shook her head. "It was a gift from my husband. He knew I had been eyeing it for a while. We're not from around here. We, um..." She paused, her gaze glossing over for a moment. "We had a death in our family."

Bianca touched a hand to her chest. "I'm sorry to hear that. I know there was a model in town who—"

"My stepdaughter. Sherry." She gave a faint smile. "I'm sorry. I'm Joan Wilson." She extended her freckly hand.

Bianca accepted the handshake. "Bianca Wallace."

Joan bobbed her head, as if the name rang a bell in her mind.

Bianca continued. "I was... actually there when she collapsed. Sherry may have mentioned my sister. Melanie Wallace."

Joan blinked as if realization hit her. "I knew that last name sounded familiar, but I didn't pick up on it. Sherry didn't... share with me too much about her friends. Or boyfriends."

"No?" Bianca pressed, hoping the woman would tell her more.

"Blended families are never easy. I already had a daughter when I married Clark. Sherry... didn't take to me very well."

"I'm sure with time, she..."

Joan shook her head. "Not Sherry." Her gaze raised upward, enough for Bianca to notice a small mole underneath her left eye. "She was always an independent child. I did my best, but she had a mind of her own. And now... she's..."

"I am sorry for your loss. I can only imagine how your husband feels," Bianca added, while keeping an eye out on the two guys drying off her car.

"As good as expected. It's terrible what happened, but the timing couldn't be worse."

"Worse?" Bianca asked.

"Clark is running for reelection for mayor of our city back in Cliffston, Georgia." She sighed. "He's worked so hard and this has broken his heart."

Bianca wondered. Wouldn't the death of his daughter be more important than him being reelected mayor? She kept that part to herself. "I hope the best for you with all of it."

Joan gave a faint smile. "His campaign manager is working on it. We've tried to keep the press out of family affairs as much as possible, but with her death broadcasted the way it was..."

Bianca had read a few articles online discussing Sherry's mysterious death. The question was, why? Who had been responsible? Bianca kept her composure, watching Joan flip her hair.

"To be honest, I can't get it out of my mind." It was true. Bianca could still see Sherry, eyes rolling to the back of her head, collapsing from the runway, practically into her and Melanie's laps.

"It's tragic," Joan added. "So young. Life ahead of her. Her career unstoppable."

"I'm sure you and your husband were proud of her," Bianca said.

Joan shrugged. "She talked to her father more than me. I tried calling to stay in touch, but I couldn't get past the wall she put up."

Bianca recalled Sherry's attitude towards Joan that day she'd called while they'd all been in her dressing room. Sherry hadn't been overly rude, but she hadn't been in the best mood for her stepmother. "Some people don't know how to open up like others."

Joan tilted her head to the side, practically giving Bianca the side eye. "I love my husband, but he doted on Sherry." A huff escaped her mouth. Her expression pinched now. "I did everything I could to be nice to her. Trying to be a mother to her and Jacqueline. The way she treated my daughter was questionable, but with me trying to keep the peace with my husband, I didn't speak up as much as I should have."

Bianca didn't respond. This lined up with what Jacqueline said, that even her mom didn't stand up for her against Sherry. Joan's annoyance showed further, with her gaze flicking upward.

Shaking her head, she added, "I've said too much, but it's been so overwhelming. One moment she's here and the next she's... gone." Joan blew out her cheeks as if to recompose herself. When a buzzing sound came through her phone, she held up a long finger. "Give me a moment."

Bianca bobbed her head.

Joan gasped. "Oh, no. I have to go. Excuse me." The woman walked to her Mercedes-Benz. The young man who'd finished drying her car gestured, letting her know he'd finished. He wiped his sweaty brow with the back of his hand.

Bianca bit the inside of her lip. Something didn't sit right with her regarding Sherry's stepmother. Was she genuinely grieving Sherry's death, or was it an act? If she and Sherry hadn't gotten along for years despite her own efforts, would she have got rid of her for good?

Blinking, Bianca knew her thoughts were far-fetched, but she'd heard their conversation. The women had tolerated each other, and Sherry hadn't treated Jacqueline as well as she could have. Then again, Bianca didn't live in a blended family. Some were not on as good terms as others. Had that been the case here? Even to the point of... murder?

Chapter 11

Later that same Thursday afternoon, Bianca twirled a curl loose from her high ponytail with her index finger. The meeting with the real estate company had gone without a hitch. They'd hired her to update their business logo. Going for a more modern look, Bianca bit her bottom lip. Their primary colors were ruby red, but she pondered going with a lighter shade.

Moving her mouse to the corner of her screen, she browsed through her colors. Rose or blush? She stared upward. Though blush would suffice, she chose rose so it wouldn't be that huge of a change.

When her phone rang, Bianca looked over at her phone on her desk. Melanie. She answered. "Hey, what's up?"

"You'll never guess who I found," she said.

Bianca had no clue. "Who?"

"Paris Deveraux. She's downtown at the antique shop. I don't know how long she's going to be there, but this may be our chance to talk to her."

Why would a high-class model go to an antique shop in a small town? Was it her day off from the fashion event? "Are you sure that's her?"

"Positive," Melanie answered with unwavering assurance in her voice.

"Okay. I'm practically finished with my project, anyway. I'll be there soon." She hung up. Thank goodness her sister had dropped off Casper at their mother's house already. Saving her work, she changed her shoes, grabbed her keys, and headed for the door. The thought of renting more office space crossed her mind again when she clicked on her seatbelt inside her car. Turned out the real estate company renting it out, she updated their company's logo six months prior. Tapping her fingers to the wheel, she thought about it more while driving into downtown.

Traffic was never an issue in Edenville, but Bianca had trouble finding a parking space. Once she parallel parked on the street, she called Melanie to see where she was. Colorful welcome signs hung in front of businesses while some had welcome displays on windows. People chatted as they walked, while a few old trucks chugged along down the street. Cinnamon filled Bianca's nose. They weren't too far from Richard and Judy's restaurant and bakery. Perfect choice for lunch.

Melanie caught her eye and waved her over to her. Bianca didn't hesitate, practically sprinting to meet her.

"She still there?" Bianca asked.

Melanie bobbed her head. "I don't know what she's looking for, but she's taking her time."

"Maybe it's a hobby of hers. It's interesting that she's even in there," Bianca commented. "Well, let's go."

Melanie followed her inside, and the bell chimed above them. They met narrow aisles with table displays on both sides. Sunlight glimmered off of silver and crystal pieces, antique wood cabinets filled with dainty figurines, collectible plates, and china cups. A grandfather clock ticked behind them and the air was mixed with oil paint and potpourri.

"You see her?" Melanie whispered.

Bianca whispered back, "Not yet." Browsing the store, Bianca noticed the silver and bronze candlesticks, pitted oil lanterns, and hand-carved dressers with warped drawers.

"Bianca." Melanie tapped her shoulder and pointed ahead.

Paris Deveraux stood holding a vintage hairbrush. Her long red hair cascaded over one shoulder, a green V-neck lantern sleeve belted solid jumpsuit, and black pumps.

"What's the plan?" her sister asked.

Bianca exhaled. "I don't know, but follow my lead." Both ladies walked closer, but they didn't announce themselves. Turning her back, Bianca admired an old wooden chest. Pivoting, her shoulder bumped Paris'. "Excuse me. I'm so sorry."

Paris' sea-blue eyes blinked at Bianca. "No problem. Wait a minute. I've met you, haven't I?"

Bianca extended her hand. "Yes. We met the day before the fashion show in town."

"Nice to see you again," Melanie chimed in.

Paris bobbed her head and placed the hairbrush back on its shelf. "Yes. The fashion show. So tragic what happened. I was backstage, so I didn't know what had happened until I heard the crowd screaming. There was so much commotion."

"When Sherry collapsed..." Melanie said. "She practically fell in our laps."

Paris touched a hand to her chest. "That's what I heard, that she fell on some people in the audience." A *tsk* sound escaped her thin, red lips. "It is a shame."

"We weren't expecting to see you here, though. I'm assuming you're a part of the extended Clique Classic fashion event in town?" Bianca asked.

Paris beamed. "Yes. I couldn't turn that down. It's been a needed distraction with everything... going on. I hate what happened to Sherry, but..." A huff escaped her mouth. "She could be a nuisance. Our careers took off around the same time, and everyone *loved* her."

Melanie's lips parted. "Did you know she would be in the fashion show with you?"

"I knew, all right." Paris replied. "Like I said, I was civil, but that was it. I wanted to back out, but my manager didn't think that was a good idea. Hunter always thinks he knows the answer to everything."

"Hunter Graham? We heard he was Sherry's manager too for a while," Bianca mentioned. Would Paris take the bait?

"Now *there* were two people who got along perfectly," Paris commented. "Anyway, I don't know why Sherry fired him. Hunter didn't take it too well at first, but he accepted it eventually. He's a gentleman. Now Aiden, he didn't take it well when she broke up with him."

"You knew about that?" Bianca wondered. How did Paris know something so personal about Sherry if they weren't even close? Not to mention how well she spoke of Hunter. Aiden, however, said otherwise about Sherry's former agent. Who was telling the truth? Bianca had no reason to believe any of them.

Paris laughed. "*Everyone* knew about those two. Aiden never ceased to post about their relationship on social media. Talking about how in love with her he was and how she was the best thing that ever happened to him."

Bianca would search for his social media next. Why hadn't that crossed her mind after she'd seen him at the jewelry store and gym?

"Now…" Paris looked both ways to see if anyone else was listening. "Just between us, I think there was someone else."

"Someone else?" Melanie raised an eyebrow.

"I think Aiden cheated on Sherry, which is why she broke up with him. He may have posted about their relationship online, but that didn't mean he didn't have the reputation of being a player. Rumors has is it was her stepsister."

"Jacqueline?" Bianca had never suspected that, and Sherry ended things with Aiden for lack of commitment. Was Paris making this up? Why would she assume such a thing?

Paris bobbed her head. "On top of everything else, we knew Aiden for being possessive. You know the 'if I can't have you, no one else will' type. He could move on, but I doubt he would let Sherry leave him for good."

"Wow." Melanie blinked.

"Who knew there was so much drama in the modeling industry?" Bianca commented, rubbing the back of her neck. She and Melanie did witness Aiden's attitude, even noticing the engorged vein in his forehead when they questioned him.

"It's every man for himself in our world, or *woman*." Paris cleared her throat. "Well, I just hope the police find whoever did this to poor Sherry, but if I had to suspect someone, it'd be Aiden. I've seen the man's temper." She smiled. "Nice to see you ladies again." She walked off as if she had no care in the world.

Paris left Bianca and Melanie standing in the aisle.

"Well, that went well," Melanie said.

"You think?" Bianca replied. "I'm not sure what to believe now. This puzzle keeps getting more and more complicated. Did Sherry tell you any of this?"

Melanie shook her head. "No, and I didn't ask. Sherry wanted to dump Aiden because he didn't want to marry her. She wanted to forget it and enjoy our lunch and catch up."

"There's only person we haven't talked to," Bianca said.

"Hunter Graham?" Melanie asked.

Bianca nodded. "And I wonder... if we can find him at the Stargaze Hotel. If he's here scouting new clients with this month-long fashion event in town, I know he's still here." Also, a small memorial in Sherry's honor would be in Edenville because of her model friends being so close by for the fashion event. The family would hold the funeral back in Georgia. Who would all be in attendance there?

"Following you," Melanie said.

Exiting the antique shop and walking back to their cars, Bianca cranked her engine and pulled off. Melanie kept close behind and by the time they reached the hotel, the sisters parked next to each other. Calling Melanie through her Bluetooth, Bianca stared ahead at the five-story building.

"Yeah?" Melanie answered.

"Trying to figure out how we're going to play this." Bianca tapped her fingers on the steering wheel, but when a black Jaguar pulled into the parking lot, she stared. The car parked a few feet away, and when a red-haired woman stepped out, Bianca gasped. "Mel!"

"I see her," Melanie said. "I wonder if she's..."

Bianca didn't stop staring as Paris fixed her hair, running her fingers through it while staring at herself in what appeared to be a compact mirror.

"Bianca, look." Melanie's voice echoed through the speaker.

Bianca did, only to see a short, stocky man walk through the automated doors. Hunter Graham wore dark jeans and a tanned, collared shirt. Paris smiled at the sight of him, and when he opened his arms, she met his embrace. Not the hug Bianca expected to see between manager and client. Hunter lingered, and Paris didn't seem to mind.

"There's no way," Melanie commented. "Him and her?"

"I doubt that they're..." Bianca paused when she saw Paris cup Hunter's face and kiss his lips. "No way." No wonder she raved about him and called him a *gentleman*.

"You've got to be kidding me." Melanie sighed. "Now what? Those two are together and... Bianca?"

Her mind's wheels were turning too, along with her sister's. "Let's see if she stays or goes."

"I'm not waiting out here for them to... you know... finish whatever they're doing," Melanie said with obvious annoyance.

Bianca held back a laugh. "If she leaves, we can talk to him. If not, we'll have to find another way."

Melanie exhaled.

Bianca refocused on Paris and Hunter. How long were they going to kiss? When they finally broke apart, Hunter walked with Paris to the driver's seat of her car. Opening the door, he waited for her to slide inside. Paris only let down the window once he closed the door, and she wrapped her hand around his neck. The couple kissed again, apparently not in a rush to say goodbye.

"I'm usually a romantic at heart, but this is too much, even for me," Melanie commented.

"She's leaving now," Bianca replied.

Paris waved at Hunter and he stepped away from her Jaguar. He waved back as she drove away.

"Now?" Melanie asked.

"Now." Hanging up, both Bianca and her sister stepped out of their cars. Melanie called out to Hunter.

"Excuse me, sir," she said.

Hunter stopped in his tracks, turning on his heels. He gave a bright smile. "Can I help you ladies?"

"I'm Bianca Wallace and this is my sister, Melanie Wallace." Bianca extended her hand.

Hunter greeted them both. "Pleasure. Hunter Graham. How can I help you?"

"I was friends with... Sherry Wilson," Melanie said.

He blinked, as if he didn't know what had happened. How could he not with the news of the model collapsing to her death all over Edenville?

"Terrible what happened." His chin dropped.

Okay. He knew.

Melanie continued. "I'm... doing a story on her for our town paper, *Edenville Gazette*. I was hoping you could give me some information. Word is you're her manager."

Bianca could have high-fived her sister, but she'd do that later. Melanie was getting the hang of things now.

"*Was* her manager," Hunter corrected. He shook his head slightly, but kept his warm smile. "That woman was too independent for her own good. She never listened."

"Sherry had a mind of her own," Melanie pointed out.

"Yes, and sadly... it got her killed," Hunter replied with his eyes closed. A sigh escaped his mouth. He faced them both and opened his eyes. His dark-blue eyes shimmered. "I'm sorry about your friend, but I can't help you with your story. Sherry... fired me and wouldn't reconsider."

"You wanted to work with her again?" Bianca wondered.

He cracked a smile. "Who wouldn't? She's brilliant. When the camera was on her, you could tell she knew what she was doing. She was a natural. Born to be a star. I only wanted to help get her there, but... we were too different. She had her own vision for her life. I even helped her, but... doesn't matter now."

"Did you try to talk to her? I never thought Sherry was... unreasonable." Melanie asked.

"She threatened to file a restraining order against me. I don't know why. One poor argument and suddenly, I'm dangerous to her? She's 'in fear for her life.'" A huff escaped his mouth. "It was ridiculous, especially with if affecting my business. It spread in the industry faster than I thought. All I wanted to do was talk to her. Straighten the whole thing out. Sherry wouldn't see me. Jacqueline wouldn't help me. You would think she would."

Bianca couldn't deny the earnestness in Hunter's voice. Perhaps he wanted to patch things up with Sherry.

"What do you mean about Jacqueline?" Melanie asked.

"They worked together, but I could tell they weren't close. Jacqueline and I talked a few times, and she always hinted at being in Sherry's shadow. Sherry never took her seriously. Jacqueline kept it professional the times I was around both of them, but it wouldn't surprise me if she...," Hunter explained, but paused.

It was a long shot, but Bianca asked anyway. "Do you have any idea who would want to hurt Sherry? Do you think Jacqueline was involved?" What was he trying to imply?

Hunter pulled his lips in for a moment. Then he blew out his cheeks. "If only I knew. I wish I could help you, but I can't." Then his phone buzzed in his pocket. "I'm sorry. If you ladies will excuse me, I have work to do." He walked off without another word.

"Well, that didn't help," Melanie said.

Bianca turned on her heels and back to her car.

Melanie followed. "Do you think he had something to do with it? He pointed the finger at Jacqueline."

Bianca ticked off each finger as she counted. "We have Jacqueline, who says Paris envied Sherry. Aiden thinks Hunter was resentful because of being fired, and while Hunter didn't accuse Jacqueline of murder, he hinted at something with her. We know Jacqueline didn't like her stepsister, but he pushed that further. He wasn't defensive with us either, as if he wanted to help."

"I wonder if this is the case of the evil stepsister, but even that didn't go that far in Cinderella's fairytale," Melanie said.

This was definitely not a fairytale. Those stories had happily ever-afters. Those didn't end in murder.

"Is there a reason you're here, Bianca?"

Gasping, Bianca turned to see Detective Sims walking from the right side of the parking lot. She didn't even see a car pull up. Now he was here. Blue suit, and a gray-collared shirt with no tie. The top buttons were open.

"How nice to see you, Detective Sims." Melanie answered.

"We were, um..." What excuse could Bianca make up this time? Why did she need an excuse anyway?

Melanie interjected. "Sis, thanks for meeting me. I've got to go. I'll see you at home later." Her sister winked at her and hurried to her car.

Bianca waved goodbye to her sister just as Detective Atkins joined her and Detective Sims from the same direction of the hotel parking lot. Where did they park to begin for Bianca to miss the police car?

Detective Atkins greeted her. "Ms. Wallace."

She greeted back. "Detective Atkins. Nice to see you again."

"I'll meet you inside," Detective Sims told him. His partner walked off after a last nod to Bianca.

She smiled in return and tapped her foot on the concrete. "I won't keep you." This was her chance to slip away.

"You didn't answer my question," Detective Sims repeated.

"Didn't I?" No harm in teasing him since there was no furrow in his brow. One of his tics, she'd noticed. What? She'd noticed what made him tic? Bianca blinked. "Just... meeting my sister."

"Uh-huh." He wasn't convinced.

Bianca swallowed. "I'm assuming you're here to investigate. Anybody I'd know?"

He eyeballed her.

Bianca rolled her eyes. "I'm not asking for details. I know the drill."

He exhaled. "Hunter Graham, and that's all I'm telling you." He reached out a hand and touched the middle of her back, leading her to her car.

Bianca ignored the tingles along her spine at the touch of his hand. "I was just leaving."

He raised an eyebrow. "I don't know what you're up to, Bianca, but please, let's not repeat last time."

She wouldn't make any promises. "I'll see you around."

He dropped his hand to his side and stepped back. Bianca unlocked her car and slid into the driver's seat as her mind raced. First, she wondered why the police wanted to see Hunter, and finally why her body had reacted to Detective Sims.

Despite her stomach flip at the latter, she couldn't help but wonder what the police were asking Hunter Graham. Bianca had some time before heading to her daughter's school. Stepping outside of her car and locking the door again, she sprinted to the hotel's automated doors.

Chapter 12

Once inside, Bianca bypassed the front desk. Would the police meet with Hunter in his room or the dining area inside the hotel? Taking a gamble, she walked along the tile floors toward the dining area. A large, green plant stood to the left of the open French doors, and Bianca took care to stand behind it as she scanned the room. Over to her left were marble countertops, which had probably served breakfast to the guests earlier.

On the main floor were round acacia wooden tables with cushioned wooden chairs. Bianca's eyes did a double take, noticing Detective Sims and Detective Atkins seated with Hunter Graham. The dining area only had a few others at tables. One young man typed on his laptop while another woman sat in the corner by the coffee machine, reading a book.

How would Bianca play this off? If only she had a magazine or newspaper to cover her face. She could hear Detective Sims now. *Stay out of police business.* Turning her back, she paced along the counter. Apples, bananas, and oranges were in bowls. Reaching out a hand, she pretended to choose which fruit to eat. Thank goodness Detective Sims' back was turned in his chair.

"When was the last time you saw Sherry, Mr. Graham?" he asked.

"I don't know. Right before she threatened the restraining order. I didn't want to cause more trouble so... almost a month," Hunter said.

"So why are there witnesses reporting that you showed to the dress rehearsal the day before?" Detective Sims asked.

Hunter Graham at the rehearsal? That couldn't be. The man with the mussed sandy brown hair looked nothing like Hunter. She told the police about that.

"Why visit her?" Detective Atkins chimed in.

"I didn't. I was here in my hotel room that night with a late meeting with my financial advisor. I was coming to the show but was running late." Hunter answered. "I knew Sherry wouldn't give me another chance. The plan was to find new clients. Sure, Sherry and I had our difficulties, but I let it go. Besides, no one compared to Sherry's talent. Her poise. Her grace. She had it. I wanted to take her career to the next level."

Bianca knew the man that showed up at the rehearsal wasn't Hunter. Was he being framed since people knew his history with Sherry? Who was that man, anyway? Were the police still looking for him? What was his name? Was he still in town?

"Did she find you controlling?" Detective Sims added.

Bianca's lips parted as she held an apple in her hand.

"No," Hunter replied.

"Did you put your hands on her in any way?" Detective Atkins asked.

Bianca heard a sigh. Hunter didn't answer right away. Did he?

"I didn't hurt her. She overreacted, as usual," Hunter explained.

Bianca's mouth twisted. Even if he hadn't meant it, perhaps he shouldn't have pushed so hard with Sherry. How was she supposed to know how far he would or wouldn't go? Did he even? Did Sherry overreact as he stated?

Hunter continued. "I apologized. I sent her cards and flowers to make amends. She wouldn't hear me out. You don't understand. When word got out about our argument, I lost clients. No one wanted to work with me like they used to. Sherry... it doesn't matter now," Hunter confessed.

Bianca gripped the apple tighter.

"Do I need to call my lawyer? I'm willing to comply with whatever you need." Hunter asked.

"No, Mr. Graham. We're only here to ask questions," Detective Sims said.

"We're talking to those taking part in Clique Classic's extended fashion event in town. Your name came up since you're scouting for new business," Detective Atkins added.

"Am I a suspect?" The octave in Hunter's tenor voice changed to worrisome. "Maybe I did something I wasn't aware of. If only I could... apologize to her."

Bianca's heart squeezed as she could hear the remorse in his voice.

"We'll let you know if we have any further questions," Detective Sims replied.

Bianca heard the chairs scrape the hardwood floors. She didn't move. Perhaps they would leave without seeing her. Was there another way out of here?

"Did you get lost?"

She squeezed her eyes shut, knowing Detective Sims was behind her. Bianca turned to face him. "No." She held up the apple. "Just... eating a snack." She bit into the apple, the crunch filling her ears.

Detective Sims' face tightened, but the irritation didn't reach his gray eyes.

"How did you know I was here?" she asked. Bianca would disappear into the floor if she could escape his narrowing eyes.

"Your perfume," he said.

"What?"

"Perfume or whatever it is you use. Smells like mint. I can smell it a mile away." Though the frustration was clear in his voice, his pupils dilated.

Bianca grinned. "You noticed the scent of my shampoo?"

"Shampoo, okay. No matter what it is, I knew it was you, Bianca." He inched closer. "How many times do I have to tell you to stay clear of this investigation?"

Bianca only stared, her body going completely still. A ringing took over her ears, and she barely understood as his lips moved. "Say that again?"

"You're not listening, are you?" A smile took over his face.

"I was stuck on you... noticing my shampoo," she confessed. Would it be a mistake to let him know?

His chest heaved with a sigh. "I notice a lot of things about you, Bianca." His face softened.

Bianca gripped her apple tighter in fear of dropping it. She swallowed despite her dry mouth. "I didn't realize you did."

"You'd be surprised," he said.

"Lamar?" Detective Atkins called out to him. "You coming?" He spotted Bianca and waved.

She waved back, clearing her throat.

"I'm coming," Detective Sims said.

His partner bobbed his head and headed back into the hallway.

Detective Sims stared at her again. She felt the heat between them, but didn't move.

"Go home," he said. "Please."

"I... I actually need to pick up my daughter from school and..." Her breathing slowed. Why couldn't she catch her breath around this man? "Casper. I need to pick up Casper."

The corner of his mouth perked up. "Do that and go home. Or... do I need to follow you home to make sure?"

Her mouth twisted into a grin. "I don't think so. At least... not this time."

He chuckled as she slipped past him.

"By the way," he called out.

Bianca turned to face him.

He pointed to the apple in her hand.

"Enjoy your *snack*." He winked at her.

Bianca turned and headed for the automated doors. That had been a close one, and yet the notion made her pulse race.

LATE THAT WEEKEND SATURDAY morning was Sherry's memorial service. A week after her death and Pastor Dudley agreed for Edenville Community Church to host. They would hold her funeral back in Cliffston, Georgia, but since most of her friends were in Edenville for the fashion event, Giselle suggested a short memorial for them to pay their respects.

A large, pure glass vase had held an enormous display of white roses. An enlarged picture of Sherry displayed for all her friends to see. Bianca could still hear the whimpers and sobs in the sanctuary. Even she had released a deep breath, recalling again how Sherry fell to her death in front of her. No one could have predicted such an untimely death. Sherry was vibrant, healthy, and well on her way to a lasting career. She was "gone too soon."

Now standing in the church's atrium, Bianca smelled the fresh cinnamon rolls she knew Judy had baked. The thick doors leading to the sanctuary were still open. Regular members, along with top models, greeted each other.

The cinnamon rolls practically called to Bianca from the plain white table. No harm indulging—this time. Grabbing a napkin, the sugar mixed with cinnamon filled her lungs. Some things were worth it, and Judy's baked treats were one of them.

Swallowing, Bianca glanced around the atrium. Some members had already left for the day. Her mother was standing between Alyssa, Judy and Richard Long, whose hand curled around his husky midsection, and the light reflected off his pale face.

What Bianca found interesting was Aiden Carlyle wasn't in attendance. If he planned on proposing to Sherry, wouldn't he come to her memorial? What could have been more important than paying respects to the family of the woman he supposedly loved? Bianca could understand Paris Deveraux being a no show since the woman didn't care for Sherry. No Hunter Graham either, but she didn't blame him since Sherry tarnished his reputation.

Despite her suspicions surfacing, Bianca knew she would need to take her sister and daughter home soon. She was proud of them both for attending. Especially Alyssa, who, judging by her down-turned features, didn't want to revisit the grim memories of that terrible night. When Bianca suggested her daughter stay home, Alyssa disagreed with determination in her eyes. Bianca took her word for it—for now. They needed to talk, and she'd waited long enough.

Turning on her heels, Bianca spotted Joan Wilson holding hands with her husband. Clark Wilson stood next to his wife and stepdaughter in a dark navy blue suit. Jacqueline's shoulders lowered as she stood in her black suit, and her gaze remained glazed. She even scratched at her cuticles as if she lacked interest in attending. Since she didn't care for Sherry to begin with, her state of indifference didn't surprise Bianca one bit.

Bianca found that Mr. and Mrs. Wilson were talking to Pastor Dudley, who wore a black suit and a black-and-white polka-dot tie. Dark brown skin, bald head, no taller than five-nine, and a respected pastor in the church and Edenville community.

"Enjoying that?" Jordan asked.

Bianca flinched and eyeballed her friend. "Don't do that."

He chuckled, only to hold up his own napkin. "I couldn't resist, either. I don't know how Judy does it."

"Me, neither."

Jordan inched closer. "How's Melanie holding up? I haven't talked to her yet. I came in after the memorial started, but I wanted to be here for her."

His words touched Bianca's heart. While Melanie had claimed she felt better, she had retreated to the ladies' room for a moment to herself.

"She's getting there. When was the last time you talked to her?" Bianca asked.

"I called last night. She didn't answer, so just giving her the space she needs," Jordan replied.

Bianca bobbed her head. Her attention directed back to Sherry's father and stepmother. She hadn't seen Joan since that day at Luther's car wash, and even then, the woman hadn't looked as distraught as she did now. Was it an act? Bianca bit at her bottom lip. She hadn't left church yet and was already suspecting someone of a crime? With Sherry's memorial over, she was sure they wouldn't stay in Edenville much longer.

"Bianca," Jordan called out.

Bianca blinked, refocusing her attention on him. "I'm sorry. What did you say?"

"I asked if Melanie was going to Sherry's funeral. I heard it's back in Georgia," he repeated.

Bianca turned and saw the softness in his speckled eyes. "I don't know. I'm sure she will if her work schedule permits."

He nodded. "That's good."

Then her sister walked out of the ladies' room. Jordan's shoulders relaxed, his face softened, and he didn't hesitate to go to her side. Bianca noticed her sister gave him a faint smile and welcomed his embrace. A few models that were at the show flocked to Melanie's side too. Though her speech about her friend caused her to choke back tears, Bianca was proud her sister pushed through despite her grief.

While her ears perked to get information from Jordan to learn if there was something going on between him and Melanie, Bianca's eyes flitted back to Clark Wilson. She watched as he whispered in his wife's ear. Then he shook Pastor Dudley's hand and headed out the second set of wooden doors leading to outside. She also spotted him with his phone in his hand. Phone call, maybe?

Bianca tossed her napkin into the nearby trash bin after she wiped the corners of her mouth and hands. She sprinted to the wooden doors, pushing them open, hoping to catch up with Mr. Wilson. The parking lot was almost empty, with only a few cars of the members who'd chosen to stay behind and socialize. Bianca waved to Ms. Ella from the florist's shop, who was walking to her apple-red Dodge Journey vehicle.

"Coming to the Blues and BBQ event next week, Bianca?" Ms. Ella called out with another wave of her hand.

Bianca's smile grew bigger. Combining two events, Edenville hosted a BBQ festival and live blues concert, with other musical choices in between so the band could rest and eat themselves. Home cooks in town brought their best BBQ dishes and local restaurant set up their stations. It would be on a weeknight in the coming week, but with the turnout exceeding expectations, there was no reason to change it now. "I'll be there."

Ms. Ella gave her a thumbs-up sign with her fingers and slid into the driver's seat of her car. Bianca shuffled between her left and right foot. Where had Clark Wilson gone? A couple of trees gave shade to the parking lot, and Bianca breathed easier when she spotted the middle-aged man underneath one tree. Phone to his ear, he placed one hand on his other ear as he listened to whomever he was talking to.

Bianca tapped her heeled foot on the concrete. She'd parked her car on the opposite side. When her gaze lifted, there was a billboard in her view. It was blank, with only a phone number on the bottom. Walking closer, Bianca tapped on her black screen as if she were copying the phone number. The more steps she took, the more she could hear from Clark Wilson. He was yelling now.

"I don't care!" He paced back and forth with a grunt, escaping his mouth. "It's done now."

What did that mean? Bianca didn't look at him. No sense in giving herself away too soon.

"No. My daughter is *dead*. Do you understand that?" he barked.

Bianca flinched. Why didn't that sound like a grieving father? Clark's tone sounded almost... morbid.

"You think I asked for this to happen? Do you know what this does to my campaign?" He continued to rant on the phone. "I know numbers have been down. Don't you think I know that?" He balled his fist, pressing it to his forehead. "Fix it. I don't care *how* you do it. Fix it! We need that flash drive. This will ruin my chances of running for governor!"

Bianca turned on her heels. This was a bit much. Joan had said he'd been running for reelection back in their hometown in Georgia. Numbers down? Was there a chance he could lose his position as mayor? What flash drive?

Bianca unlocked her screen, this time on her phone, and searched for Clark Wilson's name. The first link was to his website. She saw his biography, which included records of his community service and how long he'd been in office, along with his campaign plans if the town reelected him. Ruin his chances for governor? What did that mean? Bianca's mind couldn't fathom someone caring about that so soon after their child's death... Then again, what if this was all a part of some plot? How?

Just what if Sherry's death had been part of an undercover scheme? Scrolling through the pictures on Mayor Wilson's website, Bianca saw a picture of him with both Sherry and Jacqueline. With him in the middle, he wrapped his arms around his daughters into a group hug. Sherry's million-dollar smile dominated the photo. Flawless skin, petite figure, along with her red, ruffle-hem, floaty chiffon dress with matching heels.

Jacqueline stood in black-and-white striped pants and a black squared-neck blouse, along with her red glasses on her narrow nose. Her smile appeared forced. Clark Wilson gave what looked like his usual campaign smile. Anything for the camera. Bianca sighed.

To look at them, they appeared as the picture-perfect family, except for Jacqueline's awkwardness. Bianca spotted another photo, this one, including his wife, Joan. Though her smile didn't look as forced as Jacqueline's, Bianca couldn't help but question the sincerity. Clark appeared to have one mission. Get reelected and eventually run for governor of Georgia.

How far would he go? While Bianca recalled Joan saying he'd doted on Sherry, if she had impeded his campaign, how far would he... Bianca rolled her eyes. She needed evidence for this.

Threading her own fingers through her hair and then releasing her curls, she stopped in front of the wooden doors. How far had she walked as she scrolled the pictures online? Then she heard footsteps behind her, only to see Clark Wilson walking back in her direction. Bianca cleared her throat, opening her locked screen and pretending to be occupied with a text message.

"The last thing I need," his gruff voice said.

Bianca gave a soft smile. "One of those days?"

Clark stuffed his hands inside his pockets. "It's... a lot." He blinked. The wrinkles around his eyes became more apparent. "I'm sorry. I'm Clark Wilson. I don't think I've met you." He extended his long-fingered hands.

Bianca returned the gesture. "Bianca Wallace."

His eyes widened. "I know that name." His hand dropped to his side. "You were a friend of Sherry's. I loved what you said today."

Did she and her sister look that much alike? "Not me, actually. My sister. Melanie."

"Ah. That's right. Sorry about the mix-up. I don't have my glasses today." He rubbed his chin. "Her words today were... much needed. I'm glad Sherry had a friend like that."

Bianca couldn't have agreed more. "I actually met your wife at the car wash this past week."

Clark blinked as if everything came back to him. "She mentioned meeting a nice young woman. Pleasure to meet you."

"You too. I am so sorry for your loss." Bianca offered her condolences, despite her prickly skin.

"Thank you. It was a shock to the family. My wife and I flew down as soon as we could," Clark said.

"Are you planning on staying long?" Bianca asked. "I know the police are working to understand what happened."

"Only until we finish packing Sherry's things. We're going through on what to give away. A few of her friends have stopped by since we offered it to them first." Clark's shoulders dropped. "I don't trust the police with something like this."

Bianca tilted her head. "Oh... well, if it makes you feel any better, Edenville doesn't sit on justice. The whole town practically comes together when necessary, whether it's a native or a stranger in need of help. We don't take kindly to things like this."

Clark gave a faint smile. "Thank you. You rarely find that kind of community in this world."

Bianca bobbed her head. This was not what she'd been looking for. How could she ask without being nosy? "I remember meeting Sherry's stepsister. Jacqueline. I hope she's doing well."

Clark shook his head. "You know, for the life of me, I could not get those two to get along. Sherry didn't like Jacqueline around, and Jacqueline claimed my Sherry was too bossy. They didn't get into physical fights, but they could get irritated with one another."

"I remember those days with my sister. Playing Mom and Dad against each other. At least we *tried* to," she joked.

Clark chuckled for a moment, but his look turned serious. "Jacqueline never took to Sherry. Not that I saw. I knew there was jealously, but I soon discovered it went deeper."

Bianca's ears perked. Would he tell her more? "I'm sure they didn't dislike each other that much."

Clark lifted an eyebrow. "I wish I could believe that. I even recalled hearing Jacqueline say she *hated* Sherry."

Hated. That took things to another level. Though she didn't have any evidence to prove Clark wasn't lying, she could see the sibling rivalry being a factor.

He pinched the bridge of his narrow nose. "I can't think about this now. I have more important things to worry about."

He cleared his throat. "I'm sorry. It was nice meeting you. I need to go retrieve my wife and head out. I think... I've had enough for the day. Thank you again for supporting the family."

Bianca forced a smile. "Of course. Nice meeting you too."

Clark bobbed his head and opened one of the double doors. Bianca couldn't fathom what she'd just heard. He had *more important things to worry about* than *Jacqueline hating Sherry*.

Something wasn't adding up about the Wilson family. If she could describe them with one word, it would be suspicious. If only she knew the missing piece, but all Bianca needed was time. She could figure it out. Hopefully, with no one else getting hurt. Or worse.

"BIANCA? BIANCA?" DEBORAH Wallace called out.

Bianca blinked, dropping her hand from underneath her chin. "I'm sorry. What did you say?" Deborah Wallace insisted on a special family meal after Sherry's memorial service. Unfortunately, Melanie went home after an emotionally trying day. To Bianca's surprise, Alyssa came with her.

Bianca's mother ceased cutting the potatoes in front of her on her countertop. "What's got you so distracted? You've been quiet since you got here."

Bianca's lips parted at the sound of her mother's dogs, Jasper and Horas, barking in the living room. They were keeping Alyssa company for the time being. "I'm okay. A lot on my mind."

Her mother squinted her eyes at her. "If only I believed you." She resumed chopping. "If you're not telling me something about your sister, I wish you would. I'm getting worried."

That got Bianca's attention. She could spin her theories of Clark Wilson and his wife later. She straightened to her feet from leaning up against the counter. "Melanie is going to be okay. She's... dealing with this the best way she knows how. I think the memorial... was all she could take today. She has her good and bad moments, but she's getting there, Mom."

"I know. I just hate seeing her like this," her mother said. "She didn't even want to come over for at least an hour."

"Just give her time, Mom."

Her mother sighed. "My poor baby. I can't imagine what's going through her mind. I don't remember Sherry that much myself, but she was a sweet girl from what I remember."

"Her father and stepmother are in town until they finish packing her things. They're doing giveaways for the time being." Bianca wouldn't tell her mother about her conversation with Clark Wilson, but there was nothing wrong with getting her mother's insight. That was, if she didn't suspect Bianca of being nosy.

Her mother bobbed her head. "It's hard to lose a child. No matter what age they are. No parent plans on leaving this world before their child."

Bianca's own heart clenched. Her daughter meant the world to her. "I know. It's sad. Some things just happen at the wrong time."

"It's never the right time," her mother said. "There's no such thing as a perfect time, I think. We just have to go on when these things happen. There's a season for everything, but not the perfect time."

"His wife told me he's up for reelection. I wonder how this will affect... you know," Bianca added.

"He's still human. Politicians, leaders, businesspeople, life affects them too. I just hope he takes his time with that. That he's not in a hurry to get back on his campaign trail. The family needs time to grieve."

Bianca mulled over her mother's words. Clark Wilson didn't sound as if he needed time to grieve. He wanted whatever had gone wrong with his phone call fixed. He had plans to run for governor and Sherry's death hadn't seemed to impede that. If only Bianca could pinpoint what he meant by the flash drive comment?

"What's that face for?" her mother asked, transferring her freshly cut potatoes into her pot of bowling water on her stovetop.

"What face?" Bianca swallowed. She could get nothing past her mother. No wonder. It was the same with her and Alyssa. She could read her daughter's moves in her sleep.

"Bianca? That suspicious mind of yours is at work once again," her mother commented, with a hint of humor.

"I'm not being suspicious. I just find it strange..."

"What's strange?"

"All I heard was a phone conversation. That was it." That was all she would tell her mother.

Deborah moved to the front of her sink, turned on the faucet, and washed her hands. "So you were listening in?"

Bianca couldn't hide her grin. "If people are talking loud on the phone for everyone to hear, I can't help it if I catch bits and pieces of their conversations."

Her mother tried to hold back her own laugh. Drying her hands, she added, "That's how I know you're being suspicious.

Look, sweetie. I know it's in you to get involved, but I'm sure whatever you heard, there's a logical explanation."

Bianca's theory? The man possibly had his daughter killed to somehow further his campaign career. What was worse than that? Another scenario? Sherry's ex, Aiden Carlyle. Why didn't he attend the memorial today? Then again, no concrete evidence. Only her mind piecing together the information she had. "You're right." She wouldn't press the issue further. The last thing Bianca wanted was for her mother to worry about her.

"Besides..." Her mother folded the dishtowel, faced her, and folded her arms over her chest. "I have something you should know." Her mother's chin dropped for a moment, but then she raised it. "I don't know how to say this. I didn't think this would happen again."

Bianca walked to her mother's side. "What's wrong? *What* happened again?"

Her mother waved her comment away. "Nothing bad. I'm just getting emotional." Her eyes shined with fresh tears, and she dabbed them away with the back of her hand. "It's about Luther."

Bianca's grin grew. "Okay. What about him?"

"I'm past the age, Bianca, of beating around the bush. I'm old enough to know what I want and what I don't. After losing your father, I was okay with being alone for the rest of my life. I didn't think I would betray him by moving on, but... I didn't feel comfortable dating again." A laugh escaped her mouth. "It was easier to help others find love."

Bianca wrapped her arm around her mother's shoulders. "You're great at what you do. Even if... I wish you didn't use me as your guinea pig."

Her mother giggled. "I'm working on it. With time. But let me finish my point. Luther Burkes is hardworking, a man of faith, and a gentleman, generous, sweet—although he won't admit that part."

Bianca laughed. "I can see that."

"But he is." Her mother touched her hands to her cheeks. "I didn't think I would feel this way again about a man, but like I said, there's no point in dragging our feet. Especially when we both know what we want."

"So... are you two officially... together?" Bianca asked, joy bubbling inside her.

Her mother beamed. "Yes."

Bianca squealed, hugging her mother closer. "I'm happy for you, Mom. I know Dad would be too. He'd want you to open your heart again."

Her mother patted her arm. "I know he would. It wasn't easy to let go, but when genuine love comes your way, you don't run from it."

Bianca straightened to see her mother's face.

Her mother focused her gaze on her. "It will scare you. You're wondering, 'Does this person want me for me?' It requires a level of vulnerability that's difficult. Opening up. Sharing your heart. It's not something you do with everyone."

"I know that feeling." Bianca didn't want to think of her first marriage as a mistake, but that didn't change her from wishing things had ended differently. Though she'd healed, it didn't make the memories less painful.

Her mother took her hand. "I know you don't enjoy talking about it, but I believe, Bianca, if you're willing, there's someone out there ready to give you the love you deserve. You already know I love you. Your sister. Alyssa. Just remember that love is not limited. There's always room for more."

Bianca bobbed her head. Wanting to refocus the conversation back to her mother, she gave her a full embrace. "I'm happy for you, Mom. I am. Luther is an excellent choice."

Her mother patted her back. "Thank you. I think so too."

The barks in the living room got closer, and Alyssa pushed through the sliding door to the kitchen. Her daughter looked back and forth between them. "What's going on?"

"Your grandmother has a *boyfriend*," Bianca told her as she broke her embrace with her mother.

Alyssa's jaw dropped. "No way."

Bianca's mother put her hand on her hip. "I still got it. Even at my age."

Alyssa's face scrunched up in apparent embarrassment. "I love you, Grandma, and I'm happy for you, but... *eww*."

Bianca gestured to the cabinets. "Set the table."

"I'll remember that, young lady," her mother added as Alyssa carried the plates to the dining room. Jasper and Horas followed her.

Bianca draped her arm once again around her mother's shoulders. "So... I'm assuming he's coming to eat with us now?"

"That'd be correct, and I expect you and Alyssa to be on your best behavior." Her mother used her free hand to point at her.

"When have we not been the last few times he's been here?" Bianca teased.

Chapter 13

That same Saturday evening, people talked and murmured around Bianca and Alyssa during their mother-daughter dinner at Mobile Aztec. Though Bianca had invited Melanie, her sister had declined, and disclosing that she had plans of her own. Bianca hadn't pried—at least not yet. Lunch with her mother and Luther was delicious, but Bianca didn't see the harm in taking her daughter out to dinner. Just the two of them to help Alyssa get her mind off everything. Also, the perfect time to talk if her daughter would open up.

Silverware clinked, knives scraped against plates, and ice tinkled in glasses. For a Saturday evening, the wait for a table was only fifteen minutes, and there was a small crowd outside. Bianca watched a server bring a take-home container to a nearby table while the fragrance of grilled meat tickled her nose.

Bianca directed her attention to her daughter, who took small bites of her beef enchiladas. Come to think of it, Alyssa hadn't said much since they'd arrived. "Aren't you hungry?"

"Huh?" Alyssa raised her chin, blinking her brown eyes. What was she thinking about? "I'm sorry, what?"

"You're not eating." Bianca pointed to her plate with her own fork.

"Oh." Alyssa then took a small bite and swallowed. "Just thinking. I'm fine."

"About what?" Bianca asked.

"Well..." Alyssa placed her fork on the side of her plate. Staring at her mother, she bit her bottom lip. "I talked to Kendrick today."

Not quite what she thought they'd talk about, but if this was on her daughter's mind, she would listen. "And? I thought you two were okay." Bianca wondered, though she couldn't get used to the idea of her daughter having a boyfriend.

"That's just it. He said he was cool with me leaving for the summer to see Dad, but today when we were texting... he didn't sound as sure. Do you think the separation for that long will be a bad thing? What if he meets someone else and wants to break up with me?"

Bianca sighed. "So one moment he says, 'I'm cool.' The next is, 'Do you really have to go?'"

"Exactly. I want to see Dad, but..."

Bianca leaned in closer, grateful her daughter knew to confide in her.

"I don't want to lose Kendrick," Alyssa continued. "He's my first official boyfriend. Everyone in school knows about us. If we break up now, what will people think?"

This was a moment that Bianca didn't miss from her own high school days. "Sweetie, this is about you and Kendrick. Who cares what the other kids will say? Trust me, they're too busy with their own problems to be worried about yours. They should be, anyway."

Alyssa sighed. "I know. You tell me all the time to 'be your own person and not what others expect.'" She cupped her cheek in her hand. "This relationship thing is harder than I thought it would be."

"You thought it was all romance, laughs, and having fun together?"

"Well... yeah," Alyssa admitted.

Bianca smiled. "That's part of it, sweetie, but relationships take work. Actual work. There's communication. Healthy conflict. Sacrifice. Selflessness. That's not for the faint of heart, and you may not be as ready as you think you are. Maybe Kendrick isn't, either. You're both young and still discovering what you want out of life."

"You were young when you married Dad. How did you know so young?"

Bianca paused mid-bite. She *definitely* didn't miss high school. Clearing her throat, she set her fork down. "Like most young people, I thought I knew what I was getting into. I loved your dad, and he loved me. The plan was to be together forever, but... things change. People change, and unless a couple is growing together, they're going to grow apart. Or one will grow while leaving the other behind."

"This is way too complicated," Alyssa commented, sitting back in her chair.

"True." Bianca sipped her glass of iced tea. "That's why it's important to take time to get to know yourself. That way, you'll be clear on what you want. If someone doesn't want the same things as you..." She shrugged. "There's your answer."

Alyssa gave a faint smile. "Communication. Right?"

Bianca bobbed her head.

Alyssa straightened in her chair. "I guess I can talk to him again and let him know what I want to do. I'd like to visit dad for the summer." Her face dropped. "I don't want to lose Kendrick, Mom. I really, *really* like him."

Bianca reached for her hand across the table. "I know you do. You sneak off enough to make phone calls."

Alyssa giggled. "We can talk for hours sometimes. Then sometimes we say nothing at all, but it doesn't feel awkward, either."

"I remember those days," Bianca said.

"I just hope he understands. What if the separation is too much for us?" Alyssa added, pulling her hand back to grab her fork.

"If he cares about you, it doesn't matter how far you go for the summer," Bianca replied.

"You think so?"

"I know so. Just don't force it. What's meant for you is yours. No one can take it away." She winked at her daughter.

"Thanks, Mom. I'm glad I can talk to you about this."

"Even though I have to get used to it," Bianca teased her. "How do you think this all makes me feel? You're growing up so fast."

Alyssa's smile grew.

"And I'm very proud of you," Bianca said. "And... I want to ask. How are you doing?"

Alyssa blinked.

"The memorial today for Sherry. You haven't talked about... how it made you feel." Bianca explained.

Alyssa rubbed the side of her neck. "I'm... trying to get past it. It's hard though."

"I know. If you need to talk to someone, I can set up—"

"No, Mom." Alyssa's fingers scratched at her neck, and when she opened her mouth to speak, she stopped.

"Alyssa? You know you can tell me anything. Right?"

"I know that. I just... need some time. Please, Mom. Can we talk about something else tonight?" She forced a smile.

Bianca opened her mouth to respond, but their server returned to their table.

"How are we doing, ladies?" Eliza had olive skin, was no taller than five foot five, and her long, blonde hair was in a low ponytail draping over one shoulder.

"I think we're ready for the check." Bianca turned to grab her wallet inside her purse. Her gaze for a moment darted out the large window, only to see two familiar faces. Paris Deveraux and Aiden Carlyle. Bianca gasped. Was that really them?

"Ms. Wallace?" Eliza said. They'd come often enough for the server to know her name. She dyed the ends of her blonde hair pink, lip gloss covered her pouty lips, and one of her arched eyebrows lifted.

"Mom?" Alyssa waved her hand in front of her mother.

"Right. Sorry." Bianca straightened in her chair, handing her card to Eliza.

"I'll be right back." Eliza walked away, leaving Bianca and Alyssa alone.

"Mom, are you okay?" Alyssa asked as her eyebrows rose. "You look... surprised."

"I'm fine. I just saw some people I know."

"Friends of yours?"

Bianca shook her head. "No, they're... they knew Sherry."

"Oh." Alyssa's pupils dilated. "I wonder when the police will find out who did it."

"Me too." Bianca glanced behind her once more. Paris and Aiden were gone. Perhaps it was nothing. She wondered if perhaps they were different people. No. She knew what she saw. The question was, were Paris and Aiden up to something besides looking for a place to eat? Yet the knot in Bianca's belly said otherwise.

"Here you go." Eliza returned with her card and a receipt. "I hope you enjoyed your meal and come again."

"Thank you." Bianca looked at her daughter. "Ready?"

Exiting the restaurant, Bianca walked beside her daughter, past the waiting customers outside. Music blared through the speakers at the entrance through the double doors, and by the time they entered the parking lot, Bianca's eyes scoped the area to see if she could find Paris and Aiden. Nothing.

Bianca's eyes wandered about her surroundings, walking past the cars to hers. She hoped she wasn't being followed, as she had been before. Her car beeped as she clicked off the alarm, and she and Alyssa slid into their seats.

Maybe it was nothing. Her mind kept repeating the possibility. Her face scrunched as she further scrutinized the situation. She couldn't figure out why Aiden didn't attend Sherry's memorial.

BIANCA DROVE HOME THAT Saturday night with the radio playing in the background. Alyssa scrolled through social media on her phone, and Bianca could only hope her daughter took to heart what she'd shared at their mother-daughter dinner.

Tapping her fingers on the steering wheel, Bianca drove them home, speculating why Aiden had been with Paris.

She considered they worked in similar industries in places like California and New York. With the fashion event lasting all month that explained them remaining in a small town in Texas. Who could blame them?

What top model would pass up the opportunity to be associated with Clique Classic? They were growing in notoriety and trending on social media. Even Bianca squealed on the inside when Giselle hired her for the graphics. If Paris had worked in the same fashion shows as Sherry, it was possible they ran in the same circles.

Alyssa sat her phone down a few times in her lap, looking into the right side mirror. When she looked back behind them, Bianca's eyebrows etched together.

"You okay?" she asked her daughter.

"Uh... yeah," Alyssa said, returning her attention back to her phone.

Something was off with her daughter, and it was more than her relationship with Kendrick. Bianca could sense it as only a loving parent could with their child. Why wouldn't Alyssa tell her? Then her own phone buzzed in her purse. It was probably her mother or Melanie. She would call them back, but if they called again, it could be an emergency. Not wanting to take the chance, Bianca reached into her purse beside her left leg once she came to a red light.

Staring at the screen, she didn't recognize the number from her missed call. Then her phone buzzed once more, alerting her she had a voicemail. If this was a scammer, she was blocking their number without remorse.

"Everything okay, Mom?" Alyssa asked.

Bianca stuffed her phone back inside her purse as the light turned green. "Yeah. Sure." She didn't say another word as she drove to their neighborhood. Her garage clacked and grinded when she pushed the remote button to open it. Once parked, she cut the engine, and Alyssa slid out the passenger door and went inside the house.

Grabbing her phone again, Bianca played the voice message from her missed call.

"Hi, it's Jacqueline. Sherry's stepsister." Jacqueline sighed. "I got your number from your website. I need to talk to you. It seems as if you're the only one who'll listen to me. Please call me back. Please." She hung up.

Bianca blinked once inside her house. Her body went still as she replayed what Jacqueline had said.

"What happened?" Melanie came from the hallway with Casper trotting beside her. "Bianca?"

"She called," Bianca said.

"Who? Mom?" Her sister's softened voice contained wonder.

"Jacqueline. Sherry's stepsister," Bianca corrected her.

Melanie's forehead furrowed. "For what?"

"I'm going to find out." Bianca set her purse on her dining table and called Jacqueline back. The woman answered on the second ring.

"Hello?"

"It's Bianca Wallace. You called me?" Taking a seat at her table, Bianca ran a hand down her pant leg.

"Yes. I remembered something from before Sherry died. I've gone to the police but..." She groaned.

"Slow down. What are you talking about?" Bianca asked. She waved Melanie over. Her sister didn't hesitate to take a seat next to her.

"The day of the fashion show was such a blur. Everyone was in a hurry to get ready. I left Sherry to take a call. I told the police that, and... I think I remember seeing someone go into her dressing room after I left."

Bianca exhaled. "Do you remember who it was? Could you describe the person?" The sandy mussed hair man?

"I was on the phone. I barely saw a shadow. It didn't come to me until today. I must have blocked it out."

Bianca had to know. "Why tell me, Jacqueline? If you went to the police, didn't you—"

"They dismissed me since I couldn't tell them who went in the room, so they told me that information 'wasn't helpful.'"

Bianca ran a hand down her neck. It didn't take long for news to spread in Edenville. "If what you're saying is true, they'll look into it eventually. But... that is hard to go by if you don't know who you saw."

Silence.

"Jacqueline?" Had she hung up?

"Okay." she replied, with a hint of doubt in her voice.

"Give it time, Jacqueline. I've had the same thing happen to me and I remembered something long after it happened. Maybe something will come to you and you're able to give more information to the police. You remembered this much now. I'm sure it's only a matter of time," Bianca encouraged her.

"Okay. You're right. Anyway, thank you for listening, Bianca."

"Glad I could help," Bianca said.

With that, she hung up. Bianca did the same and placed her phone on the table.

Melanie motioned for her to talk. "Well?"

"She thinks she saw someone go into Sherry's dressing room the night she was poisoned," Bianca explained.

Her sister's eyes widened. "You're kidding? She's just now remembering this?"

Bianca raised her hands in a gesture of surrender. "She claims she must have blocked it out somehow. It's coming back to her now."

Melanie jumped to her feet and paced the floor. "That sounds too *convenient* to me."

"Mel?"

"They practically hated each other, Bianca."

"That doesn't mean she would..."

Melanie pointed at her. "You're thinking it too. Aren't you?"

"I don't know." Bianca sighed. "I honestly don't know." She gestured at the chair. "Sit down, please."

Melanie did, exhaling.

"I saw Paris Deveraux with Aiden Carlyle tonight."

Melanie jerked in her seat. "Where? At the restaurant?"

"I saw them out the window of Mobile Aztec before Alyssa and I left tonight. Something didn't feel right about seeing them together."

Melanie rubbed at her chin. "Sherry mentioned they would hang out sometimes."

"The three of them?"

Melanie shook her head. "No, but if a group of models went out after a show or gig, Paris would be there. Maybe they talked now and then."

Bianca's mouth twisted. "Maybe, but you remember how she acted at the antique shop?"

"She wasn't too heartbroken, either," Melanie commented. Then her sister snapped her fingers. "I forgot to tell you. You have a delivery from Produce Fresh."

Bianca's forehead wrinkled. "What? I didn't order groceries."

Melanie rose from her seat to grab a plastic bag from the counter, bringing it over to her sister.

Bianca pointed to the bag. "I didn't order this. There must be some mistake." She looked inside, hearing the plastic crinkle, and found a bag of apples. Apples. "Who would...?"

Melanie had her phone in hand. "You should get a message about... now."

Bianca's phone buzzed on the table. Staring at the lit screen, she spotted Detective Sims' number, along with his text:

In case you need another snack.

"No, he didn't!" Bianca exclaimed.

"Want to explain to me what this is all about?" Melanie's eyes squinted, lit with a glow of inner mischief.

"Want to tell me why you're playing along with this?"

Melanie giggled. "I thought it was funny. You should see the look on your face."

Bianca pushed the bag to the side. "Okay. Laugh all you want, but the next time Jordan comes over to *check on you*..." She raised an eyebrow.

"Fine," Melanie said. "I won't say another word tonight."

"Thank you," Bianca replied. Taking the bag, she placed it back on the kitchen island. She wouldn't let Melanie see her smile. That would give away her own amusement at Detective Sims' antics.

Chapter 14

A person could never have enough books. That was Bianca's philosophy behind buying new books for her growing collection at the store in town. The new owner, Margo Parks, a thirty-five-year-old with dark brown skin and ringleted curls, had taken over when Mr. and Mrs. Hart retired to Miami, Florida at the start of the year. Bianca chatted with Margo now and then during her frequent visits. Plus, it gave her a break from work for at least an hour, and on an early Monday afternoon, it was what she needed. Bianca was thinking more and more about the vacant office space in town.

Pulling her lips in as she clasped a paperback, her thoughts scrambled. Not just about expanding her business further, but also seeing Aiden and Paris with each other. Not to mention Jacqueline's phone call. Clark Wilson's conversation too.

As Bianca's fingers fanned the pages of her paperback, Lucy Kevin's *The Wedding Song*, the dry smell of paper filled her nose. Customers murmured around her as they stood in other aisles. The voices mixed in with the grinding and blending of the in-house coffee shop.

Bianca wandered from the romance and contemporary books to the adult fiction. She wouldn't stay much longer, as she had some emails to catch up on once she returned home. Scanning the aisle, Bianca's eyes flitted to the sign above, noting the adult fiction was in the same aisle as the thriller genre. Bianca didn't mind the genre, even if it didn't have a romantic subplot. Smiling to herself, her fingers tapped her new book, only to pause her steps when she saw Aiden Carlyle walk down the action/adventure end of the aisle.

Browsing the bookstore wasn't a crime, especially if he had a legit reason for still being in town with Clique Classic's extended event. Was reading a hobby of his? Bianca's nose wrinkled. She didn't want to catch him off guard, but then again, he hadn't minded answering some of her questions with Melanie at the gym. Would he be open to talking with her now? He left abruptly the last time.

Only one way to see. Bianca turned around and walked backwards, glancing behind her to see if he was still there. Her hand reached and grazed the books on the shelf. Pausing once she was close enough, she grabbed a book from the shelf.

Aiden, today dressed in dark jeans and a buttoned-down sky-blue shirt, dropped his chin as he read the back of one book. Bianca licked her lips, giving herself another minute to build her nerve. The last thing she wanted was to chase him away with too many questions. While keeping her own book at her hip, she attempted to slide the other one back into place.

PLOP! It plummeted to the carpeted floor.

"Oops." She bent to pick it up

"I'll get it," Aiden said, kneeling next to her. When he straightened to his feet, his eyes blinked. "You look familiar... Bi..."

She smiled. "Bianca. I met you with my sister at the gym. Melanie."

He bobbed his head. "Ah... I remember."

"How are you doing?" she asked, placing the action book back in its place.

Aiden rubbed at his forehead. "Good, I guess. It just... doesn't seem real still."

Might as well. "I'm surprised that we didn't see you at Sherry's memorial at the local church this past weekend. I saw almost everyone from the fashion show." Except Paris.

Aiden's chin dropped, giving into a slumped posture. "I... I couldn't. I stayed in my hotel room."

Was he at the Stargaze Hotel too, or Edenville Suites? Bianca didn't think to check the other hotels in town since Stargaze was the most popular, but Edenville Suites had great reviews too. Then again, for her to see him with Paris later that day, he didn't stay in his room all night.

She continued. "I'm sure you have the support of your friends through this, especially with Clique Classic still in town. I heard that you and Sherry would hang out with Paris Deveraux sometimes," she said.

Aiden straightened, rolling his eyes. "Paris Deveraux? If I didn't need this gig, I wouldn't stay in this town any longer." His voice was stern, but at least she didn't see the engorged vein in his forehead.

Taken aback, Bianca wanted him to explain. Still, she would try not to push too far. "Or perhaps... I heard that wrong?"

"Paris wasn't a friend to either of us. If she told the truth instead of focusing on how she looked all the time, maybe she'd *book* more jobs."

"She was difficult to work with?" Bianca asked.

"Sherry could be what they call a diva, but she was always professional." He sighed at the obvious memory of her. "A class of her own. Paris is a nightmare half the time. Demanding. Never courteous. The only reason she got picked for the fashion show here was because another top model had to drop out."

Bianca listened intently, hoping to get another clue. "That must have... been hard. Being in Sherry's shadow."

"Not to mention their argument," he pointed out.

"Sherry and Paris?" Bianca's eyebrows lifted.

"I heard they got into it right before the show. Someone broke it up before things got physical," Aiden explained. "I... only wanted to make things right and... propose to her after our breakup."

He told the truth about that. Bianca's mouth twisted further as she tried to recall that night. She, Alyssa, and Melanie had arrived a few minutes before the show had started. Would they have been able to hear an argument backstage? Not possible. Not with the amount of people who'd shown. The backstage manager must have kept things under wraps, so no one noticed.

"I don't have room to criticize Paris." Aiden folded his arms over his muscular chest. "I realize now that I wasn't that supportive of Sherry. But I got most of my jobs because of her. Paris pulled a few strings for me too, but I preferred Sherry."

Pulled a few strings? Was that why he'd been with her the other night? "Have you... talked to Paris since Sherry's death? Perhaps the shock has changed her attitude."

Aiden blinked. "No. Why would I talk to Paris? The woman is a parasite. Everything she touches gets ruined, eventually. I can't believe I even..."

Bianca swallowed. He hadn't seen Paris? Clearly, he was lying, but he did it with such a stern face. If she hadn't seen them together, she would have believed him. Still, Bianca wanted him to finish his thought.

Aiden pinched the bridge of his nose. "I'm sorry. I don't know why I'm telling you this." He blew out his cheeks. "The sooner I leave this town after this job, the better."

Bianca had no words. Did the police know about the argument? She didn't hear around town if the police had named yet a suspect, and they couldn't hold out-of-towners for weeks. Even if they were here for a job, surely the police asked everyone involved with Clique Classic. Was Paris an official suspect?

Aiden continued. "Anyway. It was nice seeing you again..."

"Bianca," she reminded him with a faint smile.

Aiden smiled back. "Have a good one." He walked away.

Releasing a breath she hadn't known she'd been holding, Bianca hurried to the ladies' room in the back of the bookstore. Once she pushed through the sliding door, she bent to see if anyone was in the stalls. Nothing.

Blowing out her cheeks, she called Melanie.

"On your way back?" her sister asked. She didn't sound as solemn as she had when Bianca had left earlier.

"Do you remember hearing any yelling at the fashion show before it started?" Bianca paced the floor.

"No. Why?"

"Guess who I ran into just now?"

"Who?"

"Aiden Carlyle."

Her sister choked. "You're serious? A bookstore is the last place I'd expect—"

"Let's stay focused." Bianca filled her sister in on their conversation.

By the time she'd finished, Melanie groaned. "This is getting more and more complicated. You think Paris would go that far to get rid of Sherry?"

Bianca tapped her foot on the vinyl floor. "I don't know. It's possible, but I'm not ruling Aiden out, either."

"Why?"

"She broke up with him. His career is shaky, so maybe... he returned with a proposal to make 'things right' as he said. But also... he could have conspired with Paris."

"You and your imagination," Melanie commented.

"I know we don't have all the answers yet, but something just doesn't sit right," Bianca replied.

"Well... I don't know, either, but whoever did this to Sherry needs to be held accountable," Melanie said.

"I agree." Eventually, Bianca would piece this puzzle together.

SINCE CHLOE, ALYSSA'S best friend, would drop Alyssa off home from school, Bianca called the number that same day for the vacant office building in town. Mr. Arden, the realtor, was more than happy to meet with her for lunch and offered to show her the space. She then told her virtual assistant, calling her for a quick video call.

"I love it, Bianca!" Veronica exclaimed, her face beaming on the screen through FaceTime. "I can't wait until I move there." Two months and counting.

Bianca moved the camera, panoramic style, for her virtual assistant to see the bare walls, but there was enough square footage for Wallace Designs. Bianca could picture contemporary furniture, an L-shaped desk, sea-foam or mint-green painted walls, black-and-white checkered curtains. Holding back her smile, Bianca realized she'd probably gotten too many ideas from searching the internet the night before. Besides, it gave her a break from investigating Sherry's murder.

"I love it too," she replied to Veronica. "I'd need another local assistant for more hands-on work until you get here. If they do well enough, I may keep them on as we expand our staff."

Veronica made a note of it. She pulled her blonde hair into a low ponytail draped over her shoulder. Black mascara on her long eyelashes made her dark-blue eyes pop that much more, but her lipstick had a tint of coral this time as opposed to the red she usually wore.

"I haven't decided yet, but this would be the next step." Bianca tapped her wedged heel on the beige nylon carpet. "This would be something. An actual office space."

"It gets my vote." Veronica's enthusiasm was clear in her singsong response.

Bianca giggled. "I'll talk to you later." With that, she hung up the video call and pivoted to see Mr. Arden outside. He was in his late fifties, stocky in stature, and only five-foot-eight. The man wore a brown suit with a yellow-and-black dotted tie. He'd stepped outside for a phone call, long enough for Bianca to call Veronica.

Blowing out her cheeks, Bianca headed for the glass doors to meet him outside.

"What do you think?" His voice was gravelly, low, but his blue-gray eyes sparkled.

"The space is perfect. Not too big, but enough for me to meet with clients. I can even picture a desk. Curtains," Bianca answered. Her chest fluttered. Despite her excitement, her mind wasn't fully convinced this was the right move.

"Well, this place has been vacant for a while. I'd like to have someone in by the end of this month," Mr. Arden replied.

A three-year lease. That was another factor. It was better than a five-year lease, but three years would be a huge commitment for her. While her list of clients was growing, would the momentum only increase for her?

"I understand." She bobbed her head.

"Why don't you give it a few days and get back to me? I know this is a huge decision," he said.

Bianca smiled, but she knew his offer wouldn't last for long. Mr. Arden was a business and respected family man in town with a wife and two grown children. While Bianca believed he would give her time, if another prospect came along and was ready to sign the lease, she would be out of a prospective office.

Yet, despite the empty feeling in her stomach, Bianca wanted to make a rational decision. She didn't want to sign a three-year lease on impulse. She was a businesswoman, and she wanted to do what was best for her and Wallace Designs.

"Thank you, Mr. Arden. I'll get back to you on what I decide." Blowing out her cheeks once more, she walked alongside him to his black Lincoln.

"I heard you were at the fashion show when the model collapsed. How are you dealing with that? I... wasn't sure about asking you before." Despite the wrinkles along his mouth, eyes, and forehead, there was a softness in his gaze.

Bianca squinted. "Did your wife put you up to asking me?"

He chuckled. "Perhaps... Gretchen wanted me to check since she knew I was meeting you today for lunch." Then his look turned serious. "Honestly, are you all right?"

Bianca released a cleansing breath. "I'm getting there. I think my sister took it the hardest, though. She was friends with her."

Mr. Arden rubbed at his goatee. "I'm sorry to hear that. I didn't think something like that could happen in a place like Edenville."

"Me, neither," Bianca agreed.

Mr. Arden continued. "My wife—she follows the fashion trends since our daughter is a designer herself—told me there was an interesting story about... Sherry, right? Sherry Wilson?"

"Right." Bianca edged closer to him.

"Rumor had that Sherry was... adopted, I think." He explained.

Bianca blinked.

"But we know how rumors can spread around town."

"How would her being adopted affect her death?" Bianca asked. Adoption wasn't uncommon. Did Melanie know this? The most she thought was Sherry's father had married her stepmother when she'd been at least a teenager and she hadn't gotten along with her stepmother or her stepsister, Jacqueline.

"That was another rumor my wife claims my daughter told her. Sherry kept her life under wraps, barely sharing about her personal life. If I remember correctly, I think my wife mentioned... addiction at some point. Perhaps if her adoption story got out, they'd find out about her addiction?"

Sherry addicted? To what? Then again, there were models who suffered from substance abuse or other ailments. But wouldn't Bianca have noticed something off with her? Wouldn't Melanie have?

Then again, had Sherry been that embarrassed to tell her friend about her problem? Even if that had been the case, who would have poisoned her? Had the medical examiner found traces of drugs in her system? The rumor didn't feel quite right. Bianca gasped. She spotted Hunter Graham walking in front of Ms. Ella's Flower Shop.

"Bianca?" Mr. Arden called out. He tilted his square face and raised a thick, salt-and-pepper eyebrow.

She cleared her throat. "Yes. I'm sorry. I just realized I have to meet up with someone. Thank you so much for showing the space. I'll get back to you. You can count on it."

His eyebrows squished together. "Okay. Sure. Have a good one." His car beeped, and he slid into the driver's seat of his car.

Bianca gave a last wave, only for her eyes to shift to find Hunter. Thankfully, he was still strolling along the sidewalk, but then he disappeared inside Parks Deli. As Bianca sprinted in her wedged heels, she heard brakes squealing and cars driving past her, along with a driver calling out to someone else on the street for a quick *hello*.

Approaching Parks Deli's front, she inhaled the scent of yeasty breads along with the cured meats. When she spotted Hunter's secluded table inside, she slowed her stride. His chin dropped as he scrolled on his phone. He wasn't in much of a hurry, in her opinion. Was he eating alone? With Paris? Was he meeting with a new client? Did anyone sign with him yet, or was he still on the hunt?

Hunter held the phone to his ear. Was he taking a call? Bianca paused in front of the large window of Parks Deli. She grabbed her own phone from her off-the-shoulder purse to keep herself occupied—for a while. Then she walked inside the deli, hearing the pop music blare through the speakers. Despite the background noise, she was in earshot of Hunter.

"Paris, it's me," he said. "I had a meeting with a potential client, and I knew you were busy on location with the photo shoot, so... anyway. Call me back when you get a chance." He sighed, dropping the phone to his side. Then he reached into his back pocket and pulled out cash from his brown wallet to pay for his meal.

Trouble in paradise? There was no point in just watching him. Who did he meet with as a potential client and where? Who considered working with him? Bianca needed answers. "Did you enjoy your turkey sandwich?" She could tell by the yellow wrapping paper in front of him. "I was thinking of getting the same thing. Though I love their roast beef deluxe."

Hunter pivoted in his chair to face her. His forehead wrinkled as if her question confused him, but when his eyes shifted to the deli menu on the wall sign above, his shoulders dropped. He gave a faint smile. "Yes. The cashier behind the counter recommended the turkey sandwich. For this to be my first time eating here, Parks is amazing."

"Have you tried Judy and Richard's Restaurant and Bakery? They have the best pastries," Bianca said. Hopefully, that would help break the ice.

He stuffed his wallet back in his pocket. A *hmm* escaped Hunter's throat as he obviously took in her suggestion. "Maybe next time. I'm... waiting on someone." Then he extended his hand for her to sit in the plastic chair across from him.

Bianca complied with a smile. He didn't seem bothered by her at all. "Well, I hope you get to stop by there before you leave town. Or do you plan on staying a little longer in Edenville?"

"I... don't plan on staying in town much longer, but this month-long fashion event is a goldmine for new clients. With everything going on, though, the sooner I'm out of Edenville, the better."

Bianca replied. "I'm sure the police are doing everything they can to find the truth."

His stare went blank at first, but he kept a faint smile. Was he trying to put on a brave face? "It's been a... stressful time."

"I understand," Bianca said. "I couldn't help but hear the rumors. It must be difficult for you."

He linked his hairy-knuckled fingers together and pressed them against his lips for a moment. "My career will never be the same. The police are asking me questions. When the whole time they need to pay attention to Aiden Carlyle."

"Aiden, huh?" She was sure the police had questioned him. He was Sherry's latest boyfriend. Did he even have a legit alibi where he was during the show? Did they dismiss it involved him at all? Where was he really on the day of Sherry's memorial? He wasn't off of Bianca's list of suspects, either.

"The man obsessed over her. They argued all the time. The only reason he got the gigs was because of Sherry. Paris even got him booked sometimes."

That fell in line with Aiden's story. So there was some truth, but not the entire story for sure. "So when he and Sherry broke up… they were no longer this power couple," Bianca wondered out loud.

Hunter inched closer across the table. "The man is a ticking time bomb. I don't know everything that happened, but I wouldn't be surprised if he… was involved in her death."

"Did you two get along at all?" she wondered.

He used his left hand down his face. Judging by the paler skin along his ring finger, Hunter had worn a ring. Was he still married even though he was seeing Paris Deveraux? How did his wife feel about his career down spiraling? The threatened restraining order? More research for Bianca to do, but she didn't see photos of his wife with him.

"Only for Sherry's sake," Hunter said. "But I stayed away, hoping she'd changed her mind and work with me again. I was going to take her places. Getting her deals she never considered before. It was *me* who landed her the…" He stopped.

"Go on." Bianca encouraged him. How did he make Sherry's career as he claimed?

Hunter swallowed. "It doesn't matter. She wouldn't reconsider."

When Bianca heard his phone ring, Hunter didn't hesitate to hold up his hand to her to excuse himself.

"What happened?" he said, walking out the door, not even bothering to say *hello*.

Bianca stood herself and walked out the door. She glanced up now and then, walking slowly to stay within earshot of Hunter's conversation.

"Don't worry about the police," Hunter said.

Bianca jerked but didn't make a sound.

"Where are you?" Hunter dug into his pocket, and keys jingled in his hand.

Bianca gasped. What did Hunter know? Was he going to the police? He stalked off without another word to her, leaving her biting the inside of her cheek. Checking the time on her phone, Bianca sprinted back to her car. She had time for one more stop before heading home.

YOU'RE KIDDING.

Bianca didn't respond to her sister's text, but she cut the engine to her car. Sitting in the parking lot, she released a deep breath. One last stop before calling it a day, and today had been a Monday she'd never forget. She hadn't been back to the venue since Sherry's collapse. Her death, but what better place to return to than the scene of the crime?

Unclicking her seatbelt, she rehearsed her strategy. What was she looking for? Something out of place? That was a start, but she wouldn't stay long. Not only did she want to avoid getting caught, but what if the killer returned? Sometimes that was a slip-up and the last thing Bianca wanted was to come face to face with another killer.

There were no security guards in front of the double doors, so she slid out of her car, locked the door, and bypassed the few cars that were in the parking lot. Her heels clicked along the concrete, and a rush of cold air hit her face when she opened the door.

Not the same place once filled with fashion designers, adoring fans and models, when it had been filled with smiles and the atmosphere loud with laughter. Bianca's eyes drifted to the stage. The runway was still there, and a few of the chairs were stacked together along the wall. No doubt another event would book the facility, whether it was a banquet, a wedding, or even another matchmaking event with her mother's business.

Twiddling with her charm bracelet, Bianca undid the clasp, stuffing it inside the pocket of her jeans.

"Can I help you?" a woman's voice called out. She wore a flowy, white shirt over light-blue jeans and flat sandals, and her strawberry-blonde hair draped over one shoulder. "Bianca? Yes, welcome back! I didn't get to speak to you at the memorial."

As Bianca hugged the woman, she stared past her, spotting a few people working at tables. At the memorial, she'd been distracted by Sherry's stepfather, wondering about his phone call. Pulling back from the brief embrace, she focused back on the woman in front of her. Giselle. "It's good to see you again. How's the month long event going?"

Giselle tilted her head. "We've been busy. Trying to keep going despite... losing a great model and friend."

"I'm sure you have. My sister was a friend of Sherry's. Melanie Wallace?"

Giselle snapped her fingers. "Melanie? I think I recall meeting your sister. Sherry said she was the best friend she could have asked for."

Bianca smiled. So far, so good. "I actually..." Rubbing at her bare wrist, she put on her best acting face. "I wasn't able to come back with the ongoing investigation, but I think I misplaced my bracelet that night. I've been in such a daze, I didn't notice. Has there been anything reported missing?"

Giselle shook her head. "No, not that I know of and the police have released the scene so we can continue working here. We've shot photos at a few locations around town, but we had a shoot here this morning."

"You don't mind if I look around, do you?" Bianca asked. "The bracelet means a lot to me." Not a complete lie. Alyssa had bought it for her the previous year for Mother's Day.

Giselle gestured around the ballroom. "Sure. Go ahead. Do you need any help?"

"I think I got it. Thank you very much, Giselle." Bianca walked over to where her chair had been the night of the fashion show. What was she looking for? With her nose wrinkling, she leaned as if looking for her bracelet.

Glancing to the left of the room, she saw the opening that led to the hallway. She had been back there when she and Melanie had visited Sherry the day before. While she heard the chattering of Giselle and others behind her, she inched her way to the doorway, glancing once in a while along the floor.

Her phone buzzed with another text. It had to be Melanie, since she hadn't responded to the last message.

Well. Anything?

Bianca responded. *Not yet. Don't worry. Not staying long.*

Be careful.

I will, she replied.

Approaching the hallway, she bypassed the men's and women's restrooms, only to approach another room that she was certain was Sherry's dressing room. The door was cracked, so Bianca had no trouble getting inside. She knew the police had blocked off the room and for it to be open now, they must have cleared it for evidence. Was there a point in looking now? Bianca didn't see why not, even if it was to satisfy her own curiosity.

The clothing rack from last time was gone, Sherry's makeup counter was bare, and though the couch still looked worn, Bianca didn't think anyone had sat on it since that weekend. Rubbing her lips together, she browsed. What was she expecting to find since Sherry's father and stepmother came to pack up her things? According to them, Sherry never packed light. Had they finished between loading her things from here and her hotel room? What all had they given away already?

Walking closer to the couch, Bianca leaned over to check behind it. Grabbing on to the back of the simple two-seater taupe couch, her eyes scanned the carpet. Nothing. Blowing out her cheeks, Bianca straightened to her feet. Her attention stopped on the black wastebasket in the room's corner. She peeked inside. Empty. Turning on her heels, she knew it was time to leave, but she paused. Did she see something?

Pivoting once more, Bianca inched closer to the wastebasket and squatted for an eye-level angle. Squinting, she spotted a lens from someone's glasses. There was no way the police had missed this. Had the room been used recently, and the lens was something someone threw in there? Maybe it had nothing to do with the case.

Bianca's forehead wrinkled. The only person she knew of recently who wore glasses was... Jacqueline. Her red glasses had sat on her narrow nose when she'd first met her. Taking her phone out, she snapped a few pictures of the lens. It was probably nothing, but at least she had proof just in case she needed it.

Hearing the voices increase in volume in the main room, Bianca took her bracelet out of her pocket and she clasped it inside her hand. Straightening to her feet, she headed for the door, leaving it cracked open the same way she'd found it. She heard Giselle's voice getting closer, so Bianca bolted for the ladies' room, pushing through the swinging door. She exhaled, but put her ear to the door. Giselle wasn't alone.

"Thank you for your help," a deep voice said.

Detective Sims? No doubt he would return to the scene of the crime too. Bianca held back her groan. Bad timing, though.

Tapping her fingers to the door, Bianca devised a plan to escape. Sneak out once he was down the hallway? Would he spot her car in the parking lot, anyway? Did he see her car already, and that's why he came inside? Might as well faced him now. Opening the door, she met both his and Giselle's gaze.

"Did you find it?" Giselle asked with a smile.

Bianca allowed the bracelet to dangle for a moment from her hand. "I did. Thank you."

"I'm glad," Giselle replied. "Thank goodness no one saw it and stole it." Then she turned her attention to Detective Sims, who hadn't stopped staring at Bianca with a blank face. "Is there anything else you need?"

"No, thank you," he said.

"Okay. If you change your mind, I'll be in the main room with the others." Giselle left Bianca and Detective Sims in the hallway alone.

"Bianca," he said, though he didn't appear happy to see her.

"Detective." She adjusted her off-the-shoulder purse.

"Lost… your bracelet?" He raised an eyebrow.

"I can't help it if this place is a crime scene and I couldn't get back here until now to look for it," she explained.

He inched closer. "Or... you could tell me the truth." Had his voice dropped?

Bianca found herself literally with her back against the wall. His familiar woodsy cologne filled her lungs. "Well... it depends on what you want to know. If I remember, you prefer evidence and not theories."

"Exactly." He tilted his head to the side. "So unless you have concrete proof of something, I'd appreciate it if you—"

"Go home," she said, finishing his sentence for him.

"That'd be ideal." He smirked.

"Well... if I want to go somewhere else, that's my decision. Don't you think?"

"As long as it doesn't relate to a murder case, go where you please," he countered.

"I see. Then I won't keep you from doing your job." She shifted from standing against the wall.

"I doubt that, Bianca," he said. His face softened somewhat, but she knew he was being serious.

"Have a good one." Slipping out into the hallway, giving a goodbye wave to Giselle, Bianca headed for the front doors. She would tell Detective Sims about the glass lens if she needed to, but like he said, he didn't want theories. Bianca needed something more concrete. She didn't want to accuse anyone, especially if they were innocent. Right now, Bianca didn't know whom the lens belonged to.

Chapter 15

Edenville's Community Blues and BBQ festival, late Wednesday afternoon, hosted on Main Street. The kids had a ball with the bounce house on one end of the street, while the other had long tables covered with potluck BBQ meals with other side dishes. These included, but weren't limited to: potato salads, bread and cornbread, baked beans, macaroni and cheese, pasta salads, coleslaw, corn on the cob, and grilled vegetables. What else was on the menu? Bianca had all evening to find out. She spotted the men, including Richard Long, gathered at the grill, cooking every piece of meat she could think of. Alyssa stood on the sidewalk with her best friend, Chloe.

Bianca's curls draped over one shoulder in a low ponytail. Eighty-eight degrees, cloudy, but at least it wasn't humid. The wind picked up the hem of her floral sundress, but she'd chosen flat shoes today for the occasion. For a weeknight, the turn out surprised her, but Edenville never failed to show for special events. Bianca had filled the previous day with work, with no recent developments in her investigation. Alyssa appeared herself again, so she dropped any other suspicions with her. Perhaps her daughter just needed time like Melanie to cope emotionally.

"Enjoying yourself?" Judy Long asked. She had pulled her red hair into a bun on top of her head. She looped her arm through Bianca's.

"These are always fun." Bianca's eyes scanned the crowd.

"Looking for someone?" Judy asked.

"Please don't start."

"I'm not, but... there's word around town that they spotted you with Detective Sims. Cupcakes on a bench?" Judy raised an eyebrow. "You could have at least stopped by the bakery."

Bianca laughed. "Cupcakes?" The joys of living in a small town. Everything got misconstrued. "It was ice cream. We stopped by the ice cream truck for dessert and I went home."

"Think there could be something there?" Judy asked.

Bianca knew her friend wasn't one to pry, and she didn't mind sharing with Judy. She was one of the first friends she had made when first moving to Edenville. "I don't know," she admitted.

"Do you like him?" Judy wondered.

Bianca's chest fluttered. "He's attractive. Funny. Hard-working."

"But do you *like* him?" Judy repeated. She stopped walking.

Bianca paused her steps too. "Even if I did, I don't know if I'm ready to date again. It's too..."

"Risky?" Her friend finished her sentence.

Bianca didn't answer.

Her friend tilted her head. "I understand. If you remember, I didn't marry Richard until ten years ago. I was thirty-eight. It wasn't easy to let my guard down, but I'm so glad I did. I get to walk through life with him. I'm not saying you need someone, but don't write people off without giving it a chance."

Bianca mulled over her words. "I'll think about it."

"I understand." Judy bobbed her head.

"You're not going to tell me, 'Don't take too long,' like my mother?" Bianca joked.

Judy shook her head. "No, but I *will* say: Don't stay away because of fear. You'll never know until you try." Her friend winked at her.

"Excuse me, Judy, but did you hear?" Ms. Ella from the floral shop appeared. No hat today to cover her honey-blonde hair.

"No, what?" Judy asked.

Bianca folded her arms, intrigued herself.

"The police arrested Jacqueline Wilson. Sherry's stepsister."

"*What?*" Bianca and Judy asked at the same time.

"I heard they found a small bottle of poison in her hotel room," Ella whispered to them both.

Bianca wondered if that was true. Had the police found such a thing, or had she turned herself in? Why did Jacqueline call to tell her about the person who visited Sherry right before the show? Was it to throw the heat off herself? Why tell Bianca? It wasn't as if Bianca was a pro at solving mysteries. She only had one case under her belt, and even that risked her life. "I talked to her," she whispered to herself. Thankfully, neither Judy nor Ms. Ella seemed to hear her.

"Did you hear anything else?" Judy continued.

Ms. Ella shook her head. "Only that it's enough evidence to prove her guilt."

"Excuse me, ladies." Bianca sprinted down the street to find her sister, bypassing parked cars, fellow townspeople, and blocking out the blaring music in her ears. She needed to focus.

What did all of this mean? Had Jacqueline deceived everyone and killed her stepsister?

Why was she even still in town? Sure, they were packing Sherry's things, but weren't they finished by now? Bianca noted the extra time Jacqueline spent in the hotel. Unless, was she working at the fashion event too, like Hunter? Looking for another top-notch client to assist as she did Sherry?

Bianca spotted Melanie with Jordan, sitting on a bench in front of Ms. Ella's floral shop. She gestured at her sister. "Do you have a minute?"

Melanie touched Jordan's arm. "I'll be back."

"I won't ask what you two are up to now," Jordan commented with a smirk.

Bianca could have kicked him, but she declined. Instead, she led Melanie to the other side of the street, cupping her sister's elbow in her hand. "The police arrested Jacqueline."

Melanie blinked. "What? Why? What did they—"

"They found the poison in her hotel room."

"That's stupid. Why leave it around for the police to find?" And practically almost two weeks after the murder. Why stay in town at all when she could have easily slipped away? Was staying to pack her things with their parents a cover up? Did she slip up, leaving the poison in an obvious place?

Bianca's thoughts scrambled to understand. "I wonder if that was the reason she called me."

Melanie rubbed the back of her neck. "This doesn't make any sense. I thought for sure it was Paris."

"Why her?"

Melanie shrugged. "She has this mean spirit about her. Being Sherry's rival and all, I assumed she did it to further her career.

Having Sherry out of the way may have increased her chances of booking better jobs. Everyone knew Sherry was the best."

"I can agree with that, but the police don't go on theories. They need concrete evidence," Bianca commented.

"So Jacqueline poisons her stepsister for... what? What was her motive?" Melanie asked.

"We've heard that they didn't get along. Perhaps she didn't enjoy working for Sherry and being in her shadow. Not to mention... how she looked at the memorial. She looked as if she didn't care to be there."

"Then quit," Melanie replied. "Move away and get your own life. You don't need to poison anybody, especially family members."

"I wonder if they'll let me see her," Bianca said.

"You're going to the police station?" Melanie's jaw dropped.

"The only person who can tell me the truth is Jacqueline. That's if she's honest about it. Will you keep an eye out for Alyssa? I'll be back as soon as I can," Bianca said.

"What about Detective Sims? You know how he doesn't want you involved," Melanie pointed out.

"I can at least try," Bianca answered. Wasn't family only allowed to visit a murder suspect in questioning?

Melanie hugged her. "You're amazing. Going the extra mile for others."

She patted her sister's upper back for a moment and then broke away. "I'll be back. If Mom asks, tell her I forgot something at the house."

Melanie eyeballed her. "Like what? You know I can't lie to Mom."

Bianca bit her bottom lip. "My, um... hat." She snapped her fingers. "Tell her I got too hot and went to the house to pick up my hat."

"Don't take too long then," Melanie said.

Bianca winked at her. With that, she sprinted to her car. Hopefully, the police would let her see Jacqueline. Her car beeped at the sound of her alarm turning off, but Bianca paused when she recognized a middle-aged woman. She knew the long face and silky brunette hair.

The woman stepped out of a mountain-gray Mercedes-Benz. Flat beige shoes covered her feet, and she wore a floral full-length dress and a short-sleeved cardigan that covered her shoulders. Bianca played with her keys in her hand, hearing them clink together. Did Joan Wilson know about her daughter being questioned by the police?

Turning her back, Bianca faced her reflection in the mirror. The last thing she wanted to do was get caught staring. Didn't they have to get back to Georgia for Sherry's funeral? Strange, though, that her husband wasn't with her. Was there a reason she'd come to the festival?

"Excuse me?" an alto voice said.

Bianca turned on her heels. "Yes." Her smile grew. "Nice to see you again."

"Yes! You're... Bianca. I remember." She gave an exasperating sigh. "I'm still getting used to this place during our stay.

"I didn't expect to see you here still," Bianca mentioned. "I thought after the memorial—"

"I wanted to know if there's something special going on in town. Now that Sherry's stuff is just about packed, I wanted a break, you know? Though Clark says something is missing with Sherry's things. So... I hear it's a party?"

"Yes, it's Edenville's community Blues and BBQ festival event." What was missing among Sherry's things?

"That's why I had to make a U-turn. I couldn't get through because they blocked the street off." Joan snapped her fingers. "That's where the music was coming from."

Bianca pushed her luck. "Your husband didn't join you?" What did he want to find?

The woman sighed. Her shoulders dropped. Then a *tsk* escaped her lips. "No, he wasn't in the mood." She paused. "He has his good days and bad days, but... he's still in shock. Who could do such a thing to Sherry?"

Bianca played along. Would she give her any vital information? "The police are doing everything they can to find out why." So would she once she could see Jacqueline in jail. Did Joan know where her own daughter was? Based on her soft expression, she didn't appear too worried about anything. Perhaps this was her way of coping with her stepdaughter's death. A complete one-eighty from her attitude at Luther's car wash.

"I hope they do, and soon. It's a shame for this to break the heart of our family," Joan explained, taking a handkerchief from her small black purse. She wiped at her nose and exhaled. Her strong jawline clenched.

Bianca kept the conversation as casual as possible. "Again, I'm sorry for your loss."

Joan pressed a freckly hand to her chest. "Thank you. We settled the official funeral arrangements back home. I didn't realize how many people Sherry knew, so I'm glad most could come to the memorial since they were already here with the fashion event." Pausing, she exhaled. "I still can't believe it."

Bianca continued. It didn't seem like Joan knew where her daughter was. Could she tread lightly? "You mentioned your husband, but... how's Jacqueline holding up?"

Joan's brow wrinkled. "She... Jacqueline has always had a mind of her own. She shares what she wants."

What did that mean? Did Joan know something but wasn't telling her? Bianca fiddled with her right hoop earring. "I guess every mother-daughter relationship is different."

"What do you mean?" Joan asked.

Bianca shrugged. The last thing she wanted to do was offend the woman and ruin her chances of finding out the truth. "I guess... it's assumed in society that you're automatically close to your family, but every dynamic is different. Sometimes it's not safe, circumstances strain the relationships... you know."

Joan's wrinkled neck stiffened, with a noticeable vein standing out. "No. Not every family is close."

Would she continue? Bianca didn't flinch.

"When I married my husband, I knew he came with a daughter. So did I. We agreed to be one family, but... Sherry never accepted me. Clark saw the tension and somehow it hurt their relationship too. No matter how hard I tried, and I guess... Jacqueline felt disregarded. Even now she..."

"I'm sorry?" Bianca tilted her head. That was new. Clark and Sherry's relationship strained? Though she witnessed his conversation at the memorial, she never guessed there was possibly bad blood between him and his daughter. While she suspected he cared more about his political status than Sherry's death, Bianca didn't give it more thought. Then again, was there truth to the rumor Mr. Arden told her?

Joan shook her head, her pale cheeks flushing with a hint of pink. "I've said too much. I thought driving around town would take my mind off things, but it hasn't." She gave a faint smile. "Thank you again for your hospitality. I'll have to check out other town events another time."

"I hope you can." Bianca bobbed her head.

With that, Joan stepped back, turned on her heels, and returned to her vehicle. Where was she going? The police station to see her daughter?

Would Jacqueline want to see her mother? If the police were holding her as a prime suspect, she would need all the help she could get. Now would be the time to put aside differences to seek the truth. Unless... Jacqueline *had* done it.

Bianca slid into the driver's seat of her car. The lens picture was still on her phone. Would a jealous stepsister actually kill? Despite the evidence pointing to her, had Jacqueline really poisoned her step-sister? There was only one way to find out.

BIANCA PULLED INTO the parking lot of Edenville's police station. She drove past a few cars while searching for a closer parking space. Blue paint designated a handicapped spot, while fading white paint marked the other spaces. She parked her Kia Soul in the next available spot, cutting the engine. Would they let her see Jacqueline? Bianca wasn't family.

Exhaling, she slid out of her driver's seat, clicked on her car alarm, and sprinted to the glass doors. Would she run into

Detective Sims? Was he on duty today or was he off work? If he was off, wouldn't he have shown for the BBQ event? Bianca shook her head. Not the time to be thinking about what he did outside of work. Even if he was off, she was certain he would be present for the arrest of his suspect.

Once inside, Bianca came to the waiting area with hard plastic chairs. She heard echoes from sparse waiting room, the quiet murmur of dispatchers speaking in headsets, and doors opening and closing. Bianca gave her name at the front desk. The receptionist's hazel eyes blinked.

"Are you related to Jacqueline Wilson?" she asked. Her medium-length, light-brown hair pulled into a mid-ponytail.

"She's adopted, but yes," Bianca said.

"One minute. Have a seat, please." The woman directed her to the chairs in the waiting area. Then she picked up the phone.

Bianca stepped back with a sigh. She didn't sit but tapped her foot on the fortress-white vinyl floor. She wrung her fingers together, willing her heart to stop racing.

"You're here to see Jacqueline Wilson?" Another officer she didn't recognize stepped out from behind a desk and computer.

"Yes. Is Detective Sims here?" she asked. Her palms were sweating.

"He'll be out in a minute." The fair skin man raised a thick dark brown eyebrow. Crow's feet showed around his cornflower blue eyes, and his muscular filled his dark blue uniform. "Do you have information we can use?"

Bianca patted her purse. She prayed the lens didn't belong to Jacqueline's red glasses, but if she needed to show Detective Sims, she would. She couldn't deny the frame size, but it didn't prove Jacqueline was at the scene when the police went through Sherry's dressing room for the first time.

"I'll just wait for Detective Sims. Thank you." She added a nod.

"Okay. Well, he'll be out soon." With a nod, he returned to his desk.

Bianca released a deep breath.

"Want to give me a good reason you're here? Seriously. You told the front desk you're family to the suspect?" a familiar voice asked.

Bianca pivoted to see Detective Sims. He'd unbuttoned the top button of his blue shirt, his dark pants hugged his waist, and despite his firm stance, his gray eyes twinkled.

Bianca held back her giggle. "Seemed clever."

He blinked and the next thing she knew, he chuckled. Bianca laughed along with him.

He rubbed at his forehead. "I'll ask again why you are here. There's nothing you can do, Bianca."

Her shoulders dropped. "I'm here to see Jacqueline. Word around town is she's been... arrested."

His mouth dropped. "I have to get used to word traveling fast in this town."

"I'm sure everyone knows by now at the BBQ festival," she said. While Ms. Ella was a sweet woman running her floral shop, she might as well have been a news reporter.

Detective Sims rubbed at his chin. "First. She wasn't arrested. Only brought in for questioning, which we just finished before I was summoned out here."

"So there's a chance she's innocent? Has she left yet?" Did Bianca miss her?

He tilted his head towards her. "Bianca?"

"I know you can't give me details."

"Is there something you want to tell me?" he asked.

Bianca took a moment to collect her thoughts, but reached into her purse. Taking out her phone, she scrolled to the picture of the lens. "I don't think it's relevant, but I found this in Sherry's dressing room."

He leaned in, taking in the photo. "Impossible. We searched the room."

"I think this must have been afterwards unless..."

"What?" He pressed her for the answer.

"Someone said they weren't there to begin with and... this proves they were. Or... someone came back," she said. "Whose alibi said that—"

"Bianca?" He stopped her once again.

"Fine." She rolled her eyes.

He pinched the bridge of his nose. "Send the picture to my phone, okay. I, or either Detective Atkins, will look into it."

At least he didn't dismiss her. With a quick scroll and the tap of a button, she sent the photo. "Thank you. Can I see Jacqueline?" she asked once more.

His muscular chest heaved a sigh. He gestured her toward the rooms in the back. It was the same room she'd visited the last time when investigating Martin's death. Bianca didn't have to wait too much longer as Jacqueline emerged from the hallway. With her purse clenched to her chest, she wiped her nose. Had she been crying?

Jacqueline stopped in her tracks when she spotted her. "Bianca?"

Bianca moved quickly to embrace the woman.

Detective Sims left them alone.

Bianca patted the Jacqueline's back. "Are you okay?" Breaking her embrace, she walked beside her outside the police station and into the parking lot. With phones ringing and people chattering, outside was better. Maybe Bianca could convince her to talk some place else until she had to return to the BBQ event.

Jacqueline sniffled. "Coming back from shopping to the police outside my hotel room?" She rubbed her eyes. "I hardly think I'm okay. My parents leave tomorrow. I only stayed to help pack Sherry's things and to see if I could land another assistant job. With Clique Classic still in town, I couldn't pass that opportunity up to network."

Bianca figured that much. "I heard they found the poison with your things."

Jacqueline groaned as they approached her car, an apple red Toyota RAV4. "I don't know how it got there." She scrambled inside her purse for her keys. "Yes, I ran errands for Sherry. I knew her favorite foods. How she took her coffee, and yes, we didn't get along. We had our arguments, but why would I do this? This was the only steady job I could keep."

"Why?" Bianca wondered. "Did you tell the police everything?"

"I... can't... It'll ruin my family's reputation." Jacqueline shook her head, finally grabbing her keys. They jingled in her hand. "I can't."

"Jacqueline. If the police found the poison, there's no telling what they'll find next unless you tell the whole truth. Can you remember where you were before Sherry left for the stage?"

Jacqueline wiped a stray tear from her face with her free hand, still clutching her piece of tissue. "I was on the phone with... my nanny." She blew out her cheeks.

Bianca blinked. "Nanny?" Jacqueline was a mother? Judging by the bare ring finger, she wasn't married—or was she? More than enough reason to leave town as soon as possible.

"He's three, and the doctors already think he's showing signs of autism," Jacqueline explained. "That's why it's been hard for me to find work. I didn't want to leave him, so Dad thought working for Sherry would be best to keep it in the family. I moved to California to be near her for work, taking my son with me. Thankfully, I could afford a nanny and my apartment with what Sherry paid me. I can't lose that now. I was finally stable on my own."

Bianca's heart squeezed, going out to Jacqueline.

"With Dad in politics back in Georgia, the slightest scandal would ruin his campaign. Sherry was the poster child. Perfect. Beautiful. Smart. Everyone loved her. Her dad adopted me officially a year after he married my mother. I begged them to let me take a summer trip to Venice with some friends. I'd just turned eighteen. I met a man there, and the next thing I know... I'm pregnant with Charlie."

Bianca listened without judgment.

Jacqueline leaned against the driver's door of her car. Thank goodness they were a way off from the front door, but Bianca knew Detective Sims was monitoring her.

Jacqueline continued her story. "I was told to keep him a secret. I disappointed my mother, along with my stepdad. Technically, my dad." Her bottom lip trembled. "I don't know how he convinced Sherry to let me work for her, but I did what

I had to do. The hours were long and unpredictable, with her on demand for jobs, but I made enough to find a nanny to take care of Charlie."

"So why not tell the truth, Jacqueline? Tell the police so you can prove your alibi. If not, and this gets any worse, you could go to prison. Where would Charlie be then?"

Jacqueline covered her mouth as if in shock. "I didn't... Oh, no. They'll take him away from me, won't they?"

"I don't know, but I can tell you as a mom, I would do whatever I could to keep my daughter safe and with me, even if it meant scandalizing the family name," Bianca said.

"How could I...?" She scrunched her eyes closed. "This is too much. I haven't had time to think through all of this. I've held on to this guilt for so long." Then she opened her eyes and gave Bianca a soft smile. "Thank you. Thank you so much."

"You're welcome. I'm not saying it will be easy, but Charlie deserves to stay with his mother. Is his father in his life?" Bianca asked.

Jacqueline shook her head. "He... No."

"Then he's going to need all the love and care you can give him."

"That means a lot to me."

"You're welcome." Bianca winked at her.

She tossed her tissue into her purse. "I guess I should go back inside." Jacqueline turned her head to stare at the police station.

"I would. The sooner you do, the sooner you can get back to Charlie."

Jacqueline hugged her once more. She sniffled once more after breaking their embrace and walked back to the entrance of the precinct.

Bianca watched after her, glad she could help. *Buzz. Buzz.* Bianca dub into her own purse for her cell phone. Was it her mother? How long before Melanie cracked under their mother's questions and told Deborah Wallace where Bianca was? When she checked her phone, she saw a message from her sister.

Mom's looking for you.

Bianca giggled and replied.

Coming.

Chapter 16

"Where were you?" Deborah Wallace had her arms folded and raised an eyebrow at her daughter. "You had to get a hat?"

Bianca swallowed as she walked to one of the long tables and served herself a plate. "I had a quick errand to run. Besides, it's not too hot out here as I thought, so no hat today." She fanned herself for emphasis.

"Bianca Wallace?" Her mother only used her motherly tone when she meant business.

Bianca sighed. "I went to see a new friend. She's in deep trouble and I wanted to help."

Her mother's face softened. "You have so much of your father in you, it's not even funny."

Bianca gave her a soft smile. Her mouth watered at the BBQ chicken, coleslaw, and homemade mac and cheese on her plate. "Is that a good or bad thing?"

"Both," her mother admitted. "I just hope you're not getting overly involved. You can only do so much for people. The rest is up to them and we can't make their choices for them."

"I know that, but... this was too important to ignore." Bianca walked over to a dining table to eat. Sitting in one of the fold-out chairs, plastic crinkled in her hands as she tore apart the seal for her silverware.

Her mother followed. "Okay. I trust your judgment." Then she touched her shoulder. "Just be careful."

"I will."

The music blared once more through the speakers, and this time, Bianca heard Marvin Gaye and Tammi Terrell's "Your Precious Love." The band must have been on break, so no live blues music for the next hour. Bianca smiled at the familiar tune she would hear growing up.

"Now this takes me back," her mother said as her head swayed with the music.

"Care to dance?" Luther Burkes came from behind her mother after nodding at Bianca.

Her mother took his hand. "Of course." The older couple walked hand in hand farther into the street. Thank goodness barricades and cones blocked traffic. Bianca took a bite from her mac and cheese with her fork. She watched the crowd around her eating off paper plates, neighbors standing around chatting, sitting in lawn chairs, and kids playing in the street. A few other couples danced along with her mother and Luther, including Judy and Richard.

Scanning the crowd, Bianca wondered where Melanie and Jordan were. She hadn't asked questions in a while to give her sister some privacy in her personal life, but it didn't diminish her need to know. Then her eyes fell on Alyssa and Kendrick sitting on a bench. Though his arm was around Alyssa's shoulders, Bianca didn't feel the need to tell him to back away twenty feet.

Chuckling to herself, she swallowed the last of her mac and cheese. It satisfied her stomach with the coleslaw and BBQ chicken. Thank goodness plenty of napkins were on the table. "At least I don't have to worry about cooking tonight."

"Thank goodness you're back." Melanie took a seat across from her sister.

"Me? Where have *you* been?" Bianca asked.

Melanie tilted her head to the side. "What do you mean? *You* left, remember?"

Bianca eyeballed her. "I've practically finished my plate and had a lecture from Mom. So I ask you again. Where were you?" She grinned, giving her interrogation away.

Melanie pointed to her. "I see what you're doing. If you must know, I took a walk."

"Alone?" Bianca set her plastic fork on top of her empty paper plate.

"No."

Bianca's grin grew larger. "Fine. I'll let it go because I have news."

Melanie leaned in closer. "What did you find out?"

Bianca leaned in as well, careful not to talk too loud. "Jacqueline *has* an alibi. I don't know how the poison got into her room, but she was on the phone with her nanny the night of Sherry's death."

Melanie blinked. "She's a mom? Sherry didn't tell me."

"Jacqueline's a single mother and, according to her, it would have brought embarrassment to the family. News of an out-of-wedlock child would have hurt their father's traditional political image."

"But his adopted daughter and her child should have been more important than his reputation," Melanie countered. Her forehead wrinkled with obvious disapproval.

"It makes me wonder, though."

"About what?" her sister asked.

"While I don't think Jacqueline's guilty, what if growing up in Sherry's shadow got to her? Was it simply jealously since Sherry had this glamorous lifestyle and she had to work harder because she had a child?" Bianca explained.

"Maybe. Still... that's pretty jaded."

"It wouldn't surprise me, to be honest," Bianca added. Her mouth twisted as her thoughts turned.

"What are you thinking about?" Melanie asked.

"The father."

"Sherry's father." Melanie sat back in her chair. "Why?"

Bianca ticked off her fingers at a time as she counted the suspects. "We have brokenhearted Aiden. Envious Paris Deveraux. Hunter, who lost his top client in Sherry."

Melanie tapped her own fingers to her lips as she listened.

Bianca continued. "And I can't forget the conversation Clark Wilson had at the memorial. He worried about his campaign instead of his daughter's death, and he told Joan something was 'missing from Sherry's things.'"

"When did Joan tell you this?" Melanie asked.

"Before I left to see Jacqueline. I don't know what he's looking for, but it must be important enough to stay in Edenville longer than I think he should," Bianca said. She had heard and even read enough crime fiction books on political scandals, and the lengths candidates go to in order to win a position. Was that the case here?

Melanie rubbed at her forehead. "My brain is spinning with all of this. We still don't know who that man was at the rehearsal, do we?"

"No, we don't."

"Excuse me, ladies." A tenor voice interrupted their discussion, but Bianca's arms broke out in goosebumps.

Detective Sims stood before her. No longer in his dress pants, but dark jeans, and a taupe-collared shirt. His gray eyes shined at Bianca.

"Detective," Melanie said, the octave changing in her voice. Her mood perked up quick from rubbing at her forehead. "We didn't expect to see you here."

"I thought I'd check out the famous Edenville Blues and BBQ festival event." Then he faced Bianca just as Toni Braxton's "I Love Me Some Him," played through the speakers. "Want to dance?"

Was this a sign? Though there were times she could sense Detective Sims'—Lamar's—attraction towards her, he never voiced it. Mild flirtations here and there, but never an obvious declaration. Then again, Bianca could say something if she wanted to.

She froze for a moment, but held back a yelp when she felt a kick underneath the table. Narrowing her eyes at her baby sister, Bianca stood to her feet. She'd get her for that later. "Sure." She hoped Detective Sims didn't hear the strain in her voice. Her breathing slowed when she took his hand. Heat traveled through every one of her fingers and her stomach flipped.

Joining the rest of the couples on the street, she placed her free hand on his firm shoulder. She held back a gasp when his large hand embraced her waist. Practically a breath away from his lips, Bianca faced upward, staring at the pink-and-purple hues as the sun set. Clouds covered most of the sky, making the evening overcast.

The cool breeze chilled her skin, but it did nothing to calm her body temperature.

"Are these festivals common too?" Detective Sims asked.

"Uh-huh." Why was it so hard to breathe around him? Being this close was making her brain fuzzy like static on a radio.

"I think I could get used to it. Have you since you've lived here?"

Bianca swallowed, willing her brain to function. "I think so. Edenville's been a huge part in my life. I... needed a fresh start after my divorce." Staying in California wasn't an option after her marriage was over. Moving back to Edenville was the best decision. Her mother had made it her new home after leaving Atlanta, Georgia, behind. It wasn't the same with Bianca's father gone since he died in prison. A case of mistaken identity changed the trajectory of her family life.

"What's your favorite part?" he asked.

She could feel him staring at her, but she didn't return the gesture. "Being with family again. My mom moved here first. Melanie and I followed. That was more important than I thought, so I'm glad we're together."

"The things we appreciate later in life," Detective Sims commented.

"What about you?" she asked, hoping the conversation would distract her. Her senses were on overload as she felt the heat on her back from his hand.

"I think my family too. I tried to find acceptance with my friends, but I didn't choose well back then." He chuckled. "My mom warned me, but I didn't listen, thinking I was *grown*."

Bianca laughed. "I had those moments, too, growing up." She looked toward her daughter once more, who was walking with

Kendrick down the sidewalk. What did teenagers talk about these days? "I think I'm getting a taste of that with my daughter. She's so much like me and I...."

"You what?"

Bianca returned his gaze this time. Exhaling, she admitted the truth. "I just don't want her to get hurt. I made some decisions that I thought were best, but I'm... paying for them now."

"I don't think you regret being a mother," he said.

She shook her head. "Never. So I can't say I regret everything." She rolled her shoulders back. "Can't dwell on the past. I've learned to put some things behind me."

Detective Sims spun her and brought her back to his chest. "I'm glad."

"Nice move." Her smile grew wider. "Wasn't expecting that from..."

"A detective?"

She pressed her lips together for a moment. "No, it's just... well, I can understand your need to take your job seriously. It's... nice to see this side of you, though."

"We all have layers, don't we?" He licked his lips. "We choose who we want to let in, right?"

Bianca tuned out the music and the surrounding people, focusing only on Lamar's voice. "That takes... vulnerability."

"It's risky on both sides. Both people are taking a chance," he added. Was this a general conversation, or was he talking about them?

Bianca's hand trailed to his neck, brushing her fingers along the nape. "That can be easier said than done. What if one doesn't... think they're ready? Should the other person wait for them to be? Is that fair?"

He fixed his gaze on hers. "People wait for what they *want*."

Bianca's heart skipped. "Some things... are worth waiting for."

Had he tilted his head towards hers? Bianca couldn't tell. His words spell bounded her. His grip on her hand tightened, and while a part of her wanted to run for her car, she couldn't move if she'd wanted to. Then her eyes drifted to his lips. Would he kiss her? Would she let him?

Then thunder boomed hard enough to rattle windows. When Bianca felt a drop of rain on her cheek, her eyes widened. Shouts and yells permeated from the townspeople as they scrambled to grab the food from the tables. Bianca didn't realize Detective Sims had such a firm grip on her hand, but he led her to the covered sidewalk. Bianca didn't care to see what her soft curls looked like now. Her dress now practically drenched.

"Mom! We—" Alyssa blinked at the sight of her with Detective Sims. She shook her head slightly and finished her thought. "Let's get out of here!" Alyssa shouted, using her wristlet to cover her head. It didn't help.

Kendrick's father struggled with a black umbrella in his hand. He obviously couldn't open it despite his efforts. For a tall and muscular man, this umbrella gave him a run for his money. Kendrick stood next to his mother, who wore a floral sundress herself, flattering her petite frame. Her son used his plaid shirt to help cover her and Alyssa's heads.

"I didn't bring an umbrella." Bianca could kick herself for not bringing it, but the weather report had only predicted a ten percent chance of rain. So much for that.

"We can make it, Mom," Alyssa said. She pointed to the car. "We're parked right there."

Bianca watched as Jordan draped an arm around Melanie. Her teeth chattered. They needed to get home. "Where's Mom?"

Alyssa pointed to her grandmother, who sprinted along with Luther under a purple umbrella.

"Luther!" Bianca called out over a crackle of more thunder.

He turned and waved back. "I'm coming back! Don't worry."

Bianca sighed with relief, but noticed she was still holding Detective Sims' hand. Alyssa's eyes widened even more in response, but she said nothing—yet. It was a matter of time before her daughter asked questions. Bianca pulled back, rubbing her chilled fingers together. "Sorry."

"It's okay, Bianca," he said, stuffing his hands inside his pockets.

"Sorry it rained on your first BBQ event with us," she commented.

He smiled. "Best one I've ever been to."

"Mom!" Alyssa called out again.

"I've... got to go." Bianca backed further away from him.

He nodded in agreement.

The thunder rolled once more, and though she didn't plan to leave this soon, Bianca dug into her purse for her keys. She watched Alyssa run for the car, so she and Melanie did the same, giving a thumbs-up sign to Luther. He returned the gesture, and helped instead Ms. Ella, covering her with the umbrella as they dashed to her floral shop. Bianca's feet splashed in the water, as small puddles developed on the street. Unlocking her car, it beeped, and the doors slammed close once all three women were inside.

"Turn on the heat." Melanie rubbed her hands together.

"Here, Aunt Mel." Alyssa handed her a towel.

Bianca never traveled without towels in the car, especially on days like this. She cranked the engine and turned on the heat at her sister's request. She watched a few other townspeople scatter to their cars, while others ran into buildings with the trays of food. Sheets of rain splattered on her windshield and lightning pierced the sky above.

"Can we go now?" Alyssa asked with a shaky voice, turning to look out the back window.

"I'm waiting for it to lighten some. It's pretty heavy out there," Bianca said. Was her daughter in a rush?

Melanie towel dried her damp hair. "Are you okay Alyssa?"

Alyssa's eyes widened. "Sure why?"

Why was she so jumpy? Wasn't her daughter just with her boyfriend and his parents? Now Alyssa fidgeted in the backseat.

"Is something wrong? Is everything okay with Kendrick?" Bianca wondered.

Her daughter cleared her throat, running a jerky hand through her own damp curls. "We're fine, Mom. It's nothing. I just want to go home. That's all." She faced the back window once more, but straightened in her seat and put on her seatbelt.

When the rain lightened, Bianca put the car and pulled out slowly from her paralleled parking spot on the main street.

"Okay. I'll go for it now," Melanie said, though she didn't sound convinced.

Bianca wasn't either.

Chapter 17

"ACHOO!" Melanie covered her mouth.

Bianca handed her sister a nearby tissue box on her coffee table. "Bless you." At least she hadn't caught a chill from getting caught in the rain. Once they'd arrived home, Bianca had changed her clothes and made some hot tea. At least most of the food had been spared from the Blues and BBQ event. Some Wednesday evening, this turned out to be.

Her mother had gotten home safe thanks to Luther Burkes, and Alyssa was in her room. Though Bianca tried talking to her as soon as they arrived home, her daughter insisted on being alone. So, she didn't pry. She figured it had to do something with Kendrick again, as summer break was approaching fast. The best she could come up with was Alyssa still not wanting to leave him behind.

"Thank you." Mel blew her nose. "I hope I'm not getting sick."

"I don't think so. It could have been worse." Bianca sipped her chamomile tea, relishing in the warm liquid.

"Some party. We never get rained out," her sister pointed out.

"First time for everything, I guess." Then she nudged Melanie's shoulder.

"What?" Melanie's forehead furrowed.

"Jordan. He barely left your side."

Melanie replied, "I could say the same about your *slow dance* with Detective Sims. For a second, I thought he was going to kiss you."

Me too. Though she didn't admit it aloud. "I'll tell you what. You share with me, and I'll tell you what's going on with me."

Melanie bit at her bottom lip. Then a sigh escaped her. "I don't know, to be honest. I've always liked Jordan as a friend, but... something's changed. He's sweet. Generous. Understanding. I enjoy getting to know this side of him."

"Has he said that he likes you?" Bianca wondered, turning in her seat on the sofa to face her sister.

Melanie bobbed her head. "Even then, I didn't think nothing of it because some men have said that to me before." She tucked a curl behind her ear. "Then they say all the right things to get what they *want*. I know not all men are the same, but..."

Bianca didn't dare ask, but she knew of only one man who had broken her sister's heart. Calvin Wade. Her ex-fiancé. "Does this have anything to do with...?" She wondered if her sister would open up. She hadn't talked about Calvin in a few years.

Melanie rested her head back against the couch. "It was all about him. His law career. His practice. What I would gain by being his wife. If I hadn't been so caught up in the wining and dining he did, I would have broken up with him sooner. He said all the right things. I didn't... realize how insecure I was, looking for validation from a relationship."

Bianca reached for her hand. "You've grown so much since then. You're an amazing journalist. I'm glad you live here with me and Alyssa. I know Mom loves us all, being so close."

Melanie gave a faint smile, turning her head to her sister. "I don't regret it. You're right. It took walking away from Calvin to make me see I needed to work on my heart. And now with Jordan... I can't help but wonder if I'm ready." Sitting up, she faced her sister. "Sis, I've never talked to a man before who I felt truly understood me. It's a connection I can't explain, but it's too early for wedding bells."

Bianca tilted her head as she listened.

Melanie used her free hand and ran it down the side of her cheek. "I can't figure him out. He feels too good to be true, but..."

"But what?" Bianca asked.

"Though a part of me wants to run away before anything gets started, I... I think I'm curious enough to want to try." She shrugged. "I'll never know if I don't, right?"

Bianca blew out her cheeks. "No, you won't."

Melanie adjusted to crisscross applesauce position on the couch, releasing her sister's hand. "So? What about you? I've poured my heart out, so what's the scoop with you and Detective Sims?"

Bianca wrung her hands together. "Same as you, I guess, though we talked about dating and taking risks."

"Do you enjoy talking to him?" Melanie asked.

Bianca bobbed her head. "I do."

"Do you look forward to seeing him? Even if it's only for a moment?"

Bianca pulled at the V-neck of her cotton T-shirt. "I... Yes."

"So... why not give it a shot?"

"I'm not the type of woman to..."

"To what? Make the first move? Do you know what year it is?" Melanie lifted a single eyebrow. "I don't think there's nothing wrong with initiation. It's not like you're forcing anything to happen. You're gaging to see how he feels or doesn't feel about you."

"That's not me, Mel. I don't care what year it is. I can make small talk with strangers, but I haven't seriously... dated in a long time."

"That was my biggest fear." Melanie's chin dropped.

"What?"

"I prayed Malcom didn't damage you too much." Lifting her gaze, her eyes shined. "I hated when you told us you were divorcing him. I hate what it did to you."

Bianca reached for her hand again. "I won't say it was easy, but I've healed. A part of me will always wonder why it happened, but that's past me now. You don't need to worry about that."

Melanie blew out her cheeks. "Thank God."

Bianca gave her a brief hug, patting her back. Pulling away, she said, "Sometimes I wonder who's the oldest. You're always trying to protect me."

Melanie winked. "Always. You're my sister and my best friend."

Bianca could have cried, but she fanned her face with her hands. "Stop it."

"Okay." Melanie pressed her hands to her own cheeks, as if to calm her own emotions. Then she placed her hands together in a steeple. "Back to Detective Sims. I don't think there's any harm in initiating. If he takes it from there, fine, let him pursue you. I'll never tell you to chase a man, but at least by saying something, you'll know for sure."

"I wouldn't even know what to say," Bianca admitted. "I haven't had time to think, really, with us trying to figure out who killed Sherry."

"I still don't see who could do something like that. Especially for everyone to see her fall to her death," Melanie added. "And you're certain you don't think it's Jacqueline?"

Bianca shook her head. "I don't see it. I could be wrong, but I just don't see it."

Melanie narrowed her eyes. "You did it again."

"What?" Bianca asked.

"Changed the subject," her sister pointed out.

"I'll think about it, okay? I need time to figure out what I'm feeling. The last thing I want to do is lead him or any man on," Bianca said.

"Okay." Melanie gave her a pleased look. "In the meantime, let's see if we can crack this case."

Bianca grabbed her tea cup. Melanie did the same, and the sisters clinked cups.

THAT FOLLOWING THURSDAY afternoon, not much had changed in Sherry's investigation. At least the police cleared Jacqueline, her alibi, checking out with her nanny. That made Bianca breathe easier, but there were so many questions left unanswered. Sitting at her table in the corner of R&J's Restaurant and Bakery, she wiped her mouth with her paper napkin. She figured a walk afterwards in downtown Edenville would help burn a few calories, especially since she'd indulged in a couple of Judy's homemade chocolate chip cookies. Nothing compared to her friend's homemade recipe.

Unlocking her phone screen once more, she saw there wasn't anything new that she read about Sherry's history. All the recent articles had only reported her collapse and that the police were still investigating her untimely death. Even scrolling through the photos, Bianca stared once again at the picture with Jacqueline, Sherry, and Sherry's father. Or... adoptive father. How true was that? She found nothing contrary to him being her biological father. Was there a reason to keep it under wraps?

Since she'd paid the check, Bianca sipped the last of her iced tea, waved goodbye to Judy, and walked outside. Then her eyes shifted to her phone screen once more. Clark's smile, but Jacqueline looked stiffed once again. *Scandal.* That was the word Jacqueline had used when talking about her unplanned pregnancy. Was the fact that Jacqueline had been so young and unwed the only scandal... or was there more kept in the dark?

Searching for more photos, Bianca stopped when she noticed a picture of Paris Deveraux with Clark Wilson and Sherry. Why take a photo with her archrival and her father in the first place? To save face with the press?

Then there was another picture with only Clark and Paris. The ballroom behind them appeared to be in a banquet setting, and they stood very close, with his arm wrapped around her waist. Why so close and where was his wife, Joan?

Did he know Paris well enough? Had Sherry introduced him to her? Did Paris support him as a politician? For a man that cared about his reputation, he would have known not to pose in a photo like this. The press must have had a field day with it.

Then again, perhaps it was nothing to be too concerned about, but Bianca would keep it in mind.

Bianca's fingers grazed her smooth chin as she paced down Main Street.

When her phone rang in her hands, she answered. It was her mother. "Hi, Mom."

"I want you to know I can pick up Alyssa from school today. My client had to reschedule."

"Thanks Mom. Do you think...?" Worth a shot. Her mother knew how to connect with Alyssa, even when the girl didn't want to talk. Deborah Wallace had a gift to make people feel at ease and open up to her. "Can you try talking to her when you see her? Something is up, but she's not talking to me about it. I thought it was about her and Kendrick, but I think something else is going on."

"What else do you think it is?" Her mother asked.

"Not sure. I thought she was getting better since Sherry's death. Now I don't know."

"Well, I do what I can," her mother replied. "I'm sure she's fine. Nothing I didn't go through with you and Melanie as teenagers."

Bianca hoped she was right. Otherwise, perhaps she needed to find a counselor for Alyssa. No harm in getting the extra help if needed. "Thanks. So, who's on your list now to match?" She tapped her foot on the sidewalk.

"You know I keep my clients' personal lives confidential, but this man called, saying he found my name online and my ninety-five percent success rate impressed him. He's model. This could be big, Bianca!" Her mother practically squealed.

Bianca giggled. "Anybody I would know? I don't think you've had a model before that I remember. He's local, I'm assuming."

"Yes. He's still making a name for himself, but I'm sure people will know his name soon. Not to mention he's part of Clique Classic's event in town. This is his first major gig, so I got to see them in action when I drove by the park this week," her mother said.

Bianca pulled her lips in. Any chance this up-and-coming model knew Sherry? If her mother told her this guy's name, would he answer a few of Bianca's questions? Then again, she was sure the police questioned him already. Why tell her anything? Perhaps it was a dead end. "That's great, Mom."

"Thank you. Aside from you, he's going to put this town on the map."

Her mother was her biggest cheerleader. "Thanks Mom."

"You're welcome." Her mother replied. "So where are you? How was your lunch date?"

"You mean my solo lunch date? It went well. Just taking a short walk before I head back to the house," Bianca said.

A black Jaguar caught her eye as it drove past her on Main Street. Bianca's mouth dropped open. She knew that car. Paris Deveraux. No harm in seeing where she was going. Right?

Bianca sprinted to her car with her phone in her hand. "Mom, I have to go. I'll pick up Alyssa up tomorrow afternoon." Perhaps a night with her grandmother would do her some good.

"Has she decided about getting her driver's license?" her mother asked. "I don't mind picking her up, but I think it's time."

"I'll talk to her. I have to go now." Bianca slid into her driver's seat and cranked the engine.

"You sound like you're in a rush. Is anything wrong?"

"Nothing's wrong." Bianca clicked on her seatbelt.

"Okay. I'll talk to you later." Her mother hung up.

Bianca looked between her rearview and side mirrors before pulling out of her parking space. Thank goodness a red light had stopped Paris, so it didn't take long for Bianca to catch up with her.

Chapter 18

Tapping her fingers against the steering wheel, Bianca followed the black Jaguar in front of her, careful not to be too obvious. She even took her foot off the accelerator a few times, but she kept up with Paris Deveraux. Where was the model headed? Did she finish her photo shoot for the day? Was she meeting someone afterwards? Hunter, perhaps?

Bypassing railroad tracks, Bianca slowed hearing the shaking of rubber underneath her car. The Jaguar turned left at the next light, so Bianca followed. Thank goodness she didn't have to dig too far inside her purse for her phone. The least she could do was take pictures for evidence. Turning her car again to follow, Bianca saw Paris had entered a parking garage. Parking garage?

Bianca tapped her brakes, but Paris only turned into the space with gray pillars and a low roof. She did the same, ascending to the next level. There were a few cars parked, stripes lining the pavement. No one was in sight, so perhaps they were all inside the commercial building next door. Where were they, anyway? Bianca didn't see a sign. Perhaps they came around the backside of the building.

When her phone rang, she quickly connected it to her Bluetooth. Melanie was on the line.

"What's up?" Bianca asked, driving less than twenty miles per hour.

"I thought you'd be home by now," her sister pointed out.

When a bark sounded, Bianca figured Casper was close by. "I am," she said. "But I had to check something first."

"Like what?"

"Paris Deveraux. I think she's meeting someone, and I want to know who." Bianca pulled her lips tightly closed in anticipation. Paris turned a corner again, going to the third level of the parking garage.

"Bianca? Please be careful," her sister urged her.

"I will. Don't worry. I'm not even getting out of the car. I only want to see. I wonder if it'll be Hunter or... Aiden."

"Why Aiden, though? You haven't seen them together since the restaurant, right?"

"Right, but that means nothing. Perhaps there have been phone conversations."

"There you go, being nosy again," Melanie commented, but there was a hint of teasing in her voice.

"What?" Bianca raised an eyebrow. "I'm not nosy. If I were nosy, I'd spread the news around town like Ms. Ella. No offense to her, but she's worse than the news on television."

Melanie giggled. "That's true. I don't know how she does it, but she knows everything in town."

Bianca tapped her brakes to slow down. Paris' brake lights were on. Why? Scanning the parking area, Bianca looked to see if someone was getting out of their car to meet the model. No one. Then Paris pulled forward again, once more turning to ascend to the next level. Bianca waited for a few moments in case the woman had spotted her.

"What's she doing now?" Melanie asked.

"She stopped for a second. I'm not sure if she saw me." Bianca exhaled.

"Get out of there, Bianca. If she turns out to be dangerous, you don't need to be her next victim," Melanie said.

Bianca eased on the gas. "I'll leave soon, but I'm too close to leave now." Turning to the next level, Bianca spotted Paris' Jaguar parked ahead. Paris got out of her car. She was wearing a long, black, strapless jumpsuit with heels, and her red hair flowed down her back. She walked forward and Bianca's lips parted.

"Aiden?"

"He's there?" Melanie asked.

"Yes, he is." Bianca grabbed her phone to take pictures. "I wonder why. What's going to be even more surprising is if these two worked together to get rid of Sherry."

"I don't get it. Why?"

"I don't know."

Bianca cracked a window to see if she could hear them talking, and she parked alongside a concrete pillar in the garage. She snapped a picture of the duo.

"What's so important that you keep calling me?" Aiden's voice asked.

"I did my part, so what are *you* going to do?" Paris countered, folding her arms.

"I'm not doing this anymore. It's gotten too messy," he said.

"You refused to tell her. It's not my fault," Paris replied.

Aiden pointed at her. "If you did anything—"

She slapped his hand away.

Bianca gasped and listened further. Thank goodness she'd turned her phone volume down, so no one would hear her sister on the speakerphone in her car.

"We had a deal. I kept my end, and you didn't, so unless you want me to tell the world how you really made it in the modeling business, we'll *never* be done, Aiden Carlyle," Paris threatened, with a hint of edge to her voice. "How would that *help* your image?"

"I don't take kindly to threats, Paris. Cross me and I'll ruin you." Aiden had a bite to his own voice. "I didn't find what you're talking about."

"Don't lie to me. You know where that flash drive is," Paris said.

"Bianca, get out of there," Melanie said.

This was the second time Bianca heard a flash drive mentioned. First Sherry's father and now Paris. What was so important that both she and Clark wanted it? "I'll call you back later, sis." She didn't give her sister a chance to respond. Bianca hung up. Then she watched Aiden storm off to what looked like a Chevrolet pickup truck.

Paris stomped her feet to the ground, but then she dug into her pocket, taking out her phone. "What!" she yelled, with one hand on her hip and pacing back and forth.

Who was it this time? Hunter? Did he know she was here with Aiden?

Bianca opened another browser on her phone to search for Paris' name.

A mirthless laugh escaped Paris' mouth. "You don't think I will, Clark?"

Bianca covered her mouth. Clark? What was going on between them? Did Sherry know? Bianca groaned. If only she had a clue where this supposed flash drive was. Who else was looking for it? How did this all tie together, leading up to Sherry's death?

"Unless you want the world to know the *truth*, I suggest you give me what I want. I've given you enough time," she said. Then Paris walked to her car, and Bianca lost sight of her.

Bianca let her window up, put her car in drive, and turned to follow the exit signs out of the parking garage. An engine revved and passed by her. She stopped, not wanting Aiden to hit her.

"He must be in a hurry to get out of here." Bianca exhaled once more, calming the adrenaline coursing through her body. Would this be valuable information to share with the police? No. She had no concrete proof.

Chapter 19

With her nerves rattled from the scene in the parking garage, Bianca needed a treat before heading home. Not able to resist Judy's homemade chocolate chip cookies, Bianca bought a dozen from her friend. The comfort much needed.

Alyssa was with her mother for the rest of the evening, which gave Bianca and Melanie an opportunity to discuss Paris' meeting with Aiden. Not to mention the call with Sherry's father. There was still something missing from the puzzle about Sherry's death. The case of the wanted flash drive.

Pulling onto her street, Bianca noticed a police car in her driveway. Her lips parted as the sweat built on her palms. Had something happened to Melanie? Her mother? Alyssa? Her heart thudded inside her chest, but she wouldn't assume the worst. What had happened?

When she pulled into her driveway, she hit the remote for her garage. Melanie was standing on the porch talking to two officers. Bianca knew the broad shoulders of one of them. If Detective Sims was here, that meant Detective Atkins was with him. Both men turned to see her, but Bianca pulled forward.

Swallowing the lump in her throat, Bianca breathed easier, knowing that her sister was all right. That only left her daughter and mother. She cut the engine, grabbed the apple-red paper box of chocolate chip cookies, and stepped into the garage.

"Bianca," Melanie called out. Detective Sims and Detective Atkins were right behind her, dressed in collared shirts and dress pants, their badges hanging off their hips.

"What's going on?" Bianca secured her purse strap on her shoulder while balancing the box in her hand. "Something happened?"

"We need to ask you a few questions," Detective Sims said. The smolder in his gray eyes wasn't apparent. This wasn't the same man who'd held her close when they'd danced at the town Blues and BBQ festival. The man in front of her had strong eye contact and a set jaw.

"Okay." She gestured to the house. "Won't you come inside?"

Both men and Melanie followed Bianca inside, and she closed the garage door. Melanie led both detectives to the living room once they'd passed through the dining area. Bianca set the box of cookies on her dining table, setting her purse next to it. She wrung her hands together. Two police officers wanting to talk to her? Something was wrong.

Rolling her shoulders back, she joined the rest of the group in the living room. "Can I help you with something?"

Detective Sims laced his fingers together. "Ms. Wallace." He was being formal again. This had to be serious. "I need to know where you were exactly an hour ago. What did you do this afternoon?"

Bianca blinked rapidly. Had he seen her follow Paris today? Had someone else spotted her and told the police? Her muscles twitched. The joys of living in a small town. It wasn't a crime to follow someone and though she'd followed Paris, it wasn't as if she'd attacked the woman.

"I had lunch at R&J's Restaurant and Bakery. I walked a few blocks downtown. Called my mother. Why?" She wouldn't volunteer too much information.

"Paris Deveraux is dead. We found her body in a parking garage. It appears someone had strangled her," Detective Atkins said.

Bianca gasped. "What?" That was impossible. She'd just seen the woman. Had Aiden come back and killed her? Had someone followed Paris aside from her? "That can't be."

Detective Sims exhaled. "If you know something, Ms. Wallace, we need you to tell us. A witness in town says they saw your car follow hers."

Bianca bit back her rebuttal. Ms. Ella never ceased to amaze her. Who else would spread town gossip that quick in Edenville? "I spotted her car when I got off the phone with my mother."

"What time was that?" Detective Sims asked.

Bianca shrugged. "It was close to one o'clock this afternoon."

Detective Atkins jotted down the information in his notepad.

Bianca looked over at her sister, who stood a few feet away with her arms folded. Based on her fidgeting, Melanie wasn't taking the news too well.

"You followed her to the parking garage?" Detective Sims asked.

"Yes." Bianca gestured to Melanie. "I had my sister on the phone with me."

Detective Atkins asked Melanie. "Is that true?"

Her sister bobbed her head. "Yes."

"What did you see?" Detective Sims continued.

"She met someone there." Bianca didn't want to point the finger at Aiden. He'd left, but if he'd returned and killed Paris, what else could she do?

"Who? Did you recognize the person?" Detective Sims pressed her further.

Bianca swallowed. "Aiden Carlyle." Might as well confess, since another person was dead. "I had Melanie on speaker and I let down the window so I could hear. I don't think anyone saw me."

Detective Sims dragged a hand down his face. "What did you hear?"

Bianca continued. "All I remember is Paris saying what Aiden owed her. I didn't know what that meant, but it wasn't a friendly meeting. She mentioned a flash drive, but he didn't know where it was. Next thing I know, Aiden gets into his truck and drives off. Then... I heard her on the phone with Clark Wilson, Sherry's father. Paris sounded angry talking to him too. I... took pictures of her and Aiden on my phone."

"We're going to need you to come down to the station and give your statement, Ms. Wallace." Detective Atkins stood to his feet, placing his notepad in his back pocket.

"Can I have a moment with you, Ms. Wallace?" Detective Sims gestured to her kitchen.

Bianca agreed.

"I'll walk you out, Detective Atkins." Melanie led him to the door.

Bianca sighed, waiting for a lecture from Detective Sims.

"Do you realize that you're one of the last people to see Paris Deveraux alive?" He ran his hand down the back of his neck.

"Am I a suspect?" she asked. There was no way he believed she'd killed Paris.

He didn't confirm or deny. "Just come to the station to give your statement. Send the pictures too."

"You know I didn't do anything," she said. Did he? They hadn't known each other long enough for him to know her. Would he even want to? Was it only surface-level attraction between them?

His face softened. "It doesn't matter what I think. In my work, we deal with evidence. Right now, I know someone spotted you following Paris to the parking garage. Your sister was on the phone, so her story confirms your whereabouts." He paused and exhaled. "I'm not saying we can't clear this up, but I need you to work with me so I can help you if I can."

Bianca folded her arms. There was no point in arguing. The facts were obvious. She'd followed Paris and now another person was dead. "I'll come to the station and tell you everything I know."

"Thank you, Bianca."

She tilted her head to the side. "So it's only 'Ms. Wallace' when you're being serious?"

"How would you act if I showed up, and you were meeting a client?" he asked. There was a hint of humor in his eyes.

"Okay. I'll buy it. For now."

He stared for a lingering moment, but then he resumed his professionalism. "I'll see you at the station." With that, he backed away and acknowledged her sister on his way out the door.

"Well, this just got a lot worse," Melanie commented. "Do you want me to go with you?"

Bianca shook her head. "No, it's okay. I'll be back as soon as I can."

"What do I say in case Mom calls?" her sister asked.

Bianca groaned. "Tell her... I'm at the police station and I'll explain later."

SOME THURSDAY AFTERNOON. Bianca hadn't planned to visit the police station again until she'd found enough evidence to convict Sherry's killer. She twiddled her thumbs on top of the plain table in the interview room. Finding it difficult to keep still, she cupped one elbow with one hand while tapping her lips with the other. Paris Deveraux was dead, and she'd been one of the last people to see Sherry before she'd walked on stage. Had Bianca missed something in the parking garage?

Aiden had left. He'd practically almost ran her down, cutting in front of her to exit the garage. She hadn't looked back to see if Paris had left. Bianca exhaled. What about Clark? Had he been on his way during their hostile conversation? Did he snap on Paris? If only she had stayed a few minutes longer, perhaps she could have seen who attacked Paris. Who would do such a thing? What if Bianca could have saved her?

Her pool of suspects was dwindling. Joan Wilson hadn't slipped up in her behavior that Bianca knew of. According to Jacqueline, her parents were leaving town. Besides, Joan wasn't at the fashion show at all. Unless she hired someone to do the job for her. Would Clark go as far as having his daughter killed? Bianca couldn't forget his behavior at the memorial. The flash drive still bugged her.

"Thank you for your patience." Detective Sims entered the room with a notepad and pen.

"Sure." Bianca wished time sped up so she could leave.

His chair scraped the floor as he sat across from her. A faint smile grew on his face. "I seem to remember you being in here before."

Bianca narrowed her eyes at him. "I was attacked the last time and followed by a stalker. Now... I'm a suspect in a murder."

"That's what we're going to determine. Can you think of anything else that happened before leaving the parking garage?"

Bianca rested her hands once more on the tabletop. "I told you. Aside from Aiden Carlyle, the phone call Paris had with Clark. I couldn't hear him, but she sounded angry with him."

He dictated her words. "We'll check Clark Wilson and see where he was."

"Jacqueline said her parents were returning to Georgia today. They've packed all of Sherry's things, but I don't know what time their flight was. Either now or later, perhaps?" Bianca added.

Detective Sims wrote it all down. "And Aiden Carlyle?"

"This wasn't the first time I saw him with her," Bianca said. Did he dismiss her comment about Clark? Wasn't that top priority, considering their conversation? "Detective, if Clark Wilson—"

"We're doing our job, *Ms. Wallace*. When was the first time you saw Aiden with Paris?" He made another note on his paper.

"I was with my daughter at a local restaurant. Mobile Aztec. I saw them outside the large window."

"When was this?"

"This past weekend. Saturday evening after Sherry's memorial that morning." She rubbed her head. "Though I saw them, they didn't stay long enough for me to find out what they were doing together. Especially since..."

Detective Sims tilted his head to the side. "Since what?"

"I think... Paris was involved with Hunter Graham. Sherry's former manager," Bianca confessed.

"She told you this?" he asked.

"No, but I... saw them together. Kissing. It was at the Stargaze Hotel, before you and Detective Atkins showed to question him," Bianca explained.

Detective Sims rubbed at his chin. "He failed to mention that."

"Maybe they kept their relationship under wraps?" Bianca could understand keeping a relationship private.

"I'll look into that too."

Bianca's head spun with more of her theories. "Because if Hunter didn't know she was seeing Aiden, perhaps Hunter—"

Detective Sims held up a hand to stop her. "Before you start, let's stick with the facts. What were you doing following Paris Deveraux in the first place?"

Bianca sat back in her chair. "I may have been a little... curious. I didn't stay long. Once Aiden left, I did the same."

"Do you know which way he went?" he asked, making more notes on his notepad.

"No. He cut in front of me and left. We had to be on the fourth level of the garage, so I didn't see which way he went." She perked with more curiosity. "You can find him?"

"That's police business, Bianca. What else?" he continued.

At least he wasn't being formal as before. Bianca blinked. She had to focus. Another person was dead. "I told you. I heard her practically arguing with Clark, and then she had words with Aiden." Might as well ask. "Am I under arrest?"

Detective Sims replied. "No. Just trying to clear up this mess. Thank you for coming."

"I can go?" She didn't stand right away.

He gestured to the door. "You can go, Bianca."

Grabbing her purse, she scooted her chair back and headed for the door. Pausing with her hand on the shiny doorknob, she asked him, "Did you really suspect that I had something to do with this?" Turning on her heels, she faced him.

He leaned back in his chair, stretching his long legs underneath the table. "No."

Releasing her grip on the metal doorknob, she asked. "Why not?"

"It... doesn't sound like you," he said. His expression was soft and his gray eyes were bright. "What would have been your motive anyway, strangling a woman you hardly knew? While there are senseless acts of violence, I don't think that's the case here."

Her chest fluttered at the faith he obviously had in her. Bianca willed her body temperature to cool off. "Thank you. I appreciate that."

"You're welcome," he said. Was there a twinkle in his eye?

Bianca hurried out the door and down the hallway. She waved to a few faces but proceeded out the glass doors. Breathing easier, she clutched tightly to the shoulder strap of her purse. She wasn't a policewoman, so it wasn't her job to solve this case. Perhaps this was as far as she could go.

Approaching her car, her phone buzzed. Once she slid into the driver's seat and cranked the engine, she connected her Bluetooth to her car. The screen showed Malcom's name.

"Hey." Bianca clicked on her seatbelt.

"Bad time?" his bass voice asked.

"No. I was just..." She paused. He didn't need to know where she was. Another thing Bianca had to get used to since being divorced. Malcom no longer being her best friend. "Just heading home."

"I was calling because I can't reach Alyssa. Is she with you?"

"No. She's with my mom." Bianca raised an eyebrow. That wasn't like her daughter not to answer her phone. Something practically glued to her teenager's hand. "Maybe Mom has her helping in the kitchen. Or..."

"She's still with that boy? Kendrick, right?" Malcom exhaled. "I can't."

Bianca giggled, pulling out of the parking lot of the police station. "As far as I know, they're still together."

"I'm tempted to break it up."

"She's almost seventeen, Malcom. We've talked about this," Bianca said.

"Doesn't matter. I was his age before," he added.

A *hmm* escaped Bianca's lips. "So if we'd had a son, would this even be a conversation?" The double standard was real.

"Bianca?"

"I'm only asking. If Alyssa were a boy, would you be this concerned?"

He sighed.

"Exactly," Bianca continued. "Because she's a girl, you'd rather she stay single until she's thirty-five."

"Forty," he corrected her, but there was a hint of humor in his voice.

"Malcom!"

"Fine. I'm working on it, okay?"

"Good." Bianca stopped at a red light. "I'll have her call you back. It's possible she forgot. You know what it was like at her age. No need to worry."

"Right. Teenagers." He groaned.

Bianca laughed. "I'll make sure she returns your call. Everything still set for her to come to California?"

"Hope and I are ready," he answered.

Bianca ignored the twinge in her chest at the sound of his new wife's name. "Good." At least it was just a twinge. Some progress was better than none. "Talk to you later."

"Bye."

Bianca hung up, only to call her daughter. It went straight to voicemail. Not like her daughter at all. Next, Bianca tried her mother. Deborah Wallace picked up on the second ring.

"Hey, sweetie," her mother greeted.

"Mom, where's Alyssa? Malcom called, and she didn't answer. Now I can't reach her." Bianca's forehead furrowed.

"She's with Kendrick," her mother explained. "He stopped by the house after I picked her up. I think he said they were heading to the park."

"Okay, but that doesn't mean she can't answer her phone for her parents." Bianca tapped her fingers along her pant leg, while her other hand gripped the wheel. "Perhaps they're spending *too* much time together."

"I'm sure they'll be back. Give them some space. I remember another girl who was wrapped up in her boyfriend at that age." Her mother hadn't hesitated to remind her.

Bianca winced. "Okay, but as soon as she gets back, have her call me."

"What about Malcom?" her mother asked.

"She can call him afterwards. I need to talk to her first. Some more boundaries need to be set with Kendrick." A gnawing feeling overtook Bianca's stomach. Something wasn't right at all. Alyssa's behavior had been strange since the fashion show to begin with.

"Don't worry. He said they wouldn't be long. Kendrick is a respectable young man."

"Around *us*," Bianca added.

"Don't get overly suspicious," her mother warned her in her motherly tone.

Bianca couldn't ignore the knot in her belly. "I'm going to head to the park." Making a U-turn at the light, she headed in the direction of the town park.

Chapter 20

"Thank you." Bianca released a thankful breath to God as she pulled into the parking lot for the park. Since it was late afternoon, school kids played on the swing sets. People reclined on blankets or were reading books. Dogs barked, birds chirped, and a cool breeze sighed through the trees.

Bianca blinked when she spotted the athletic, round-faced boy with his phone to his ear. Alone. "Kendrick?"

He stopped in his tracks. "Ms. Wallace?" He dropped his phone to his side and cleared his throat. "I didn't expect to see you."

"Where's Alyssa? My mother said she left with you?"

He blinked rapidly. "We hung out here, but..."

Bianca's heart thudded. "What? Did you two have a fight or something?"

He shook his head earnestly. "No. Nothing like that." The mole on his left cheek apparent. "She said she was going to the restroom, but... she's not back yet."

Bianca dashed for the public restrooms and Kendrick followed suit. "Is she sick?" Was that why she wasn't answering her phone?

"She didn't seem like it." Kendrick kept up the pace beside Bianca. "I've been trying to call her, but she's not picking up."

Bianca's palms sweated. Arriving at the ladies' room, she gestured to Kendrick to stay outside. He agreed, and she didn't waste time pushing at the swinging door. She heard water dripping from the faucet next to her.

"Alyssa?" Bianca called out. She didn't hear anyone inside. There were four stalls, and she looked underneath the first one to see if she recognized her daughter's shoes. First stall, nothing. Second stall. Empty. Third stall was out of order. Bianca faced the last stall, which had a handicap sign on the front.

Bianca opened the door, ignoring the bleach cleaner in the air. Nothing. No sign of Alyssa. She backed up a few paces. "Okay. Don't panic." That was what she told herself, but as a mom, her worst fears played in her mind. Alyssa knew not to run off. She kept her phone with her, so why not answer her mother's phone calls?

Bianca exited the handicap stall and walked past the other three.

"Ms. Wallace?" Kendrick called out from outside.

No sense in keeping the boy waiting. Exiting the restroom, Bianca found Kendrick holding another phone in his hand. "This is Alyssa's phone."

Bianca reached for it. Kendrick didn't delay in giving it to her. Bianca tapped the screen, only to see the missed calls from her, Alyssa's dad, and Bianca's mom. "Where did you find this?"

Kendrick pointed to the concrete. "It was lying face down along the edge of the building." He rubbed the back of his head. "What happened to her?"

Bianca wanted to panic too, but she could do that later. This was about finding her daughter. She had to keep her wits about her. "Was there anyone following you by chance?"

Kendrick shook his head. "No, ma'am, not that I noticed. We were sitting in the gazebo, and Alyssa said she needed a minute in the ladies' room. That was probably like... ten or fifteen minutes ago, I think."

Bianca swallowed, holding back her own scream of frustration and anger. Whoever had taken her daughter was going to pay. "What else? Was there someone else going in and out of the restrooms here?"

Kendrick's hand transferred from his neck to his forehead. "I don't know. My best friend texted me, so I wasn't paying attention."

Bianca reached into her own pocket. Calling the police was the only thing to do next. Alyssa kidnapped. Who would do such a thing? Why her? Bianca called Detective Sims. The police could send out an Amber Alert.

"Hello?" he answered.

"Alyssa's gone."

"What do you mean, 'gone'?"

Bianca paced the ground. "She came to the park with her boyfriend, but she's gone. We found her phone outside the ladies' room. Someone took her. I know it!" Had Alyssa screamed? How could someone kidnap her in a park full of people? Had the person threatened her? Was a weapon involved and she couldn't scream?

"Slow down, Bianca," Detective Sims said. "Alyssa is missing?"

"Yes. I haven't been able to reach her. Her father and grandmother called too, and Alyssa hardly ever misses a call or text."

"Do you know anyone who may have taken her? Is there someone out to get you?" he asked.

Bianca gasped. "Oh, no." She'd only returned from the police station herself being questioned in Paris Deveraux's death. "I don't know. I didn't see anyone following me." She pressed her free hand against her cheek. "My poor baby."

"Don't worry. We're on our way."

"Please find her." Bianca's bottom lip trembled. "Not my daughter. God, please, not my daughter."

"Is there anything I can do?" Kendrick asked. His own forehead etched with his apparent worry.

Bianca swallowed. "Detective, I have Alyssa's boyfriend here with me. I'm going to let him tell you everything he saw."

"Okay, good," he replied.

She heard rummaging in the background, so she could only assume he was preparing to leave. Bianca handed Kendrick the phone. Between her own fidgety hands and dry mouth, she barely heard what Kendrick told Detective Sims. She had to think. Had someone found out she was investigating Sherry's death? Who was keeping tabs on her to know to even get close to Alyssa?

"Here you go." Kendrick handed Bianca back her phone. "He wants to talk to you."

Bianca gave a faint smile and held up the phone to her ear. "Yes." Her gazed flitted around the park. "I'm going to ask if anyone saw anything. I think I—"

"I'm almost there, Bianca. Wait." Detective Sims' tone changed. There was a hint of demand.

"You can't be serious," she said, pacing a few steps away from Kendrick.

"I am. I don't want you to cause any more trouble."

"Trouble? Did you hear me? Whoever this person is has my child!" She hadn't meant to shout, but who could blame her?

"I know that, but I can't have you making things worse, Bianca, by getting involved. This isn't like last time when it was only you. This is Alyssa we're talking about. I know if anything worse happened to her, you would lose it." He sighed, taking a breather. "We're almost there. I need you to call your mother or your sister. You don't need to be alone right now." Not to mention she needed to tell Malcom. She could only imagine his reaction.

She pressed a hand to her chest, choking back her tears. "But... that's my baby, Lamar. Someone took my baby." She didn't call him "Detective Sims" this time. This situation was too personal.

"I know, Bianca, and we're going to do everything we can to find her," he assured her. "And we *will* find her."

Bianca blew out her cheeks. "Okay."

"Trust me?" he asked.

She didn't know why, but there was no hesitation in her response. "Yes." Then Bianca heard sirens. "Is that you?"

"No, but I'm coming. I had Detective Atkins dispatch a nearby car first. I'll be there soon." With that, he hung up.

Kendrick, who stood with his hands inside the pockets of his dark jeans, said, "I'm sorry, Ms. Wallace. If only I had been paying more attention, none of this would have—"

She shook her head, reaching out a hand to his shoulder. "No, Kendrick. Don't blame yourself." Bianca sniffled. "The police are going to handle it. We're going to find Alyssa." Shifting her gaze, Bianca spotted two police officers sprinting through the grass, passing by barking dogs and their owners. She breathed easier knowing Detective Sims was coming, but that didn't stop the pain in her chest.

Chapter 21

Aplane flying overhead caught Bianca's attention, along with her phone ringing in her hand. Her mother's face showed on screen. When her eyes shifting back to Detective Sims, Bianca's heart raced. If only it was only because she was glad to see him, but his presence made the moment even more real.

Not wanting to make her mother wait, Bianca answered her call. "Hello?"

"I still don't think checking up on Alyssa is a smart idea," her mother lectured her. "I told you she's fine."

"Mom—"

"I know you're worried, but she's growing up, Bianca," her mother continued. "Every parent has to learn when to let their children go."

"Mom! Alyssa's gone," Bianca said. She hadn't meant to raise her voice, but Deborah Wallace was on a roll.

"She's going to be graduating soon and... wait. What did you say?" her mother asked, her voice filled with curiosity now.

"Alyssa's gone. She's not here at the park with Kendrick." Bianca threaded her fingers in her loose curls and then released them. It did nothing for the tension building inside her head.

"Where is she?" her mother questioned. Now the woman sounded just as worried as Bianca. "Where's Kendrick? Did he—?

Bianca stopped her before her mother's assumptions went too far. "He doesn't know. He said Alyssa went to the ladies' room but never came back. We found her phone, but she's... gone."

Her mother gasped. "Oh, no."

"Detective Sims and Detective Atkins are here now." Bianca stared ahead at the other police officers who'd arrived first. They were further away, questioning people around the park, including Kendrick, to see if they saw anything. The adults in the park murmured to themselves, exchanging whispers, while the children ran around chasing their dogs. Bianca swallowed. Her mind kept wandering to the worst-case scenario. Never finding Alyssa. Her only child. She had to be scared, especially not being able to reach Bianca.

"Bianca?" her mother called, breaking her train of thoughts.

"I'm here."

"I'm calling your sister. I have a few clients to call to see if I can reschedule."

"I'm sure they'll find her in no time." She only prayed for that miracle.

"I can't concentrate on work with my granddaughter missing. I'm rescheduling, calling a dog-sitter, and heading to the park now."

No sense in arguing with Deborah Wallace with her mind made up. "Okay." She spotted Detective Sims walking in her direction. "Mom, I have to go."

"I'll be there as soon as I can. Do you want me to call Malcom for you?"

Bianca couldn't think about telling him now. What could he do all the way from California? Though Bianca was sure he'd be angry for not telling him as soon as she found about Alyssa's disappearance. "No, I'll tell him. As soon as I finish talking to the police."

Her mother hung up, and Bianca stuffed her phone in her back pocket.

Detective Sims' face softened. "How are you holding up?" Though his mouth opened as if he wanted to say more, he didn't.

"I'm trying not to... fall apart." Bianca rubbed at her arms. If only it was because of the slight chill in the air.

"Is there anything else that you know?" He gestured to Detective Atkins, who paced to the bystanders standing on the grass. "We're going to question as many as we can. Someone saw something."

"What if they didn't? Did Kendrick mention hearing a scream of any kind?" she asked.

Detective Sims shook his head. "Only that he was texting his friend. He showed us his phone, so the messages check out in terms of the timeframe."

Bianca blew out her cheeks. "I just keep thinking that... they forced her to go with them. What if there was a weapon? That would keep her from screaming for help, I'm thinking. Alyssa knows not to talk to strangers. She's friendly, but I taught her to be aware of her surroundings."

Detective Sims rubbed at his stubbled chin. "I can see that, but it's still speculation." His eyes scanned the park. "Kendrick's message to his friend was at 4:30 p.m."

"That's all we know?" Bianca shuffled between her feet. "What else?" Bianca's heartbeat raced. She wanted her daughter back. To know she was safe in their house again.

Detective Sims assured her. "We're going to find her."

Bianca's eyes caught another police car pulling into the parking lot. While she exhaled with relief, it did nothing for her frayed nerves. "When? For all we know, she could be halfway to Oklahoma by now? What if this person has—?"

Detective Sims gripped her shoulders. Not too rough. He held her in place as if to steady her, but Bianca's body shook. "Bianca, listen to me."

Her vision blurred with fresh tears. "I can't lose her." She whimpered.

"Shh... I know." He soothed her.

Then he massaged her shoulders. His firm fingers caressed her skin, and while a tear from Bianca's eyes dripped to her cheek, her lips parted as she calmed herself down again. Her skin heated, and with him so close, breathlessness took over her body. Taking a step back, she cleared her throat and his arms dropped from her shoulders to his side. This was about finding Alyssa.

Bianca ran her hand alongside her neck, her skin still tingling from his gentle touches. "I needed that. Thank you." Then she dabbed her teary eyes.

Detective Sims stepped closer. "I don't need you worrying yourself to death." He sighed but continued. "I don't know what it's like to have a child go missing, but we're going to do everything in our power to find Alyssa. You said you trust me. Remember?"

Bianca nodded, taken aback by the sincerity in his voice. She could have kissed him but held herself back. Not the time when her daughter needed help. "I remember and... I do."

He gave a faint smile. "Is someone coming to stay with you?"

"My mom's on her way. She's calling my sister too." Bianca swallowed to regain her composure. Her eyes shifted to the parking lot again, and lo-and-behold, she spotted Melanie, Jordan, Judy, and Richard, along with her mother. Bianca figured her mother had recruited her own search party for Alyssa. "They're here." She gestured behind them.

Detective Sims glanced behind him for a moment, only to direct his attention back to her. "We'll check the grounds again, see who saw anything, but then I want you to go home."

"You can't expect me to go home now," she argued. He couldn't have been serious. Glancing at the skies, noticing the bright yellow turning into a deep gold, she knew the sun would set soon. Alyssa could be all alone with a stranger for the night. Bianca shivered at the notion.

"I'm asking you to let us do our job," he countered with a raise of his eyebrow.

"Bianca!" Melanie called out. She opened her arms when she reached for her sister.

Detective Sims stepped aside while her family and friends surrounded her.

Melanie patted her back as a whimper escaped her own throat. "I can't believe it." She stepped back for her mother to hug Bianca.

"Any news?" her mother asked as she directed her gaze to Detective Sims.

He shook his head. "None yet." He cleared his throat. "If you'll excuse me, I have a few more people to question before it gets too late."

"Where's Casper?" Bianca asked Melanie.

"We left him with the dog sitter at Mom's," her sister said.

"How are you?" Jordan chimed in, despite the downcast look on his face.

"I'm trying not to panic—too much," Bianca admitted. Then her eyes bugged. "I need to tell Malcom."

"What do you need us to do, Bianca?" Richard asked, his arm wrapped around Judy's shoulders.

"Look around for clues," Bianca answered. "See if Alyssa left anything else behind. All we found was her cell phone."

Jordan nodded while her mother patted Bianca's back. She gave a weak smile, but stepped away to call Alyssa's father. This would not be a pleasant conversation.

FRESH-CUT GRASS FILLED Bianca's lungs as she paced the ground with her phone in her hand. Selecting Malcom's name in her list of contacts, she held a breath she hadn't realized she'd been holding. Two rings later, he answered.

"Bianca?" he said.

"Is this a bad time?" she asked.

"About to have dinner with Hope. Why?" He sounded distracted, with a shuffling noise in the background.

"Alyssa is missing." Bianca didn't know how else to say it.

"She ran off with that Kenneth boy. Didn't she?" he retorted back as the overprotectiveness oozed from his voice.

"His name is Kendrick." Bianca face-palmed herself. "She was with him, but that's not what happened."

"Then what happened?" he asked with a hint of sternness in his voice.

"Alyssa's been... kidnapped."

"*What?!*" Malcom exclaimed. "Who took her? Where is she, Bianca?"

"She was at the park with Kendrick and stepped into the ladies' room for a few minutes. We found her phone but nothing else. The police are here, so they're asking around."

Silence.

"Malcom?" She couldn't imagine what he was thinking. Her own heart was breaking at the thought of Alyssa out there alone.

"Who was it, Bianca?" Why did his tone sound accusatory?

"What? I don't know, Malcom. If I knew, don't you think I would have told you?" Was he insinuating that she knew who did this?

He exhaled. "Sorry. I'm just worried."

"I understand. Me too." Bianca used her free hand to grab the nape of her neck. Her skin felt hot to the touch, but thank goodness the cool breeze chilled her skin. She would enjoy it for now. Summer had yet to hit hard in Edenville.

"Who would take Alyssa?"

Bianca replied, "I hope the police find out soon. I'd hate for her to be out all night with... whoever this person is."

"Have you made any enemies recently, Bianca?" Malcom asked.

"Like who? I'm a single mom in a small town," she countered. The only person who may have wanted revenge on her was Priscilla Davis, but the woman was in prison. Did she know...? Bianca shook off the idea with a shimmy of her shoulders. Talk about a bitter woman if she was still coming after Bianca.

"Well?" Malcom pressed.

"I helped the police out with a case once, but the killer is behind bars now."

"We'll get to that next. Has Alyssa had problems at school? Bullies?" he asked further.

Alyssa had never mentioned problems with any of her classmates. She and Chloe were close, as always. Speaking of her best friend, Bianca pivoted to see Chloe along with Kendrick and a few more teenagers asking around the park. She appreciated their efforts to help find her daughter.

"No." Bianca's hand drifted from her hand to her hip. She couldn't think straight with a sensitive stomach.

"God, I hope this is not a trafficking case. They could have spotted her and... not Alyssa," Malcom said.

Bianca sighed, willing herself not to cry. Tears would not find her daughter. Tears wouldn't even make her feel better. Rolling her shoulders back, it was best to hang up before she broke down. "I'll call you as soon as I know something."

He added. "I'm booking a flight out there now. I can't sit here and do nothing. I'll stay in a hotel."

"Okay," she replied with a sniffle.

"Bianca? How are you holding up?"

She pulled her lips in for a moment. "I'll be okay. We're going to find her and the kidnapper."

"Bianca?"

"I'm fine, Malcom," she reassured him. "As fine as I can be. I'm not alone. My mom and sister are with me. Once the police give us the word, we'll head somewhere else to look or call it a night." She hoped for the former. Bianca wouldn't be able to sleep until her daughter was back home with her and Melanie.

MELANIE LOOPED HER arm through Bianca's as they walked to her Kia Soul that evening. Jordan had offered to follow them home, but Melanie had assured him she could look after her sister. Deborah Wallace said goodbye to Judy and Richard, along with the other townspeople who'd helped search the grounds for Alyssa.

The day's events could have knocked Bianca over with a feather. The sun had set an hour ago, and an occasional shooting star flew across the velvet sky. Another tear cascaded down her cheek. Where was her daughter? For all Bianca knew, this person would harm her, or worse. Kill her.

Leaning in, Melanie stopped in her tracks and pulled Bianca to her. She rested her head on her sister's shoulder as Melanie patted her back.

"We're going to find her." Melanie soothed her, holding her close.

"Bianca?" her mother's voice called out. Judging by the wrinkle in her mother's brow, Deborah Wallace was beside herself with worry too.

Bianca straightened, breaking her embrace with her sister. Facing her mother, she said, "I'll be okay. I know we're going to find her." Despite her stomach clenching, Bianca prayed for it to be true. She would find her daughter. No matter whom she had to face.

Her mother took both of her hands in hers. "I know we will, and don't forget you raised a strong young woman. Alyssa is brave and she…" Her bottom lip trembled, but she continued. "We're going to find her. I'll even come over and keep Casper for the night. Luther can keep an eye out on Jasper and Horas for me. I don't want you—"

"Mom." Bianca stopped her. Releasing her mother's hands, she pinched the skin between her thumb and forefinger. "Thanks, but I'd rather you go home."

Her mother blinked, as if taken aback by her daughter's words. "I will not leave you alone."

"I know it's just… I have a lot on my mind and I think I need to be alone. Besides, it's not like Melanie won't be there."

Her mother placed her hands on her shoulders. "I'm just worried about you."

"That's why you need to go home. I can't have us both worried and pacing the floor. It's… a lot for me right now. Can you understand that?"

Her mother's shoulder's drooped, dropping her hands to her sides once more. "You'll call me if you change your mind?"

"I will." Bianca promised.

"I'll call you if I need backup," Melanie said, nudging her sister's shoulder to diffuse the somber mood. Yet, her sniffle and slackened face gave her away.

Deborah rubbed at her arms, facing her oldest daughter once more. "If you need space, I can respect that. But remember, you're not alone, Bianca. Family is here."

She knew that.

"Want me to keep Casper for you instead? So you'll know he's taken care of while you take a breather? I'm going to worry, anyway." Her mother added.

Bianca bobbed her head. Though cuddling with their dog didn't sound too bad, he was better off with her mother and her Yorkies. Bianca's brain was in a haze. All she could think about was Alyssa. "Thank you. I appreciate that, Mom."

"I'll look after her," Melanie said.

Her mother kissed Bianca's cheek. "Get some rest. I know the police will call you when they find out anything." Deborah Wallace rolled her shoulders back. "I want a few words with Alyssa's *kidnapper*. They took the wrong girl."

Melanie raised an arched eyebrow. "I don't think the police will allow that, Mom."

Bianca appreciated the moment of humor. "I agree. You're better off letting them take the person to jail."

"I know enough people in town to make that happen if I want to." Her mother faced Melanie. "I know you'll take care of your sister."

With that, her mother gave her one last hug along with Melanie. Bianca slid into the passenger's seat of Bianca's car, grateful that Melanie was driving them home. Clicking on her seatbelt, she rested her head against the headrest and closed her eyes. Melanie drove her in silence for a few moments, but Bianca exhaled, pressing her hands to her cheeks.

"It doesn't make any sense," she said.

"What?" Melanie asked as she stopped in front of a red traffic light.

"I'm questioned today by the police in connection with Paris' death. Next thing I know, Alyssa is missing." Despite lightheadedness, her brain sought to piece the mystery together.

"What are you thinking?" her sister asked.

"Was it all a... setup?" Bianca asked, as she scratched at her cheek. "Me following Paris, only for her to be killed? Was that what the killer wanted? Have they been on my trail this whole time?" She turned in her seat. "Remember how we were followed that time coming from the farmer's market after Martin's death?"

"Don't remind me," Melanie said.

"What if it's happening again, and I... didn't see it?" Bianca ran a hand down her neck. "I keep wondering: Did I miss something in the parking garage? Aiden left. Why leave only to come back and kill Paris? Why delay if that was his plan all along?"

"Maybe it wasn't. What if he didn't intend to kill her but changed his mind?" Melanie asked.

Bianca paused for a moment. "I think... this has to be connected to Sherry's death. What if..." She didn't have time to tell Detective Sims this, but he would agree since the out-of-town victims were both models and knew each other.

"What if what?" Melanie switched lanes, only to pass by the Stargaze Hotel.

Bianca flinched in her seat. Alyssa's reaction at Mobile Aztec. Her uneasiness after the BBQ event last night. Was someone following her? Is that what made her so jumpy lately? Bianca thought harder. Alyssa went to the ladies' room before the fashion show started. Didn't she say when she returned, *I thought I saw something?* What did her daughter see? Bianca didn't recall her exact statement since she'd been comforting a distraught Melanie.

"Mel? Did Alyssa talk to you any last night after we came home from the festival?"

"No. I know she was jumpy in the car, though. You saw how she was looking over her shoulder."

"That's what worries me." Bianca's muscles tightened. "I should have gotten Alyssa to talk to me sooner. This whole time I thought it was about her and Kendrick, especially with her leaving to visit her dad."

"What do you mean?" Melanie asked, obviously not following her sister's comments as she drove down the street.

She filled her sister in on her theory. "What if Alyssa saw something backstage? What if the killer is not targeting me but... her?" This just got even worse.

Melanie gasped. "But the police took her statement, didn't they? If she saw something, they would have figured it out by now. Unless... she had little details to begin with. How long was she gone?" Her sister paused. "I was in such a blur, I don't remember all the police asked me that night."

Bianca groaned. "I can't remember either." What else could she piece together? Snapping her fingers, Bianca recalled the flash drive. "Before the killer murdered Paris, she mentioned a flash drive. Clark did too at the memorial."

"If I remember correctly..." Melanie said. "Sherry couldn't have been serious, though."

"About what?" Bianca asked. Every bit of information helped if it meant finding Alyssa.

"The day of the rehearsal. Didn't she mention writing a... book?"

The only person who Bianca knew would know for sure would be Sherry's assistant. Jacqueline. She had to have had all of Sherry's appointments. Was there a book deal on the table? Grabbing her cell, she pulled up the young woman's number. "Only one way to find out."

Jacqueline picked up after the second ring. "Hello?" She sounded breathless.

"Jacqueline. It's Bianca Wallace. If you have a few moments, I have some questions for you. Wait. Are you okay?"

"I'm okay. Just looking for something," she said. "But go ahead."

Bianca put her on speakerphone. "Well... Melanie recalls Sherry mentioning wanting to write a book. Do you know anything about that? Was it true or a rumor?"

"Yeah. Hunter set up the deal for her." Jacqueline explained. "They didn't announce officially, but she was working on it."

"Do you know if she saved anything..." The flash drive. "What kind of book was she going for?"

"Autobiography or a tell-all book, I think. She wanted to share about her childhood, her rise to fame, and anything else she wanted her fans to know," Jacqueline said. "Is something wrong, Bianca?"

"Did she keep a flash drive?" Bianca asked.

Melanie tapped her fingers on the steering wheel, glancing back and forth at her sister as she listened.

Jacqueline replied. "Yes, as far as I know. I have one too to keep all of her itinerary and important information whenever we traveled. That's what I can't find right now."

"Did she show you her notes?" Bianca wondered.

"No. She kept that to herself."

"If you find something, please send it to me." Bianca dictated her email address to her.

"Sure. I don't know what this is about, but I hope this helps," Jacqueline said. "I have to go." With that, she hung up.

Bianca locked her phone screen.

"Sherry writing a tell-all book? Wow." Melanie switched lanes on the two-lane main street, stopping in front of another traffic light.

Bianca said, "Sherry's writing a tell-all book, and people are looking for the flash drive. If the deal had yet to be announced, how did they know she was writing it?"

"I'm sure her manager knew."

Bianca gripped her car's console. "Jacqueline said he set up the deal and then... Sherry fires him." Cutting him out of the commission. The man had stayed in town to recruit new clients. Did he make any progress or had Sherry's leaving him damage his reputation for good? Something to consider. "Turn around."

"Why? Bianca, I promised Mom I'd take you home."

"You will, just not now. Go back to the Stargaze Hotel." Bianca faced her sister. "Please."

Melanie exhaled and made a U-turn at the next traffic light. "What makes you think we're going to find something there?"

"I don't know." Once they entered the parking lot, Bianca's eyes flitted to see if she spotted a familiar car.

Though Bianca couldn't picture Sherry's own father behind his daughter's murder, but it wouldn't have been the first time she'd seen one family member turn on another. She couldn't deny Clark and Paris' phone call, and even though he wasn't in town during the murder, he could have hired someone to get rid of his daughter.

Pulling into the Stargaze Hotel parking lot, it was lit because of the streetlights. Bianca's eyes scanned the cars.

"Bianca." Melanie gasped.

Bianca's eyes shifted to Hunter Graham, who practically sprinted to his champagne Chevrolet Impala. She must have missed it the last time she'd been here, or he'd had it parked in the back, depending on where his room was. Hunter carried a duffle bag along with a small suitcase. Did he not have a home to go back to? She could understand him scouting Clique Classic's remaining models in town for his business, but why not leave to return to New York or California?

"Looks like he's leaving," Melanie said.

Bianca perked. Did Detective Sims know about Hunter leaving? "Let's see where he goes."

Melanie gripped the steering wheel. "I can't believe you talked me into this."

"If he knows something, maybe he can help us find Alyssa." Bianca tapped on the dashboard, and Melanie put the car in drive once they heard Hunter crank his engine. Melanie allowed for at least one car between them for space, but she did well keeping up with Hunter.

"Where do you think he's going?" Melanie asked. "This isn't the usual way to leave Edenville."

"I know. I wonder if he's meeting someone." Bianca scooted to the edge of her seat, as if that would give her a better angle.

"He's turning here?" Melanie questioned as she followed Hunter to a dirt road off the main street.

The knot in Bianca's belly increased with her suspicions. "Wait a minute."

"What?" Thank goodness Melanie had turned off the headlights. So far, they hadn't given themselves away to Hunter, so he didn't know that they were following him. Hopefully, he would help them if he knew anything that was going on in town. Then again, if he was the culprit, he could be violent.

"Is this the way to old Montgomery place?" Bianca asked. "I think there's an old barn out here."

"It's been years since Mr. Montgomery moved away," Melanie added. "I'm surprised no one picked up the property. According to Mom, it's eighty acres, but the bank owns it."

Bianca recalled the story her mother had told her when she'd first moved to Edenville. Mr. Montgomery's wife had died of breast cancer, and he had taken a second mortgage on their home to pay her medical bills. Unfortunately, he'd gotten behind and the bank had foreclosed. No one had lived on the property since then.

"I don't think we're going to find anything here," Melanie said.

Bianca didn't take her eyes off of Hunter's car. He parked outside of the worn barn, while Montgomery's house was off to the left of the property, steps leading to the front door with a fenced-in porch.

"It doesn't make sense that he's here." Bianca's stomach quivered.

Melanie stopped the car. "He's going inside."

Bianca noticed he had a small suitcase in his hands. What was he carrying in there? *Ping!* Her phone alerted her she'd received an email. "It's Jacqueline." Bianca didn't hesitate to open the message.

"What did she say?" Melanie asked.

Bianca read to herself first.

I found my flash drive thinking it was mine, but it's Sherry's. Wow. Sherry's notes for her book are on here. I can't believe it. I'm sending a copy to the police. She called it Lies the World and Hollywood Told Me. I'm attaching it for you to read!

Jacqueline

"Bianca, what did she say?" Melanie called out.

A high-pitched scream made both of them flinch. Bianca grabbed her sister's arm, forgetting about Jacqueline's email for a moment. Her heart pounded as her chest heaved. "No."

"Oh, no. Is that...? I think we need to call the police," Melanie said, shaking her head slightly.

As a mother, Bianca knew the cry of her daughter. It was the same yelp Alyssa had uttered when she'd spotted a dead mouse in her grandmother's backyard. She was inside. *Hunter* had taken her? Bianca swallowed to regain her composure, but she wasn't leaving without Alyssa. Even if she had to face a potential killer.

Chapter 22

"Bianca." Melanie gasped.

"She's in there," Bianca said. Her mouth went dry at the notion. "I know it."

"We need to call Detective Sims. The police need to get out of here. Now." Melanie pulled out her phone.

"You do that." Bianca unclicked her seatbelt and stuffed her phone in her pocket. Alyssa's safety was a priority, so reading Jacqueline's email had to wait for now. Besides, she was sending it to the police.

Melanie grabbed her arm. "What are you doing? You can't go in there."

"I'm not leaving Alyssa."

"*Stop* for a second!" Melanie reasoned with her. "We don't know for sure. All we heard was a scream, so if someone is in trouble, the police can figure it out."

Bianca eyeballed her sister, not convinced. "I know Alyssa when I hear her." Her breath caught in her throat, but she pressed forward. "Do you seriously expect me to stay in the car and wait for the police? Who knows what he's doing to her now? If he touches her, I..." She couldn't finish her thought. Her worries grew too gruesome.

She felt helpless for a moment, but there was no way she would not fight for her daughter. She wondered if Hunter would be in more danger than she would be once she got a hold of the man who'd kidnapped Alyssa.

Melanie sighed. "I'm sorry. I can't imagine how you must be feeling. We just need a plan. If he's crazy enough to take Alyssa, what else is he capable of?"

"I don't know," Bianca said. Though her mind immediately went to murder. "But we won't find out sitting in the car. Call Detective Sims and tell him where we are."

Melanie agreed. "Okay."

Bianca slipped out of the passenger side of her car and headed for the trunk.

Melanie cut the engine, and based on her murmuring, she was on the phone. Bianca bit her bottom lip as she opened her trunk, trying not to cause too much noise. The buzzing of bugs filled her ears while the earthy smell of the land filled her lungs.

She grabbed the crowbar. If she could knock Hunter out, Alyssa could get away.

Melanie stuffed her phone into her pocket. "He's on his way and he wants us to wait."

"You told him I wouldn't. Right?" Bianca raised an eyebrow.

"He said and I quote, 'I know Bianca won't wait, but tell her to anyway.'" A soft smile danced across Melanie's lips.

Though Bianca would have laughed herself, now wasn't the time for jokes. Even if the police got there in time, Hunter could escape or hurt Alyssa. She gestured to her sister in a whisper.

"I can't wait much longer for the police to get here," Bianca said.

"I think we need to wait. We don't know what we're dealing with yet." Melanie added.

Bianca bit the inside of her cheek. "If you want to wait in the car, that's fine."

Melanie groaned. "Fine." She covered her face with both hands as if to gather her thoughts. Running her fingers down her face and neck, a sigh escaped her mouth. "Let's go."

Bianca could see her sister's pained look in the moonlight. Gripping the metal bar in her hands, she hoped she wouldn't have to use the weapon. Hopefully, Hunter would let her daughter go. When they came to a rusting tractor, they ducked behind it for cover. Bianca couldn't hear anything coming from the inside. Her stomach clenched. She would probably still hit Hunter for good measure.

"I don't know how we're going to sneak inside without him seeing us," Melanie whispered.

"I know." Bianca's fingers tensed around the crowbar. "If only I could be sure." Taking a step forward, she rounded to the other side of the tractor, which had once had a red shade, but now it had more of a burnt orange appearance. Bianca and Melanie tip-toed to the barn door, listening for voices inside.

"One more scream," Hunter said. "And that's the *end* for you. Now tell me what I want to know. *Now.*"

Bianca's lips parted, but she held her composure. When they heard a phone ring, both she and her sister flinched, but thankfully, he didn't hear them. Standing up against the barn walls, Bianca and Melanie kept quiet as Hunter swung open the door.

"I can't talk right now, Kyle. I told you that. You're supposed to—what? What do you mean you grabbed the *wrong* flash drive?" Hunter argued.

Bingo. Bianca gestured to Melanie and her sister treaded lightly to head inside the barn. Her hand practically cramped at how closely she held the crowbar, but she inched forward, grateful that Hunter's back was turned.

"You idiot! If you had done your job, we wouldn't be in this mess," he grumbled. Disdain for whoever this Kyle was on the phone dripped from his mouth.

So close. Bianca could knock him out long enough for them to get away. Detective Sims would be here soon. Right? There was nothing to worry about. Then she heard the creaking floorboards behind her.

Oh, no. She swung back to hit Hunter. It was now or never, but he spun on his heels so quick to point a gun at her. His other hand hung up the call on his phone. Bianca trembled. He had found her out.

"Mom!" Alyssa shouted from behind her. Bianca would have glanced back for a second, but she wouldn't turn her back on the man with a gun. Judging my Alyssa's whimpers, she'd been crying. Bianca only prayed her daughter was in good shape overall. She focused on Hunter.

"Drop it." He motioned for Bianca's hand.

She did not take her eyes off him. His brow sweated and his nostrils flared.

"The police are on their way," Melanie called out to Hunter.

"Well, then." His eyes narrowed on Bianca. "I guess I'll have to take you with me. I've come this far. Might as well go all the way. Since your daughter won't talk, you're the next best thing."

Bianca raised her hands in a gesture of surrender. "Whatever you say. Just let my daughter and sister go."

"Get in the car! Now!" He barked at Bianca.

She flinched at the raising of his voice, but did as he'd instructed. Definitely not the mild-mannered man she'd assumed him to be.

"Bianca no!" Melanie yelled!

"Mom!" Alyssa cried again. "Don't go!"

Bianca had no choice. Opening the passenger door, she slid inside his Chevrolet Impala. Her breath hitched. Where was Detective Sims? Staring in the rearview mirror, Bianca only wished she had the keys to the car, but she kept her eye on Hunter, who sprinted to the driver's side. Opening the door, he didn't waste time in starting the car and speeding down the dirt road.

Bianca breathed easier when she heard sirens, but she knew it was hardly over. Alyssa and her sister were safe. She was a different story. How would she buy time?

Where was Hunter taking her? Why did he kidnap Alyssa in the first place? She had nothing to do with anything. What did he want her daughter to tell him? Was he the one she saw that night backstage? If he'd already killed two women, was she next?

He drove with one hand on the wheel, while he held the gun in the other. The engine hummed, and she watched the speedometer raise to fifty miles per hour. Now it was at sixty miles per hour.

Next thing she knew, they were back on the main road. Bianca exhaled, feeling around in the front pocket of her jeans. She gulped down her breaths to stay quiet. Thank goodness she was sitting or she would have fallen over because of the weakness in her legs.

At least she had her phone. The police could trace her. They'd find her. She only hoped it wouldn't be too late.

Chapter 23

Bianca's bottom lip trembled. At least her daughter was safe, but this was not the way she'd intended for her night to end. Sitting next to Hunter Graham, one hand on the wheel and a gun in his hand. His car smelled like the evergreen freshener hanging from his rearview mirror. Dust and dirt covered the floor mats, and there was a lingering odor of coffee in the air.

7:55 p.m. was the time showing on the screen on the dashboard. Had the police found Melanie and Alyssa? Her phone didn't buzz and Bianca breathed easier, grateful her sister didn't call. What if a phone call were to set Hunter off even more? Despite the glow of the screen on his pale skin, she noticed how tense his hand was as it gripped the wheel.

The engine roared, and he switched lanes, passing the cars, trucks, and SUVs on the road, heading to the main highway out of Edenville. Where was he taking her? How long would he give her before he shot her? Bianca's heart pounded inside her chest. Her palms sweated at the thought of being shot and dumped somewhere in a ditch.

Despite her anger against the man for kidnapping her daughter, Bianca had to think of a plan until the police showed.

Detective Sims was coming. She knew that deep within her clenching stomach.

"Want to tell me how you killed Sherry and Paris?" she asked.

Hunter gave a mirthless laugh. "You are clever, aren't you? Like mother, like daughter. I saw her backstage that night being nosy with her phone. Typical teenagers wanting to go live on social media. My brother, Kyle, was a decoy the night before, but I knew your daughter saw me leave Sherry's dressing room. I wanted to know what she saw. She *claims* she saw nothing."

His brother? The man with the mussed sandy brown hair? Why didn't Alyssa tell her? Was it because she knew she didn't have any business trying to film backstage? Regardless, Alyssa should have said something, and not have kept it to herself. If Hunter or Kyle had been following her this whole time, she should have confided to Bianca. "That was your getaway plan? Take an innocent kid? To kill her?"

He glanced at her for a moment with a sneer. "Almost got away with it, too." He laughed, but it wasn't out of amusement.

Bianca exhaled to keep her composure. He wasn't kidding. He'd come this far and was determined to get away with his crimes. "So... you poisoned Sherry?"

"Paris was the brains behind that one. She hated Sherry as much as I did. The woman fooled no one. She pretended to be nice and friendly, but that was only to keep up appearances for her fans. The woman was selfish. Paris agreed Sherry was better off *dead*."

Bianca folded an arm against her stomach. Paris had been in on Sherry's murder? "Then why kill Paris? I thought you two were basically... together." She had to buy time. Keep him talking and distracted. If only she could hear police sirens in the background.

"What made you think that?" His voice dropped.

"I saw you two... kissing," she said.

Hunter shrugged. "She didn't care about me. I told her my divorce would be final soon, but she only kept me as the *backup* guy. Someone who would be at her beck and call whenever she needed him. I didn't believe it at first, but the way she looked at Aiden... and Clark Wilson."

What did Clark have to do with anything? "I'm sorry?"

A muscle tic jumped in Hunter's cheek. "Their affair. Sherry found out the latter part of last year, and was going to expose them in her tell-all book."

Wow. No wonder her relationship with her father was strained. Did Joan know? Jacqueline?

"I'm the reason she got the deal with Swan Publishing, but Sherry left me. No one wanted to work with me because of her big mouth. I needed the money. Paris promised she'd refer her model friends to me. She said she'd convince them to take me on as an agent if I worked to keep her name and Clark's out of the book. That's why I stayed in town so long. I couldn't pass up Clique Classic, especially with them trending in the fashion world. With the divorce, my ex was taking me for everything I had. If only Sherry had been reasonable to keep me on her payroll."

"So you teamed up with Paris to kill her," Bianca stated. Her hand grabbed the handle of the passenger door.

"Her and Clark," he admitted. "He only wanted to scare her, but I figured it was best to get rid of Sherry. Paris wanted in because of her own hate for the woman. Clark's nothing but a wimp. He'd do anything to keep his reputation in Georgia, including getting rid of his oldest daughter. Sherry got in the way for all of us."

Bianca's breath left her lungs for a moment. The adoption was true? Is that why Sherry willed to write her book in the first place? When did she find out about Clark and Paris' affair?

Hunter's speedometer increased to seventy miles per hour. He managed not to hit any innocent drivers as he weaved in and out of the lanes, but it made Bianca's stomach quiver all the more. Though the multiple-lane highway wasn't as crowded, there were enough cars for Hunter to hit if he didn't slow down.

He continued. "She always said she was the brains of it all. I was to follow her lead. Jacqueline left Sherry's dressing room only for a moment. With her door cracked, it was the perfect opportunity. Paris switched water glasses while Sherry stepped out of her room to take a phone call in the hallway. My brother bought the arsenic online with no problem.

Within thirty minutes, it did its job. Sherry's death would shock the nation, being caught on camera like that, and I could have made Paris my next top model. I know enough people in the industry. I could have made it happen. Clark would save his political reputation too, avoiding the scandal in Georgia. Gaining the sympathy of constituents by losing his *beloved* daughter."

Bianca couldn't believe her ears. "Everything was going for you all until... Paris betrayed you."

Hunter's jaw was tight. Sweat beaded on his brow. "She called it off between us. Didn't even have the guts to tell me face to face. She left a voicemail. So I followed her to the parking garage. I saw her with Aiden." A *tsk* escaped his mouth. "I guess she figured I had a thing for Sherry too."

Attraction for Sherry? No wonder Aiden told him in the grocery parking lot to stay away from her? Did that push her into wanting a restraining order?

Hunter continued. "Once he left, I got out and confronted her. She didn't let me get a word in hardly. There I was, pouring my heart out, and she spat in my face. I thought to myself, *Sherry deserved to die, and Paris does too.*" Did he hear her phone call with Clark? If he knew about their previous affair, did that drive him over the edge too, to hear her talk to a former love interest? Did that make Hunter snap?

Bianca exhaled. "You... strangled her?"

He wet his lips. "I didn't know what to do. Seeing her on the ground. Eyes open. Breathless. I... hurried back to my hotel room. I knew it was a matter of time before they showed the security footage to the police. I didn't see the cameras at first in the garage."

Bianca gasped, finally hearing the sirens in the background.

Hunter growled. "No!" He sped around a few more cars, his tires screeching.

"Hunter." Bianca braced one hand on the dashboard while keeping her other hand on the passenger door handle. "You can't keep running."

"Shut up!" he yelled.

Bianca saw the flashing lights behind them. How had Detective Sims got here so fast? She was glad he wasn't too far behind. The question: How was he going to get Hunter to surrender? How much farther would he take her before he murdered her?

Chapter 24

Bianca braced herself, keeping one hand on the dashboard along with the other on the door handle. The police sirens rang in her ears. Tires screeched as Hunter passed by more cars in his way. They'd already passed the sign of leaving Edenville and entering the town of Belland. Horns honked while Bianca inhaled the car exhaust. Lights flashed behind them still.

"Hunter, you can't—"

"*Shut up!*" he shouted. He was the man with the gun, so there was no point in arguing with him.

Bianca's chest heaved all the more. There had to be a way to talk him down. How could she persuade him to give himself up? Best-case scenario, the police would arrest him—or worse, he'd die on the scene trying to defend himself. There was no way he could win.

"You don't get it," he barked. "You just don't get it."

"Then tell me," Bianca said. "Why put yourself through all of this?"

"I *made* Sherry's career! She was nobody until I found her back in Georgia when she was twenty. I gave her everything she needed to make a name for herself. When she asked about writing a book last year, I set it all up for her. I thought it was a great opportunity for the both of us. Then... I found out what she wanted to write about. When I saw some notes on her laptop, I knew it was a tell-all book. I advised her against it, but she wouldn't listen to me. She fired me on the spot, threatening to expose my treatment of her, claiming I wanted to control her."

Bianca didn't reply.

"I came to her in good faith. Wanting to make amends and change her mind about the book's theme. She wouldn't hear of it. She kept saying, 'the world must know.' The woman was selfish." Hunter continued.

"I'm sorry Sherry ruined your career, and I... can't imagine the pain Paris caused you."

"How would you know about pain?" he spewed at her. He shook his head slightly. "I bet you're the type of woman who can get whatever she wants. My life has been nothing but a struggle since my wife left me. I can't seem to get ahead, no matter how hard I try." He glanced behind them for a moment. "I've got nothing to lose." He faced forward, and the engine roared even louder.

Bianca's gaze flitted to the side mirror. The police were still there, but Hunter wasn't giving up. Swallowing despite her dry mouth, she tried one last measure. "You're wrong, Hunter. I may not know exactly how you feel, but I know heartbreak."

"Then tell me *all* your problems, Bianca." There was sarcasm in his voice, but she continued.

"I married my high school sweetheart. I thought we were going to be together forever, but he left me. I didn't plan on being a single mother, but I am. I moved to Edenville to start my life over. He has a new wife and life in California. It took me... a long time to forgive him."

Hunter didn't say a word, so she hoped he was listening to her.

"I was angry at everyone. Even in therapy, I had to unpack all the betrayal I'd felt when he left. There I was. My so-called perfect life pulled out from under me." Bianca sighed. "I haven't been the same since then."

Hunter admitted, "My wife was so paranoid, thinking I was seeing other women, but I was at the office working late. She became even more suspicious when Sherry threatened a restraining order. I confessed my attraction to Sherry, but I never caved while we were married. She left anyway."

"I'm sure you were," Bianca reassured him. "I wish I knew what changed with my husband, but I honestly think we grew apart. I wasn't the same girl he'd married. He never told me, but I think he preferred it when I depended on him. I didn't mean to leave him out, but I grew up. So... he sought someone else." Bianca ignored the ache in her chest. The memories of her failed marriage flashed through her mind.

"Sounds like he couldn't handle a strong woman," Hunter said.

Bianca released her grip on the door handle. "Perhaps he couldn't, but no matter how much pain I was in, I couldn't take it out on others. I needed to heal. It was the only way."

His hand clenched the wheel even harder. It might as well have been a part of his hand. "It's too late."

"It's not, Hunter. You can pull over and admit your crime. Trust me, I—"

"No!" Hunter shouted.

Bianca screamed as the car swerved. Was that a deer in the door? A large crunch flooded her ears, shaking the car. The tires screeched as Hunter attempted to control from hitting other cars. The gun fell from his hand and Bianca's gaze fell to the floor. She reached for it, but Hunter grabbed at her hair. A high-pitched scream escaped her mouth.

Thud. He threw her back against the passenger door. She squeezed her eyes shut to hold back another scream. Pushing herself back up in her seat. She caught Hunter looking behind him. He had better control of the car, but the gun was next to his thigh.

Bianca moved quick, taking the gun in both of her hands and pointing it to him. "Pull over, Hunter! Now!"

"You won't shoot me." He sneered, followed by a bark of laughter. There was no reasoning with a man with nothing to lose. He'd already killed two people. In his eyes, his life was over.

POW! Bianca pulled the trigger, and Hunter yelped, but he maintained one hand on the wheel. The tires screeched as the car swerved, but they didn't veer off the road. Bianca only grazed his forearm, but she saw the blood soaking his dress shirt.

"You shot me?" He sounded shocked.

"Pull over, Hunter." She squared her shoulders. "I won't miss you twice. Not only have you endangered me, but you've traumatized my daughter. I've tried reasoning with you, but *don't* underestimate me."

The police sirens rang in her ears. Hunter's gaze bore into hers, but his eyes weren't as tight as they'd once been. He did as she asked and pulled over. The car came to a stop.

"Unlock it," she said, gesturing at the door. She didn't take her eye off him for one minute. When she heard the click, she opened her door and stepped outside, still pointing the gun at him. Her heart pounded all the more. Sweat built along her hairline, but she stepped backward from the car.

"Bianca!"

She knew Detective Sims' voice, but she didn't turn to face him. Bianca was *not* turning her back on Hunter. Did he have another gun?

"Bianca!" Detective Sims repeated. "Drop the gun!"

She heard the padding of feet along the pavement, but she kept her focus on Hunter. He didn't get out, but next thing she knew, his tires spun into action one more time as he sped off ahead. His car burned rubber, flooding her nose with the stench, and with a barricade ahead, he wouldn't get far. Then again, a desperate man would at least try to keep running from the law.

"Get him!" Detective Sims shouted.

Bianca dropped the gun to her side as she watched the scene unfold. Next thing she knew, arms wrapped around her shoulders, guiding to her a police car. She knew Lamar's touch anywhere, but what had her eyes glued ahead of her were the two cops chasing Hunter. He only crashed into a barricade.

Slowing her breathing, Bianca sat in the backseat of the police car. She didn't even realize when she'd given the gun to Detective Sims, but he knelt in front of her now. Turning her head slightly, she saw Detective Atkins had Hunter handcuffed. His arm still bled from where she shot him, but there was another bleeding scratch on the side of his face.

"Bianca?" Detective Sims called out to her.

She didn't reply. Bianca could only lean forward and rest her head on his shoulder. Thank goodness he didn't turn her away, but he cradled the back of her hand. She would be fine, but that had been another close call with a killer.

BIANCA STARED AT THE concrete in the back of the police car, wrapped in a blanket. When her eyes shifted to the night sky, she spotted blinking satellites and airplanes. Clouds blocked a portion of the sky, but thanks to the breeze, they blew along their path.

Sniffling, she rubbed at her nose and tightened her grip of the blanket around her shoulders. She was okay. Alyssa was okay, too, according to Detective Sims. Hunter was going to jail. That was all that mattered.

"Bianca?" Detective Sims walked back over to her after talking with Detective Atkins.

Glancing up at him, the lights from the police car flashed, illuminating his face.

She answered. "Yes?"

"How are you doing?" He knelt in front of her again. His eyebrows drew together and his eye contact was strong.

"Relieved." Closing her eyes, she heard the *POW* of the gun again in her mind. She hadn't intended to shoot him. Bianca had hoped her threat would be enough, but Hunter wouldn't listen to her. Would she have killed him? Bianca shivered at the thought. "Did he confess?"

Detective Sims bobbed his head. "He did."

"Good." She exhaled. "That was close."

He gave a faint smile.

"What?" she wondered.

"He didn't think you were going to shoot him," he said.

Bianca tried to hide her grin. "He left me no choice. Where was he going, anyway? Did he say?"

Detective Sims shook his head. "To meet his brother in Belland. According to him, he wasn't planning on you and your sister showing up. The plan was to kill Alyssa in the barn. She was his next target to find out what she knew."

"I remember him saying that." Bianca cleared her throat. "Look, um... I know you didn't want me to get involved, but..." she faced him. "As a mother, I couldn't—"

"You don't have to explain that to me, Bianca." His eyes softened. "I don't have kids, so I can't imagine what went through your head. When your sister called again saying you'd found Alyssa, but Hunter took you... I didn't blame you for going after your daughter. Even *if* I think you need to step aside."

She brushed a few stray hairs behind her ear. "Thank you for understanding. I have to say... I don't think I want to do this again. He came too close to my child."

Detective Sims nodded, but he didn't say a word.

"Thank you. For being here," she said truthfully. To know he hadn't been too far behind brought Bianca peace of mind.

"I'm glad you're okay," he answered, his eyes focused even more intently on her face.

Suddenly, the blanket made her too hot, so she loosened her grip on it. "Did you... find Clark Wilson? He was in on this too."

Detective Sims rubbed the back of his neck. "Jacqueline forwarded us a copy of Sherry's notes for her book. The line that stood out was, 'I'm telling my story even if they kill me.'"

Bianca's mouth fell open.

Detective Sims continued. "Jacqueline found the flash drive you were talking about. Hunter had his brother, Kyle, plant the poison in her room to frame her and to get the flash drive, but he grabbed Jacqueline's instead, which had Sherry's itinerary on it.

Sherry's drive had everything from Hunter's job as her manager and her father's affair with her archrival. According to Sherry's notes, she felt 'no loyalty to the man she called father,' since he always put his career ahead, anyway.

Paris wanted Sherry dead, since the affair leaking to the public would tarnish her image. Clark claims she was going to use the flash drive to blackmail him for ending things between them, so he had no problem with Hunter killing her. Thankfully, because of severe thunderstorms, his plane brought him and Joan back to Edenville. We arrested him at the airport, along with Hunter's brother in Belland."

Bianca blinked. "Wow." Wrapping her mind around the events made her skin tingle. She'd seen the photos between Clark and Paris, but never guessed a full-fledged affair between them. Hunter appeared so well-mannered, trying to make amends with Sherry. She never imagined him wanting her dead because she'd fired him and he didn't want her tell-all book to launch. "What about Aiden?"

Detective Sims exhaled. "In his case, Paris loaned him money."

"For what?" Bianca's eyebrow arched.

"When he and Paris dated, they lived together," Detective Sims informed her.

"But if they lived together, why—"

"He claims that's how petty she was with their relationship. A few of her modeling checks covered the rent, but when they broke up and she found out about him and Sherry, she wanted her money back."

Bianca wrapped her arms around her middle. "This was a mess. Who would have guessed all of this?"

The corners of Detective Sims' mouth turned up. "It's over. So you can rest easy tonight knowing you and your daughter are both safe."

"Mom! Mom!" Alyssa's voice called out. Detective Sims stood to his feet and Bianca jumped to stand.

"Alyssa!" She dropped the blanket around her shoulders and spotted her daughter running to her with Melanie at her heels. An unexpected release of tension left her body, and she opened her arms to her baby girl. Alyssa slowed her pace, but wrapped her arms around her mother's neck.

Bianca held her daughter close, noticing her daughter trembling. She cradled her daughter's head along with her back. "It's okay. I'm okay." Pulling back, she cupped her daughter's tear-stained face. "Are you okay? What happened?"

Alyssa whimpered. "All I remember was coming out of the restroom and someone grabbed me from behind. He said, 'scream and I'll shoot.' I heard my phone drop to the ground, but I was too scared. So... I went with him."

"Why didn't you tell me what you saw at the fashion show that night?" Bianca asked.

Alyssa's eyes welled with more tears. "I knew I wasn't supposed to be back there anyway, Mom. I can't even remember what I saw, but I saw... a man come down the hallway. He kept looking over his shoulder, and then I think he saw me. I left without saying anything, thinking it was nothing. I didn't know he was going to... kill someone." Her breath caught. "I didn't realize someone was following me this whole time. But then at the park he... he..."

Bianca hugged her daughter again. No sense in lecturing her. The point was, she was back with her now. "It's over now. You're safe."

"What about you?" Alyssa pulled away again to face her mother. "I was so scared when he pointed that gun at you."

Bianca brushed Alyssa's curled hair behind her ears. "I'm okay. I tried not to panic when you went missing, but you *knew* I would find you. Didn't you?"

Alyssa's eyes shined again with more fresh tears, and she hugged her mother once more. Bianca held her tight, only to spot Melanie standing a few feet away, her own eyes glistening with tears. Bianca reached out a hand and her sister joined them in a group hug.

"I'm so glad you're safe," Melanie said. "For a moment there... I thought we wouldn't see you again."

Bianca pulled back and gave a faint smile. "I'm just glad you two are okay." She touched Alyssa's cheek. "Did you talk to your father?"

Alyssa wiped at her eyes. "I did. He couldn't get a flight here with the storms, but he's glad we're all okay."

"Mom knows too." Melanie added. "I had to calm her down when I said you were gone."

Bianca only hugged her sister and daughter again. This had been some night. A night she would never forget.

"Excuse me, ladies," Detective Sims said behind them.

Bianca pivoted to see him with his hands on his hips, his badge attached in front of his left hip.

"I hate to break up a family moment," he said, "but I'm going to need you ladies to come with me to the station to get your official statements." He gestured to Detective Atkins, who waved over Melanie to him.

Epilogue

Two weeks later, Bianca stood next to her daughter in front of a large window at the airport. She was leaving to spend the summer with her father, and after being kidnapped, Alyssa thought it was best to get out of town for a while, anyway. Bianca didn't blame her. Malcom suggested Alyssa see a counselor for PTSD while she was in California. Though she claimed to be fine, Bianca knew it was a good idea after everything her daughter had been through.

Hunter was behind bars. He'd already struggled to gain new clients, but after his arrest, he ruined his chances for good. Staying in Edenville as long as he did for Clique Classic's month long fashion event didn't profit him anything. Bianca also heard Aiden Carlyle returned to New York and was filming a hot chocolate commercial. It was good to know he was moving on with his life without Sherry.

Jacqueline, according to Detective Sims, had returned to California to be with her son after Sherry's funeral back in Georgia two weeks prior. Turned out, when she'd returned to pack up Sherry's things left in her dressing room, she'd dropped her glasses, causing one of the lens to pop out. So, no harm done, especially since there was never a need to prove she hadn't been there, anyway. Clark Wilson lost his position as mayor and his wife Joan left him.

Bianca only wished there was a way she could have saved Paris. Hunter had shown up not long after she'd left, argued with Paris, and then he'd strangled. Despite the hollow feeling in her stomach still, Bianca knew there was nothing she could have done to prevent another murder. When her phone rang inside her purse, she saw her sister's name on the screen. Melanie had left Edenville on another journalist assignment in Oklahoma, but she attended Sherry's funeral in Cliffston, Georgia.

"Hey." Bianca greeted. She held up a finger to her daughter as she stood from her seat.

"Has Alyssa left yet?" Melanie asked.

"Not yet. Still waiting. How are you?"

Her sister sighed. "I know it's been two weeks, but I'm still trying to wrap my mind around everything that's happened."

Bianca shuffled her feet back and forth. "Who knew a month long fashion event would bring all of this to the small town of Edenville," Bianca said.

"I'm still speechless." Melanie replied. "But I am going to write a tribute story for Sherry. My boss thinks it's a great idea since we were friends. I just... wish she would have shared more with me, but I've accepted the fact that maybe she wasn't ready to tell me some things. I can't imagine how she must have felt finding out her father... had an affair. Then he's in on her murder?"

"I know." Bianca had no explanation for that one. "At least he's behind bars too. And Kyle. Who knew Hunter had a criminal brother."

"And he slipped up, grabbing the wrong flash drive," Melanie added. She released a deep sigh. "I hope readers enjoy my tribute to Sherry. She was... a great friend. I'm glad I knew her for the time I did."

"I know they will, sis. I'm sure Sherry would have loved it." Bianca agreed.

"So..." Melanie changed the subject. "Are you excited about moving into your new office space?"

Bianca's grin grew wider. She'd signed the papers last week with Mr. Arden. Wallace Designs had a new home. A three-year lease was a commitment, but she knew it was the best decision. Her home was wonderful starting out, but in this new season of her life, she wanted to take things to a new level.

"I am." Now all she had to do was choose the furniture, add curtains, her sign. Bianca's mouth twisted. Thank goodness she wrote everything down at home. *More office supplies too.*

"Mom, I think that's it," Alyssa said, stuffing her phone back inside her small purse.

Bianca looked over at her daughter. "I have to go, Mel. I'll talk to you later."

"Love you," her sister said.

"Love you too." She hung up and walked back over to where Alyssa was sitting.

Her daughter had already said her goodbyes to Bianca's mother. Deborah Wallace hoped she had a great time with Malcom. Bianca's eyes flitted around at the other passengers sitting lounging in the surrounding chairs, texting and talking on their phones, and some were sleeping. They called names over the intercom while other voices made small talk. A mixture of cleaning products and coffee filled the air.

Thank goodness she had her airport escort pass. With this being Alyssa's first solo trip, she wanted to see her off at the gate. Bianca knew eventually she wouldn't have to anymore, but this time was an exception, so she'd called ahead, making the process that much smoother when she and Alyssa had checked in at the front desk.

Wringing her own hands together, Alyssa stared out the large floor-to-ceiling window across from them, overlooking planes loading and unloading, luggage trains, ground crew, and runways.

Bianca stared up at the gate, showing number seventy-one. Then she gave a faint smile. "Ready?"

Alyssa met her gaze and returned the gesture. "I think so. I just..."

"Just what?" Bianca tilted her head, wanting her to finish her thought.

"I want everything to go okay. This will be the most time I'll be spending with my... stepmother," her daughter explained.

"Don't worry." That was the best Bianca could muster up to say. She didn't care for the new wife, but she was civil.

"Are you going to be okay? This is the entire summer," Alyssa said.

"I have plenty to do with my time," Bianca said, although she wasn't sure what that meant. This would be a long summer. The withdrawals hadn't kicked in yet.

"I'll call you as much as I can." Alyssa winked at her. She and Kendrick agreed to be long distance for her stay over the summer.

Bianca smiled and hugged her baby girl. Not so much a baby anymore.

"Calling passengers for gate seventy-one," the intercom announced.

Bianca pulled back and rubbed her daughter's shoulders. "That's you." She choked back tears, but Alyssa's face only softened.

"Mom, don't cry. Please." She hugged her mother again.

Bianca patted her daughter's back. "I'll be fine." Pulling back, she dabbed at her eyes, grateful she'd chosen to wear waterproof mascara. "You go. Have a good time with your dad."

Alyssa leaned in and kissed her mother's cheek. "I love you."

Bianca cupped her daughter's chin. "I love you too." With that, Alyssa adjusted her small purse on her shoulder and backed away. With a last wave, she turned on her heels and headed for gate seventy-one.

Waving back, Bianca exhaled as her daughter disappeared among the other passengers, boarding the same flight. Blowing out her cheeks, Bianca headed for the automated doors. Pacing back to her car, she held back the tears that blurred her vision, but she reminded herself things would be fine.

When her phone buzzed, she wondered if it was her sister calling to see if she had fallen apart now that Alyssa was leaving. Sniffling as she stared at her screen, she saw it wasn't Melanie. Not even her mother. It was Detective Sims.

Unlocking her car, Bianca slid inside and connected her Bluetooth to the speaker.

"Detective Sims?" Surprised by his call, her mouth hung open. Still, it brought a faint smile to her face.

"Is this a bad time?" he asked, his deep voice filling her car.

Bianca tapped on her steering wheel. "I just dropped Alyssa off at the airport. About to head back home. Is something wrong?"

He cleared his throat. "No, nothing's wrong. I, uh... stopped by your house this morning, but no one was home."

True, and Casper was with the dog sitter. Why would Detective Sims have stopped by her house unless something was wrong? "Are you sure there's nothing wrong?"

"Nothing's wrong, Bianca. I just wanted to have this conversation in person."

What conversation? The case was closed, right? "About what?"

"You... hopefully agreeing to a date with me," he said. "I wanted to ask you face to face, so this is the next best thing. So... I'm asking. Will you go on a date with me?"

Bianca gasped, swallowing despite her dry mouth. This wasn't what she'd expected today at all...

To be continued in *Lather. Rinse. Murder* (A Bianca Wallace Mystery, 3)

THANK YOU FOR TAKING the time to read my book! If you enjoyed *Killer Runway*, please leave a review at any of your favorite retailers.

Best Regards,

Daria

About the Author

Daria started writing as a teenager. Since she loves romance novels, she figured why not write them too? She graduated with a degree in healthcare management, so writing was not in the cards for her. It's rare that you won't catch her reading. Aside from that, she loves Turner Classic Movies, painting, Pilates, the piano, and chocolate.

More Books by Daria

Christmas Therapy
The Wedding Report
Christmas Connection
Wish for Love

Stay in Touch

My website: www.dariawhite.com[1] Subscribe to my newsletter! Here you'll also get invited to my exclusive Facebook Group, **Daria's VIP Circle**. Want to interact with me more? Get on my mailing list for a VIP invite! I'd love to have you!

Follow me on Twitter: www.twitter.com/Daria_White15[2]

Follow me on Instagram: www.instagram.com/dariawhite90[3]

Bookbub: https://www.bookbub.com/profile/daria-white

---

1. http://www.dariawhite.com

2. http://www.twitter.com/Daria_White15

3. http://www.instagram.com/dariawhite90

Thank You from Daria

Thank you again for reading *Killer Runway*. When I tell you this story took a turn, it did. If you were surprised, so was I. Lol. Believe it or not, the final ending came to me just one month before the release date. Yes, sometimes that happens to me. I hope you enjoyed it and are looking forward to book three. I'm excited!

If you enjoyed this story, please take a few minutes to leave a rating or a review. If it's only a few words, it's perfectly fine with me. Unbelievably, it helps other readers to decide if they want to read my work or not. I look forward to sharing the next story with you. There's more to come!

God Bless,

Daria

Shout Outs!

WWW.VILADESIGN.NET[1] (Tatiana, you're the best and deliver every time!). To my family, your support and belief in me means so much. To my writing partners, you rock! I love

1. http://www.viladesign.net

bouncing ideas with you and you're always willing to give me amazing feedback. To my ARC team, I appreciate you taking the time to read *Killer Runway* in advanced. Your early reviews make such a difference!

To all of my fans, your support is a blessing. It's my pleasure to bring a new story to you. Thank you for reading whatever I choose to write!

Don't miss out!

Visit the website below and you can sign up to receive emails whenever Daria White publishes a new book. There's no charge and no obligation.

https://books2read.com/r/B-A-YNYJ-XVJUB

BOOKS 2 READ

Connecting independent readers to independent writers.